switched

switched

Amanda Hocking

St. Martin's Griffin New York

This is a work of fiction. All of the characters, organizations, and events portrayed in this novel are either products of the author's imagination or are used fictitiously.

ISBN 978-1-61793-578-7

To Pete—fellow Aardvark, comrade,
and original cover model

ACKNOWLEDGMENTS

First and foremost, I have to thank the readers and book bloggers. I've said it before but it bears repeating—I could never have gotten this far without all your support and encouragement. I want to thank you all by name, but if I did that, the acknowledgments would become a novel itself. So I just want to say thank you to every person who read *Switched,* told their friends about it, left a review, tweeted about it, blogged about it, or liked it on Facebook, thank you a million times over.

I want to thank my mom for being ridiculously supportive and understanding in all my endeavors, no matter how insane or far out they might be. The actions of the mothers in this book—namely, Kim and Elora—in no way reflect my experiences with my own mother or my stepmom. Both of them are caring, intelligent, strong women who have always had my back and loved me even when I didn't deserve it.

I need to thank my platonic lifemate/roommate Eric

Goldman for being the only person in the whole world who can tolerate my random but frequent obsessions, the sheer volume of my voice, and the fact that I spend more time with people I make up in my head than with people in the real world.

I can't forget the rest of the Clique—Fifi, Valerie, Greggor, Pete, Matthew, Bronson, and Baby Gels. You guys are the greatest friends in the whole world. Seriously. I have no idea why you're friends with me, but I'm grateful for it every day.

The whole writing process I've gone through to get here has allowed me to meet other fantastic authors, including the Indie Author Mafia: Daniel Arenson, David Dalglish, David McAfee, Robert Duperre, Sean Sweeney, Mike Crane, and Jason Letts. Not only are these guys awesome writers (and if you haven't checked out their books, you definitely should), but they are funny, smart, fiercely loyal, and incredibly nice. They've definitely helped me keep a saner head in times of insanity. I have to give a shout-out to the rest of my author support team: Stacey Wallace Benefiel and Jeff Bryan, and to everyone over at the Kindleboards.

Last but not least, I have to thank my current writing team. People often ask me if I feel bitterness or resentment toward all the agents who passed on my work before, and to that I say a resounding no. It wasn't the right time or the right place, and I needed all those no's to get to the right agent and the right publisher.

From day one, my agent, Steve Axelrod, has been working hard for my books and for me. I daresay he's the greatest agent on the planet. My new publishers at St. Martin's Press, namely, my editor, Rose Hilliard, and the SVP Matthew Shear are so tremendous. Rose has believed in me since long before I signed with them.

And finally, I want to thank you for reading this. Without the support of readers like you, I'd just be a dreamer. You're the ones who make my dreams come true every day.

switched

PROLOGUE

eleven years ago

A couple things made that day stand out more than any other: it was my sixth birthday, and my mother was wielding a knife. Not a tiny steak knife, but some kind of massive butcher knife glinting in the light like in a bad horror movie. She definitely wanted to kill me.

I try to think of the days that led up to that one to see if I missed something about her, but I have no memory of her before then. I have some memories of my childhood, and I can even remember my dad, who died when I was five, but not her.

When I ask my brother, Matt, about her, he always answers with things like, "She's batshit, Wendy. That's all you need to know." He's seven years older than I am, so he remembers things better, but he never wants to talk about it.

We lived in the Hamptons when I was a kid, and my mother was a lady of leisure. She'd hired a live-in nanny to deal with me, but the night before my birthday the nanny had left for a family emergency. My mother was in charge of me, for the first time in her life, and neither of us was happy.

I didn't even want the party. I liked gifts, but I didn't have any friends. The people coming to the party were my mother's friends and their snobby little kids. She had planned some kind of princess tea party I didn't want, but Matt and our maid spent all morning setting it up anyway.

By the time the guests arrived, I'd already ripped off my shoes and plucked the bows from my hair. My mother came down in the middle of opening gifts, surveying the scene with her icy blue eyes.

Her blond hair had been smoothed back, and she had on bright red lipstick that only made her appear paler. She still wore my father's red silk robe, the same way she had since the day he died, but she'd added a necklace and black heels, as if that would make the outfit appropriate.

No one commented on it, but everyone was too busy watching my performance. I complained about every single gift I got. They were all dolls or ponies or some other thing I would never play with.

My mother came into the room, stealthily gliding through the guests to where I sat. I had torn through a box wrapped in pink teddy bears, containing yet another porcelain doll. Instead of showing any gratitude, I started yelling about what a stupid present it was.

Before I could finish, she slapped me sharply across the face.

"You are not my daughter," my mother said, her voice cold. My cheek stung from where she had hit me, and I gaped at her.

The maid quickly redirected the festivities, but the idea percolated in my mother's mind the rest of the afternoon. I think, when she said it, she meant it the way parents do when their child behaves appallingly. But the more she thought, the more it made sense to her.

After an afternoon of similar tantrums on my part, someone decided it was time to have cake. My mother seemed to be taking forever in the kitchen, and I went to check on her. I don't even know why she was the one getting the cake instead of the maid, who was far more maternal.

On the island in the kitchen, a massive chocolate cake covered in pink flowers sat in the middle. My mother stood on the other side, holding a gigantic knife she was using to cut the cake to serve on tiny saucers. Her hair was coming loose from its bobby pins.

"Chocolate?" I wrinkled my nose as she tried to set perfect pieces onto the saucers.

"Yes, Wendy, you like chocolate," my mother informed me.

"No, I don't!" I crossed my arms over my chest. "I hate chocolate! I'm not going to eat it, and you can't make me!"

"Wendy!"

The knife happened to point in my direction, some frosting stuck to the tip, but I wasn't afraid. If I had been, everything might've turned out different. Instead, I wanted to have another one of my tantrums.

"No, no, no! It's my birthday, and I don't want chocolate!" I shouted and stomped my foot on the floor as hard as I could.

"You don't want chocolate?" My mother looked at me, her blue eyes wide and incredulous.

A whole new type of crazy glinted in them, and that's when my fear started to kick in.

"What kind of child are you, Wendy?" She slowly walked around the island, coming toward me. The knife in her hand looked far more menacing than it had a few seconds ago.

"You're certainly not my child. What are you, Wendy?"

Staring at her, I took several steps back. My mother looked maniacal. Her robe had fallen open, revealing her thin collarbones and the black slip she wore underneath. She took a step forward, this time with the knife pointed right at me. I should've screamed or run away, but I felt frozen in place.

"I was pregnant, Wendy! But you're not the child I gave birth to! Where is my child?" Tears formed in her eyes, and I just shook my head. "You probably killed him, didn't you?"

She lunged at me, screaming at me to tell her what I had done with her real baby. I darted out of the way just in time, but she backed me into a corner. I pressed up against the kitchen cupboards with nowhere to go, but she wasn't about to give up.

"Mom!" Matt yelled from the other side of the room.

Her eyes flickered with recognition, the sound of the son she actually loved. For a moment I thought this might stop her, but it only made her realize she was running out of time, so she raised the knife.

Matt dove at her, but not before the blade tore through my dress and slashed across my stomach. Blood stained my clothes as pain shot through me, and I sobbed hysterically.

My mother fought hard against Matt, unwilling to let go of the knife.

"She killed your brother, Matthew!" my mother insisted, looking at him with frantic eyes. "She's a monster! She has to be stopped!"

ONE

home

Drool spilled out across my desk, and I opened my eyes just in time to hear Mr. Meade slam down a textbook. I'd only been at this high school a month, but I'd quickly learned that was his favorite way of waking me up from my naps during his history lecture. I always tried to stay awake, but his monotone voice lulled me into sleeping submission every time.

"Miss Everly?" Mr. Meade snapped. "Miss Everly?"

"Hmm?" I murmured.

I lifted my head and discreetly wiped away the drool. I glanced around to see if anyone had noticed. Most of the class seemed oblivious, except for Finn Holmes. He'd been here a week, so he was the only kid in school newer than me. Whenever I looked at him, he always seemed to be staring at me in a completely unabashed way, as if it were perfectly normal to gawk at me.

There was something oddly still and quiet about him, and I had yet to hear him speak, even though he was in four of my classes. He wore his hair smoothed back, and his eyes were a matching shade of black. His looks were rather striking, but he weirded me out too much for me to find him attractive.

"Sorry to disturb your sleep." Mr. Meade cleared his throat so I would look up at him.

"It's okay," I said.

"Miss Everly, why don't you go down to the principal's office?" Mr. Meade suggested, and I groaned. "Since you seem to be making a habit of sleeping in my class, maybe he can come up with some ideas to help you stay awake."

"I am awake," I insisted.

"Miss Everly—now." Mr. Meade pointed to the door, as if I had forgotten how to leave and needed reminding.

I fixed my gaze on him, and despite how stern his gray eyes looked, I could tell he'd cave easily. Over and over in my head I kept repeating, *I do not need to go the principal's office. You don't want to send me down there. Let me stay in class.* Within seconds his face went lax and his eyes took on a glassy quality.

"You can stay in class and finish the lecture," Mr. Meade said groggily. He shook his head, clearing his eyes. "But next time you're going straight to the office, Miss Everly." He looked confused for a moment, and then launched right back into his history lecture.

I wasn't sure what it was that I had just done exactly—I tried not to think about it enough to name it. About a year ago, I'd discovered that if I thought about something and looked at somebody hard enough, I could get that person to do what I wanted.

As awesome as that sounded, I avoided doing it as much as possible. Partially because I felt like I was crazy for really believing I could do it, even though it worked every time. But mostly because I didn't like it. It made me feel dirty and manipulative.

Mr. Meade went on talking, and I followed along studiously, my guilt making me try harder. I hadn't wanted to do that to him, but I couldn't go to the principal's office. I had just been expelled from my last school, forcing my brother and aunt to uproot their lives again so we could move closer to my new school.

I had honestly tried at the last school, but the Dean's daughter had been intent on making my life miserable. I'd tolerated her taunts and ridicules as best I could until one day she cornered me in the bathroom, calling me every dirty name in the book. Finally, I'd had enough, and I punched her.

The Dean decided to skip their one-strike rule and immediately expelled me. I know in large part it was because I'd resorted to physical violence against his child, but I'm not sure that was it entirely. Where other students were shown leniency, for some reason I never seemed to be.

When class finally ended, I shoved my books in my book bag and left quickly. I didn't like hanging around after I did the mind-control trick. Mr. Meade could change his mind and send me to the office, so I hurried down to my locker.

Bright-colored flyers decorated battered lockers, telling

everyone to join the debate team, try out for the school play, and not to miss the fall semiformal this Friday. I wondered what a "semiformal" consisted of at a public school, not that I'd bothered to ask anyone.

I got to my locker and started switching out my books. Without even looking, I knew Finn was behind me. I glanced over my shoulder and saw him getting a drink from the fountain. Almost as soon as I looked at him, he lifted his head and gazed at me. Like he could sense me too.

The guy was just looking at me, nothing more, but it freaked me out somehow. I'd put up with his stares for a week, trying to avoid confrontation, but I couldn't take it anymore. *He* was the one acting inappropriately, not me. I couldn't get in trouble for just talking to him, right?

"Hey," I said to him, slamming my locker shut. I readjusted the straps on my book bag and walked across the hall to where he stood. "Why are you staring at me?"

"Because you're standing in front of me," Finn replied simply. He looked at me, his eyes framed by dark lashes, without any hint of embarrassment or even denial. It was definitely unnerving.

"You're *always* staring at me," I persisted. "It's weird. You're weird."

"I wasn't trying to fit in."

"Why do you look at me all the time?" I knew I'd simply rephrased my original question, but he still hadn't given me a decent answer.

"Does it bother you?"

"Answer the question." I stood up straighter, trying to make my presence more imposing so he wouldn't realize how much he rattled me.

"Everyone always looks at you," Finn said coolly. "You're very attractive."

That sounded like a compliment, but his voice was emotionless when he said it. I couldn't tell if he was making fun of a vanity I didn't even have, or if he was simply stating facts. Was he flattering me or mocking me? Or maybe something else entirely?

"Nobody stares at me as much as you do," I said as evenly as I could.

"If it bothers you, I'll try and stop," Finn offered.

That was tricky. In order to ask him to stop, I had to admit that he'd gotten to me, and I didn't want to admit that anything got to me. If I lied and said it was fine, then he would just keep on doing it.

"I didn't ask you to stop. I asked you why," I amended.

"I told you why."

"No, you didn't." I shook my head. "You just said that everyone looks at me. You never explained why *you* looked at me."

Almost imperceptibly the corner of his mouth moved up, revealing the hint of a smirk. It wasn't just that I amused him; I sensed he was pleased with me. Like he had challenged me somehow and I had passed.

My stomach did a stupid flip thing I had never felt before, and I swallowed hard, hoping to fight it back.

"I look at you because I can't look away," Finn answered finally.

I was struck completely mute, trying to think of some kind of clever response, but my mind refused to work. Realizing that my jaw had gone slack and I probably looked like an awestruck schoolgirl, I hurried to collect myself.

"That's kind of creepy," I said at last, but my words came out weak instead of accusatory.

"I'll work on being less creepy, then," Finn promised.

I had called him out on being creepy, and it didn't faze him at all. He didn't stammer an apology or flush with shame. He just kept looking at me evenly. Most likely he was a damn sociopath, and for whatever reason, I found that endearing.

I couldn't come up with a witty retort, but the bell rang, saving me from the rest of that awkward conversation. Finn just nodded, thus ending our exchange, and turned down the hall to go to his next class. Thankfully, it was one of the few he didn't have with me.

True to his word, Finn wasn't creepy the rest of the day. Every time I saw him, he was doing something inoffensive that didn't involve looking at me. I still got that feeling that he watched me when I had my back to him, but it wasn't anything I could prove.

When the final bell rang at three o'clock, I tried to be the first one out. My older brother, Matt, picked me up from school, at least until he found a job, and I didn't want to keep him waiting. Besides that, I didn't want to deal with any more contact with Finn Holmes.

I quickly made my way to the parking lot at the edge of the school lawn. Scanning for Matt's Prius, I absently started to chew my thumbnail. I had this weird feeling, almost like a shiver running down my back. I turned around, half expecting to see Finn staring at me, but there was nothing.

I tried to shake it off, but my heart raced faster. This felt like something more sinister than a boy from school. I was still staring off, trying to decide what had me freaked out, when a loud honk startled me, making me jump. Matt sat a few cars down, looking at me over the top of his sunglasses.

"Sorry." I opened the car door and hopped in, where he looked me over for a moment. "What?"

"You looked nervous. Did something happen?" Matt asked, and I sighed. He took his whole big brother thing way too seriously.

"No, nothing happened. School sucks," I said, brushing him off. "Let's go home."

"Seat belt," Matt commanded, and I did as I was told.

Matt had always been quiet and reserved, thinking everything over carefully before making a decision. He was a stark contrast to me in every way, except that we were both relatively short. I was small, with a decidedly pretty, feminine face. My brown hair was an untamed mess of curls that I kept up in loose buns.

He kept his sandy blond hair trim and neat, and his eyes were the same shade of blue as our mother's. Matt wasn't overtly muscular, but he was sturdy and athletic from working out a lot. He had a sense of duty, like he had to make sure he was strong enough to defend us against anything.

"How is school going?" Matt asked.

"Great. Fantastic. Amazing."

"Are you even going to graduate this year?" Matt had long since stopped judging my school record. A large part of him didn't even care if I graduated from high school.

"Who knows?" I shrugged.

Everywhere I went, kids never seemed to like me. Even before I said or did anything. I felt like I had something wrong with me and everyone knew it. I tried getting along with the other kids, but I'd only take getting pushed for so long before I pushed back. Principals and deans were quick to expel me, probably sensing the same things the kids did.

I just didn't belong.

"Just to warn you, Maggie's taking it seriously," Matt said. "She's set on you graduating this year, from this school."

"Delightful." I sighed. Matt couldn't care less about my schooling, but my aunt Maggie was a different story. And since she was my legal guardian, her opinion mattered more. "What's her plan?"

"Maggie's thinking bedtimes," Matt informed me with a smirk. As if sending me to bed early would somehow prevent me from getting in a fight.

"I'm almost eighteen!" I groaned. "What is she thinking?"

"You've got four more months until you're eighteen," Matt corrected me sharply, and his hand tightened on the steering wheel. He suffered from serious delusions that I was going to run away as soon as I turned eighteen, and nothing I could say would convince him otherwise.

"Yeah, whatever." I waved it off. "Did you tell her she's insane?"

"I figured she'd hear it enough from you." Matt grinned at me.

"So did you find a job?" I asked tentatively, and he shook his head.

He'd just finished an internship over the summer, working with a great architecture firm. He'd said it didn't bother him, moving to a town without much call for a promising young architect, but I couldn't help feeling guilty about it.

"This is a pretty town," I said, looking out the window.

We approached our new house, buried on an average suburban street among a slew of maples and elms. It actually seemed like a boring small town, but I'd promised I'd make the best of it. I really wanted to. I didn't think I could handle disappointing Matt anymore.

"So you're really gonna try here?" Matt asked, looking over at me. We had pulled up in the driveway next to the butter-colored Victorian that Maggie had bought last month.

"I already am," I insisted with a smile. "I've been talking to this Finn kid." Sure, I'd talked to him only once, and I wouldn't even remotely count him as a friend, but I had to tell Matt something.

"Look at you. Making your very first friend." Matt shut off the car's engine and looked at me with veiled amusement.

"Yeah, well, how many friends do you have?" I countered. He just shook his head and got out of the car, and I quickly followed him. "That's what I thought."

"I've had friends before. Gone to parties. Kissed a girl. The whole nine yards," Matt said as he went through the side door into the house.

"So you say." I kicked off my shoes as soon as we walked into the kitchen, which was still in various stages of unpacking. As many times as we'd moved, everyone had gotten tired of the whole process, so we tended to live out of boxes. "I've only seen one of these alleged girls."

"Yeah, 'cause when I brought her home, you set her dress on fire! While she was wearing it!" Matt pulled off his sunglasses and looked at me severely.

"Oh, come on. That was an accident and you know it."

"So you say." Matt opened the fridge.

"Anything good in there?" I asked and hopped onto the kitchen island. "I'm famished."

"Probably nothing you'd like." Matt started sifting through the contents of the fridge, but he was right.

I was a notoriously picky eater. While I had never purposely sought out the life of a vegan, I seemed to hate most things that had either meat in them or man-made synthetics. It was odd and incredibly irritating for the people who tried to feed me.

Maggie appeared in the doorway to the kitchen, flecks of paint stuck in her blond curls. Layers of multicolored paint covered her ratty overalls, proof of all the rooms she had redecorated over the years. She had her hands on her hips, so Matt shut the fridge door to give her his full attention.

"I thought I told you to tell me when you got home," Maggie said.

"We're home?" Matt offered.

"I can see that." Maggie rolled her eyes, and then turned her attention to me. "How was school?"

"Good," I said. "I'm trying harder."

"We've heard that before." Maggie gave me a weary look.

I hated it when she gave me that look. I hated knowing that I made her feel that way, that I had disappointed her that much. She did so much for me, and the only thing she asked of me was that I at least *try* at school. I had to make it work this time.

"Well, yeah . . . but . . ." I looked to Matt for help. "I mean, I actually promised Matt this time. And I'm making a friend."

"She's talking to some guy named Finn," Matt said corroborating my story.

"Like a *guy* guy?" Maggie smiled too broadly for my liking.

The idea of Finn being a romantic prospect hadn't crossed Matt's mind before, and he suddenly tensed up, looking at me with a new scrutiny. Fortunately for him, that idea hadn't crossed my mind either.

"No, nothing like that." I shook my head. "He's just a guy, I guess. I don't know. He seems nice enough."

"Nice?" Maggie gushed. "That's a start! And much better than that anarchist with the tattoo on his face."

"We weren't friends," I corrected her. "I just stole his motorcycle. While he happened to be on it."

Nobody had ever really believed that story, but it was true, and it was how I figured out that I could get people to do things just by thinking it. I had been thinking that I really wanted his bike, and then I was looking at him and he was listening to me, even though I hadn't said anything. Then I was driving his motorcycle.

"So this really is gonna be a new start for us?" Maggie couldn't hold back her excitement any longer. Her blue eyes started to well with happy tears. "Wendy, this is just so wonderful! We can really make a home here!"

I wasn't nearly as excited about it as she was, though I couldn't help but hope she was right. It would be nice to feel like I was home somewhere.

TWO

"if you leave"

Our new house also supplied us with a large vegetable garden, which thrilled Maggie endlessly. Matt and I were much less thrilled. While I loved the outdoors, I'd never been a big fan of manual labor.

Autumn was settling in, and Maggie insisted that we had to clear the garden of its dying vegetation to prepare it for planting in the spring. She used words like "rototiller" and "mulch," and I hoped Matt would deal with them. When it came to work, I usually just handed Matt the necessary tools and kept him company.

"So when are you hauling out the rototiller?" I asked, watching as Matt tore up dead vines. I'm not sure what they used to be, but they reminded me of grapevines. While Matt pulled things up, my job was to hold the wheelbarrow so he could throw them in.

"We don't have a rototiller." He gave me a look as he tossed the dead plants into the wheelbarrow. "You know, you could be helping me with this. You don't need to physically hold that at all times."

"I take my job very seriously, so I think it'd be better if I did," I said, and he rolled his eyes.

Matt continued grumbling, but I tuned him out. A warm fall breeze blew over us, and I closed my eyes, breathing it in. It smelled wonderfully sweet, like fresh-cut corn and grass and wet leaves. A nearby wind chime tinkled lightly, and it made me dread winter coming and taking this all away.

I'd been lost in the moment, enjoying the perfection, but something snapped me out of it. It was hard to describe exactly what it was, but the hair on the back of my neck stood up. The air suddenly felt chillier, and I knew somebody was watching us.

I looked around, trying to see who it was, and this weird fear ran over me. We had a privacy fence at the back of the yard, and a thick row of hedges blocking our house on either side. I scanned them, searching for any signs of crouching figures or spying eyes. I didn't see anything, but the feeling didn't go away.

"If you're gonna be out here, you should at least wear shoes," Matt said, pulling me from my thoughts. He stood up, stretching his back, and looked at me. "Wendy?"

"I'm fine," I answered absently.

I thought I saw movement around the side of the house, so I went over there. Matt called my name, but I ignored him. When I rounded the house, I stopped short. Finn Holmes stood on the sidewalk, but oddly enough, he wasn't looking at me. He was staring at something down the street, something out of my sight.

As strange as it sounds, as soon as I saw him, the anxiety I'd felt started to subside. My first thought should've been that it was him causing my uneasiness, since he was the one who always stared at me in such a creepy fashion. But it wasn't.

Whatever I'd felt in the backyard, it wasn't because of him. When he stared, he made me self-conscious. But this . . . this made my skin crawl.

After a second, Finn turned to look back at me. His dark eyes rested on me a moment, his face expressionless as always. Then, without saying a word, he turned and walked off in the direction he'd been staring.

"Wendy, what's going on?" Matt asked, coming up behind me.

"I thought I saw something." I shook my head.

"Yeah?" He looked at me hard, concern etched on his face. "Are you okay?"

"Yeah. I'm fine." I forced a smile and turned to the backyard. "Come on. We've got a lot of work to do if I'm gonna make it to that dance."

"You're still on that kick?" Matt grimaced.

Telling Maggie about the dance may have been the worst idea I've ever had, and my life is made up almost entirely of bad ideas. I hadn't wanted to go, but as soon as she'd heard about it, she decided it would be the most fantastic thing ever. I'd never gone to a dance before, but she was so excited about it, I let her have this small victory.

With the dance at seven, she figured she had enough time to finish the coat of paint in the bathroom. Matt had started to voice his complaints, mostly about my interacting with the opposite sex, but Maggie shut him down. To keep him from getting in her way, she ordered him to finish the yardwork. He complied only because he knew that there was no stopping Maggie this time.

Despite Matt's attempts to slow us down, we finished the garden pretty quickly, and I went inside to get ready. Maggie sat on the bed and watched me as I rummaged through my closet, offering suggestions and comments on everything. This included an endless stream of questions about Finn. Matt would grunt or scoff every now and then at my answers, so I knew he was listening nearby.

Once I had decided on a simple blue dress that Maggie insisted looked amazing on me, I let her do my hair. My hair refused to cooperate with anything I tried to do it, and while it wasn't exactly obedient for Maggie, she outwitted it. She left some of it down, so the curls framed my face, and pulled the rest of it back.

When Matt saw me, he looked really pissed off and a little awed, so I knew that I must look pretty awesome.

Maggie gave me a ride to the dance, because we both weren't convinced that Matt would let me out of the car. He kept insisting on a nine o'clock curfew, even though the dance went until ten. I thought I'd be back well before that, but Maggie told me to take all the time I wanted.

My only experience with dances was what I had seen on

TV, but reality wasn't that far off. The theme appeared to be "Crepe Paper in the Gymnasium," and they had mastered it perfectly.

The school colors were white and navy blue, so white and navy blue streamers covered everything, along with matching balloons. For romantic lighting, they had strung everything with white Christmas lights.

Refreshments covered a table on the side, and the band playing on the makeshift stage under the basketball hoop wasn't that bad. Their set list appeared to include only songs from the films of John Hughes, and I arrived in the middle of a "Weird Science" cover.

The biggest difference between real life and what films had taught me was that nobody actually danced. A group of girls stood directly in front of the stage swooning over the lead singer, but otherwise the floor was mostly empty.

People sat scattered all over the bleachers, and, attempting to fit in, I sat in the first row. I kicked off my shoes immediately, because for the most part I hate shoes. With nothing else to do, I resorted to people-watching. As the night wore on, I found myself feeling increasingly lonely and bored.

Kids actually started dancing as the gymnasium filled up, and the band moved on to some kind of Tears for Fears medley. I decided that I'd been here long enough, and I was planning my escape when Finn pushed through the doors.

Wearing a slim-fitting black dress shirt and dark jeans, he looked good. He had the sleeves rolled up and an extra button undone on his shirt, and I wondered why I never realized how attractive he was before.

His eyes met mine, and he walked over to me, surprising me with his direct approach. As often as he seemed to be watching me, he'd never initiated contact before. Not even today, when he'd walked past my house.

"I didn't peg you for the dancing kind," Finn commented when he reached me.

"I was thinking the same thing about you," I said, and he shrugged.

Finn sat down on the bleachers next to me, and I sat up a bit straighter. He glanced over at me but didn't say anything. Already he looked annoyed, and he'd just gotten here. An awkward silence settled over us, and I hurried to fill it.

"You arrived awfully late. Couldn't decide what to wear?" I teased.

"I had stuff with work," Finn explained vaguely.

"Oh? Do you work somewhere near my house?"

"Something like that." Finn sighed, clearly eager to change the subject. "Have you been dancing?"

"Nope," I said. "Dancing is for suckers."

"Is that why you came to a dance?" Finn looked down at my bare feet. "You didn't wear the right shoes for dancing. You didn't even wear the right shoes for walking."

"I don't like shoes," I told him defensively. My hem landed above my knees, but I tried to pull it down, as if I could get it to cover my bare-feet embarrassment.

Finn gave me a look I couldn't read at all, then went back to staring at the people dancing in front of us. By now the floor was almost entirely covered. Kids still dotted the bleachers, but they were mostly the headgear kids and the ones with dandruff.

"So this is what you're doing? Watching other people dance?" Finn asked.

"I guess." I shrugged.

Finn leaned forward, resting his elbows on his knees, and I moved so I was sitting up straighter. My dress was strapless, and I rubbed at my bare arms, feeling naked and uncomfortable.

"You cold?" Finn glanced over at me, and I shook my head. "I think it's cold in here."

"It's a little chilly," I admitted. "But nothing I can't handle."

Finn would barely look at me, which was a complete 180 from his constant creepy staring. Somehow, I found this worse. I don't know why he had even come to the dance if he hated it so much, and I was about to ask him that when he turned to look at me.

"You wanna dance?" he asked flatly.

"Are you asking me to dance with you?"

"Yeah." Finn shrugged.

"Yeah?" I shrugged sarcastically. "You really know how to sweet-talk a girl."

His mouth crept up in a hint of a smile, and that officially won me over. I hated myself for it.

"Fair enough." Finn stood up and extended his hand to me. "Would you, Wendy Everly, care to dance with me?"

"Sure." I placed my hand in his, trying to ignore how warm his skin felt and the rapid beating of my own heart, and got to my feet.

Naturally, the band had just started playing "If You Leave" by OMD, making me feel like I had walked into a perfect movie moment. Finn led me to the dance floor and placed his hand on the small of my back. I put one hand on his shoulder while he took my other hand in his.

I was so close to him I could feel the delicious heat radiating from his body. His eyes were the darkest eyes I had ever seen, and they were looking at only me. For one unspoiled minute, everything in life felt perfect in a way that it never had before. Like there should be a spotlight on us, the only two people in the world.

Then something changed in Finn's expression, something I couldn't read, but it definitely got darker.

"You're not a very good dancer," Finn commented in that emotionless way of his.

"Thanks?" I said unsurely. We were mostly just swaying in a small circle, and I wasn't sure how I could screw that up, plus we seemed to be dancing the exact same way as everyone else. Maybe he was joking, so I tried to sound playful when I said, "You're not that great yourself."

"I'm a wonderful dancer," Finn replied matter-of-factly. "I just need a better partner."

"Okay." I stopped looking up at him and stared straight ahead over his shoulder. "I don't know what to say to that."

"Why do you need to say anything to that? It's not necessary for you to speak incessantly. Although I'm not sure you've realized that yet." Finn's tone had gotten icy, but I still danced with him because I couldn't come up with enough sense to walk away.

"I've barely said anything. I've just been dancing with you." I swallowed hard and didn't appreciate how crushed I felt. "And you asked me to dance! It's not like you're doing me a favor."

"Oh, come on," Finn said with an exaggerated eye roll. "The desperation was coming off you in waves. You were all but begging to dance with me. I *am* doing you a favor."

"Wow." I stepped back from him, feeling confused tears threatening and this awful pain growing inside of me. "I don't know what I did to you!" His expression softened, but it was too late.

"Wendy—"

"No!" I cut him off. Everyone nearby had stopped dancing to stare at us, but I didn't care. "You are a total dick!"

"Wendy!" Finn repeated, but I turned and hurried through the crowd.

There was nothing in the world I wanted more than to get out of here. Patrick, a kid from biology class, stood by the punch bowl, and I rushed over to him. We weren't friends, but he'd been one of the few kids here who had been nice to me. When he saw me, he looked confused and concerned, but at least I had his attention.

"I want to leave. *Now,*" I hissed at Patrick.

"What—" Before Patrick could ask what had happened, Finn appeared at my side.

"Look, Wendy, I'm sorry," Finn apologized sincerely, which only pissed me off more.

"I don't wanna hear anything from you!" I snapped and refused to look at him. Patrick looked back and forth between the two of us, trying to decipher what was going on.

"Wendy," Finn floundered. "I didn't mean—"

"I said I don't want to hear it!" I glared at him, but only for a second.

"Maybe you should let the guy apologize," Patrick suggested gently.

"No, I shouldn't." Then, like a small child, I stomped my foot. "I want to go!"

Finn stood just to the side of us, watching me intently. I clenched my fists and looked at Patrick directly in his eyes. I didn't like doing this when people watched, but I had to get out of here. I kept chanting what I wanted over and over in my head. *I want to go home, just take me home, please, please, just take me home. I can't be here anymore.*

Patrick's face started to change, his expression growing relaxed and faraway. Blinking, he stared blankly at me for a minute.

"I think I should just take you home," Patrick said groggily.

"What did you just do?" Finn asked, narrowing his eyes.

My heart stopped beating, and for one terrifying second

I was certain he knew what I'd done. But then I realized that'd be impossible, so I shook it off.

"I didn't do anything!" I snapped and looked back at Patrick. "Let's get out of here."

"Wendy!" Finn said, giving me a hard look. "Do you even know what you just did?"

"I didn't do anything!" I grabbed Patrick's wrist, dragging him toward the exit, and, much to my relief, Finn didn't follow.

In the car, Patrick tried to ask me what had happened with Finn, but I wouldn't talk about it. He drove around for a while, so I was reasonably calm by the time he dropped me off, and I couldn't thank him enough for it.

Matt and Maggie were waiting by the door for me, but I barely said a word to them. That freaked out Matt, who started threatening to kill every boy at the dance, but I managed to reassure him that I was fine and nothing bad had happened. Finally, he let me go up to my room, where I proceeded to throw myself onto the bed and not cry.

The night swirled in my head like some bizarre dream. I couldn't get a read on the way I felt about Finn. Most of the time he seemed weird and bordering on creepy. But then we had that glorious moment when we danced together, before he completely shattered it.

Even now, after the way he'd treated me, I couldn't shake how wonderful it had felt being in his arms like that. In general, I never liked being touched or being close to people, but I loved the way I had felt with him.

His hand strong and warm on the small of my back and the

soft heat that flowed from him. When he had looked at me then, so sincerely, I had thought . . .

I don't know what I had thought, but it turned out to be a lie.

Strangest of all, he seemed to be able to tell that I had done something to Patrick. I didn't know how anyone could know. I wasn't even sure that I was doing it. But a normal, sane person wouldn't even suspect that I could do that.

I could suddenly explain all Finn's odd behavior: he was completely insane.

What it came down to was that I knew nothing about him. I could barely tell when he was mocking me and when he was being sincere. Sometimes I thought he was into me, and other times he obviously hated me.

There wasn't anything I knew about him for sure. Except that despite everything, I was starting to like him.

Sometime in the night, after I had changed into sweats and a tank top, and after I had spent a very long time tossing and turning, I must've finally fallen asleep. When I woke up, it was still dark out, and I had drying tears on my cheeks. I had been crying in my sleep, which seemed unfair, since I never let myself cry when I was awake.

I rolled over and glanced at the alarm clock. Its angry numbers declared it was a little after three in the morning, and I wasn't sure why I was awake. I flicked on my bedside lamp, casting everything in a warm glow, and I saw something that scared me so badly, my heart stopped.

THREE

stalker

A figure was crouched outside my window, my *second-story* window. Admittedly, a small roof was right outside of it, but a person standing on it was about the last thing I expected to see. On top of that, it wasn't just anybody.

Finn Holmes looked hopeful, but not at all ashamed or frightened at having been caught peeping into my room. He knocked gently at the glass, and belatedly I realized that's what had woken me up.

He hadn't been peeping intentionally; he'd been trying to get my attention so I could let him into my room. So that was *slightly* less creepy, I supposed.

For some reason, I got up and went over to the window. I caught sight of myself in my mirror, and I did not look good. My pajamas were of the sad, comfy variety. My hair was a total mess, and my eyes were red and puffy.

I knew I shouldn't let Finn in my room. He was probably a

sociopath and he didn't make me feel good about myself. Besides, Matt would kill us both if he caught him in here.

So I stood in front of the window, my arms crossed, and glared at him. I was pissed off and hurt, and I wanted him to know it. Normally I prided myself on not getting hurt, let alone telling people they had hurt me. But this time I thought it would be better if he knew that he was a dick.

"I'm sorry!" Finn said loud enough so his voice would carry through the glass, and his eyes echoed the sentiment. He looked genuinely remorseful, but I wasn't ready to accept his apology yet. Maybe I never would.

"What do you want?" I demanded as loudly as I could without Matt hearing me.

"To apologize. And to talk to you." Finn looked earnestly at me. "It's important."

I chewed my lip, torn between what I knew I should do and what I really wanted to do.

"Please," he said.

Against my better judgment, I opened the window. I left the screen in place and took a step back so I was sitting on the end of my bed. Finn pulled the screen out easily, and I wondered how much experience he had sneaking in girls' windows.

Carefully, he climbed into my room, shutting the window behind him. He glanced over my room, making me feel self-conscious. It was rather messy, with clothes and books strewn about, but most of my stuff sat in two large cardboard boxes and a trunk on one side of my room.

"So what do you want?" I said, trying to drag his attention back to me and away from my things.

"I'm sorry," Finn repeated, with that same sincerity he had demonstrated outside. "Tonight I was cruel." He looked away thoughtfully before continuing. "I don't want to hurt you."

"So why did you?" I asked sharply.

Licking his lips, he shifted his feet and exhaled deeply. He had intentionally been mean to me. It wasn't some accident because he was cocky or unaware of how he treated people. Everything he did was meticulous and purposeful.

"I don't want to lie to you, and I promise you that I haven't," Finn answered carefully. "And I'll leave it at that."

"I think I have a right to know what's going on," I snapped and then remembered that Matt and Maggie were sleeping down the hall and hastily lowered my voice. "And what you're doing at my window in the middle of the night."

"I came here to tell you," Finn assured me. "To explain everything. This isn't the way we normally do things, so I had to make a phone call before I came to see you. I was trying to figure things out. That's why it's so late. I'm sorry."

"Call who? Figure out what?" I took a step back.

"It's about what you did tonight, with Patrick," Finn said gently, and the pit in my stomach grew.

"I didn't do anything with Patrick." I shook my head. "I have no idea what you're talking about."

"You really don't?" Finn eyed me suspiciously, unable to decide if he believed me or not.

"I—I don't know what you're talking about," I stammered. A chill ran over me and I started feeling vaguely nauseous.

"Yeah, you do." Finn nodded solemnly. "You just don't know what it is."

"I'm just very . . . convincing," I said without any real confidence. I didn't want to keep denying it, but talking about it, giving credibility to my own private insanity, scared me even more.

"Yeah, you are," Finn admitted. "But you can't do that again. Not like you did tonight."

"I didn't do anything! And even if I did, who are you to try and stop me?" Something else flashed in my mind, and I looked at him. "Can you even stop me?"

"You can't use it on me now." Finn shook his head absently. "It's really not that major, especially the way you're using it."

"What is it?" I asked quietly, finding it hard to make my mouth work. I let go of any pretense I had that I didn't know what was going on, and my shoulders sagged.

"It's called *persuasion*," Finn said emphatically, as if that were somehow much different from what I had been saying. "Technically, it would be called psychokinesis. It's a form of mind control."

I found it disturbing how matter-of-factly he talked about all of this, as if we were talking about biology homework instead of the possibility that I possessed some kind of paranormal ability.

"How do you know?" I asked. "How do you know what I have? How did you even know I was doing it?"

He shrugged. "Experience."

"What does that mean?"

"It's complicated." He rubbed the back of his head and stared at the floor. "You're not going to believe me. But I haven't lied to you, and I never will. Do you believe that, at least?"

"I think so," I replied tentatively. Considering we'd only spoken a handful of times, he hadn't had much of an opportunity to lie to me.

"That's a start." Finn took a deep breath, and I nervously pulled at a strand of my hair as I watched him. Almost sheepishly, he said, "You're a changeling." He looked expectantly at me, waiting for some kind of dramatic reaction.

"I don't even know what that is. Isn't it like a movie with Angelina Jolie or something?" I shook my head. "I don't know what it means."

"You don't know what it is?" Finn smirked. "Of course you don't know what it is. That would make it all too easy if you had even the slightest inkling about what is going on."

"It would, wouldn't it?" I agreed.

"A changeling is a child that has been secretly exchanged for another."

The room got this weird, foggy quality to it. My mind flashed to my mother, and the things she had screamed at me. I had always felt I didn't belong, but at the same time I'd never consciously believed it was true.

But now, suddenly, Finn confirmed all the suspicions I had been harboring. All the horrible things my mother had told me were true.

"But how . . ." Dazedly, I shook my head, then one key question sprang to mind. "How would you know that? How could you possibly know that? Even if it were true?"

"Well . . ." Finn watched me for a moment as I struggled to let everything sink in. "You're Trylle. It's what we do."

"Trylle? Is that like your last name or something?" I asked.

"No." Finn smiled. "Trylle is the name of our 'tribe,' if you will." He rubbed the side of his temple. "This is hard to explain. We are, um, trolls."

"You're telling me that I'm a *troll*?" I raised one eyebrow, and finally decided that he must be insane.

Nothing about me resembled a pink-haired doll with a jewel in its stomach or a creepy little monster that lived under a bridge. Admittedly, I was kind of short, but Finn was at least six feet tall.

"You're thinking of trolls the way they've been misrepresented, obviously," Finn hurried to explain. "That's why we prefer Trylle. You don't get any of that silly 'Billy Goats Gruff' imagery. But now I have you staring at me like I have totally lost my mind."

"You have lost your mind." I trembled in shock and fear, not knowing what to think. I should've thrown him out of my room, but then again, I never should've let him in.

"Okay. Think about it, Wendy." Finn moved on to trying to reason with me, as if his idea had real merit. "You've never really fit in anywhere. You have a quick temper. You're very intelligent and a picky eater. You hate shoes. Your hair, while lovely, is hard to control. You have dark brown eyes, dark brown hair."

"What does the color of my eyes have to do with anything?" I retorted. "Or any of those things—"

"Earth tones. Our eyes and hair are always earth tones," Finn answered. "And oftentimes our skin has almost a greenish hue to it."

"I'm not green!" I looked at my skin anyway, just to be sure, but there was nothing green about it.

"It's very faint, when people do have it," Finn said. "But no, you don't. Not really. Sometimes it gets more predominant after you've been living around other Trylle for a while."

"I am not a troll," I insisted fiercely. "That doesn't even make any sense. It doesn't . . . So I'm angry and different. Most teenagers feel that way. It doesn't mean anything." I combed through my hair, as if to prove it wasn't that wild. My fingers got caught in it, proving his point rather than mine, and I sighed. "That doesn't mean anything."

"I'm not just guessing here, Wendy," Finn informed me with a wry smile. "I know who you are. I know you're Trylle. That's why I came looking for you."

"You were looking for me?" My jaw dropped. "That's why you stare at me all the time in school. You're stalking me!"

"I'm not *stalking*." Finn raised a hand defensively. "I'm a tracker. It's my job. I find the changelings and bring them back."

Of all the major things that were wrong with this situation, the thing that bothered me most was when he said it was his job. There hadn't ever been any attraction between us. He had just been doing his job, and that meant following me.

He was stalking me, and I was only upset about it because he was doing it because he had to, not because he wanted to.

"I know this is a lot to take in," Finn admitted. "I'm sorry. We usually wait until you're older. But if you're already using persuasion, then I think you need to head back to the compound. You're developing early."

"I'm what?" I just stared up at him.

"Developing. The psychokinesis," Finn said as if it should be obvious. "Trylle have varying degrees of ability. Yours are clearly more advanced."

"They have *abilities*?" I swallowed "Do you have abilities?" Something new occurred to me, twisting my insides. "Can you read my mind?"

"No, I can't read minds."

"Are you lying?"

"I won't lie to you," Finn promised.

If he hadn't been so attractive standing in front of me in my bedroom, it would've been easier to ignore him. And if I hadn't felt this ludicrous connection with him, I would've thrown him out right away.

As it was, it was hard to look into his eyes and not believe him. But after everything he had been saying, I couldn't believe him. If I believed him, that meant my mother was right. That I was evil and a monster. I had spent my whole life trying to prove her wrong, trying to be good and do the right things, and I wouldn't let this be true.

"I can't believe you."

"Wendy." Finn sounded exasperated. "You know I'm not lying."

"I do." I nodded. "Not intentionally anyway. But after what I went through with my mother, I'm not ready to let another crazy person into my life. So you have to go."

"Wendy!" His expression was one of complete disbelief.

"Did you really expect any other reaction from me?" I stood up, keeping my arms crossed firmly in front of me, and I tried to look as confident as I possibly could. "Did you think you could treat me like shit at a dance, then sneak into my room in the middle of the night and tell me that I'm a troll with magical powers, and I'd just be like, yeah, that sounds right?

"And what did you even hope to accomplish with this?" I asked him directly. "What were you trying to get me to do?"

"You're supposed to come with me back to the compound," Finn said, defeated.

"And you thought I would just follow you right out?" I smirked to hide the fact that I was really tempted to do that. Even if he was insane.

"They usually do," Finn replied in a way that completely unnerved me.

Really, that answer was what completely lost me. I might have been willing to follow his delusions because I liked him more than I should, but when he made it sound like there had been lots of other girls willing to do the same thing before me, it really turned me off. Crazy, I could deal with. Slutty, not so much.

"You need to go," I told him firmly.

"You need to think about this. This is obviously different for you than it is for everyone else, and I understand that. So I'll give you time to think about it." He turned and opened the window. "But there is a place where you belong. There is a place where you have family. So just think about it."

"Definitely." I gave him a plastic smile.

He started to lean out the window, and I walked closer to him so I'd be able to shut the window behind him. Then he stopped and turned to look at me. He felt dangerously close, his eyes full of something smoldering just below the surface.

When he looked at me like that, he took all the air from my lungs, and I wondered if this was how Patrick felt when I persuaded him.

"I almost forgot," Finn said softly, his face so close to mine I could feel his breath on my cheeks. "You looked *really* beautiful tonight." He stayed that way a moment longer, completely captivating me, then he turned abruptly and climbed out the window.

I stood there, barely remembering to breathe, as I watched him grab a branch of the tree next to my house and swing down to the ground. A cool breeze fluttered in, so I closed the window and pulled my curtains shut tightly.

Feeling dazed, I staggered back to my bed and collapsed on it. I had never felt more bewildered in my entire life.

I barely got any sleep. What little I had was filled with dreams of little green trolls coming to take me away. I lay in bed for a while after I woke up. Everything felt muddled and confusing.

I couldn't let myself believe that anything Finn had said

made sense, but I couldn't discount how badly I wanted it to be true. I had never felt like I belonged anywhere. Until recently, Matt had been the only person I ever felt any connection with.

Lying in bed at six-thirty in the morning, I could hear the morning birds chirping loudly outside my window. Quietly, I got up and crept downstairs. I didn't want to wake Matt and Maggie this early. Matt got up early every school day to make sure I didn't oversleep and then drove me to school, so this was his only time to sleep in.

For some reason, I felt desperate to find something to prove we were family. All my life I had been trying to prove the opposite, but as soon as Finn had mentioned that it might be a real possibility, I felt oddly protective.

Matt and Maggie had sacrificed everything for me. I had never been that good to either of them, yet they still loved me unconditionally. Wasn't that evidence enough?

I crouched on the floor next to one of the cardboard boxes in the living room. The word "memorabilia" was scrawled across it in Maggie's pretty cursive.

Underneath Matt's and Maggie's diplomas and lots of Matt's graduation pictures, I found several photo albums. Based on the covers, I could tell which ones had been Maggie's purchases. Maggie picked albums covered in flowers and polka dots and happy things.

My mother only had one, and it was adorned with a faded brown, nondescript cover. There was also a damaged blue baby book. Carefully, I pulled it out, along with my mom's photo album.

My baby book had been blue because all the ultrasounds had said I was a boy. Tucked in the back of the book there was even a cracked ultrasound photo where the doctor had circled what they had incorrectly assumed was my penis.

Most families would have made some kind of joke about that, but not mine. My mother had just looked at me with disdain and said, "You were supposed to be a boy."

Most mothers start out filling the beginning of a baby book, but then forget as time goes on. Not mine. She'd never written a thing in it. The handwriting was either my father's or Maggie's.

My footprints were in there, along with my measurements and a copy of my birth certificate. I touched it delicately, proving that my birth was real and tangible. I had been born into this family, whether my mother liked it or not.

"What are you doing, kiddo?" Maggie asked softly from behind me, and I jumped a little. "Sorry. I didn't mean to scare you." Wrapped in her housecoat, Maggie yawned and ran a hand through her sleep-disheveled hair.

"It's okay." I tried to cover up my baby book, feeling as if I had been caught doing something naughty. "What are you doing up?"

"I could ask you the same thing," Maggie replied with a smile. She sat down on the floor next to me, leaning against the back of the couch. "I heard you get up." She nodded at the pile of photo albums on my lap. "You feeling nostalgic?"

"I don't know, really."

"What are you looking at?" Maggie leaned over so she

could peer at the photo album. "Oh, that's an old one. You were just a baby then."

I flipped open the book and it went chronologically, so the first few pages were of Matt when he was little. Maggie looked at it with me, making clucking sounds at my dad. She gently touched his picture once and commented on how handsome her brother was.

Even though everyone agreed that my father had been a good guy, we rarely talked about him. It was our way of not talking about my mother and not talking about what had happened. Nothing before my sixth birthday mattered, and that just happened to include every memory of Dad.

Most of the pictures in the album were of Matt, and there were many with my mother, my dad, and Matt looking ridiculously happy. All three of them had blond hair and blue eyes. They looked like something out of a Hallmark commercial.

Toward the end of the book, everything changed. As soon as pictures of me started to appear, my mother began looking surly and sullen. In the very first picture, I was only a few days old. I wore an outfit with blue trains all over it, and my mother glared at me.

"You were such a cute baby!" Maggie laughed. "But I remember that. You wore boys' clothes for the first month because they were so sure you were going to be a boy."

"That explains a lot," I mumbled, and Maggie laughed. "Why didn't they just get me new clothes? They had the money for it."

"Oh, I don't know." Maggie sighed, looking faraway. "It

was something your mother wanted." She shook her head. "She was weird about things."

"What was my name supposed to be?"

"Um . . ." Maggie snapped her fingers when she remembered. "Michael! Michael Conrad Everly. But then you were a girl, so that ruined that."

"How did they get Wendy from that?" I wrinkled my nose. "Michelle would make more sense."

"Well . . ." Maggie looked up at the ceiling, thinking. "Your mother refused to name you, and your father . . . I guess he couldn't think of anything. So Matt named you."

"Oh, yeah." I faintly remembered hearing that before. "But why Wendy?"

"He liked the name Wendy." Maggie shrugged. "He was a big *Peter Pan* fan, which is ironic because *Peter Pan* is the story of a boy who never grows up, and Matt was a boy who was always grown up." I smirked at that. "Maybe that's why he's always been so protective of you. He named you. You were his."

My eyes settled on a picture of me from when I was about two or three with Matt holding me in his arms. I lay on my stomach with my arms and legs outstretched, while he grinned like a fool. He used to run me around the house like that, pretending that I was flying, and call me "Wendy Bird," and I would laugh.

As I got older, it became more and more apparent that I looked nothing like my family. My dark eyes and frizzy hair contrasted completely with theirs.

In every picture with me, my mother looked utterly exasperated, as if she had spent the half hour before the picture was taken fighting with me. But then again, she probably had. I had always been contrary to everything she was.

"You were a strong-willed child," Maggie admitted, looking at a picture of me covered in chocolate cake at my fifth birthday. "You wanted things the way you wanted them. And when you were a baby, you were colicky. But you were always an adorable child, and you were bright and funny." Maggie gently pushed a stray curl back from my face. "You were *always* worthy of love. You did nothing wrong, Wendy. She was the one with the problem, not you."

I nodded. "I know."

But for the first time, I truly believed that this all might be entirely my fault. If Finn was telling the truth, as these pictures seemed to confirm, I wasn't their child. I wasn't even human. I was exactly what my mother had accused me of being. She was just more intuitive than everybody else.

"What's wrong?" Maggie asked, looking concerned. "What's going on with you?"

"Nothing," I lied and closed the photo album.

"Did something happen last night?" Her eyes were filled with love and worry, and it was hard to think of her as not being my family. "Did you even sleep?"

"Yeah. I just . . . woke up, I guess," I answered vaguely.

"What happened at the dance?" Maggie leaned back against the couch, resting her hand on her chin as she studied me. "Did something happen with a boy?"

"Things just didn't turn out the way I thought they would," I said honestly. "In fact, they couldn't have turned out more different."

"Was that Finn boy mean to you?" Maggie asked with a protective edge to her voice.

"No, no, nothing like that," I assured her. "He was great. But he's just a friend."

"Oh." Understanding flashed in her eyes, and I realized she'd probably gotten the wrong idea, but at least it kept her from asking more questions. "Being a teenager is hard, no matter what family you come from."

"You're telling me," I muttered.

I heard Matt getting up and moving around upstairs. Maggie shot me a nervous look, so I hurried to pack up the photo albums. He wouldn't exactly be mad at me for looking at them, but he definitely wouldn't be happy either. And first thing in the morning, I did not want to deal with a fight with my brother, on top of worrying about whether or not he was really even my brother.

"You know, you can talk to me about this stuff whenever you want," Maggie whispered as I slipped the albums back in the cardboard box. "Well, at least whenever Matt isn't around."

"I know." I smiled at her.

"I suppose I should make you breakfast." Maggie stood up and stretched, then looked down at me. "How about plain oatmeal with fresh strawberries? Those are things you eat, right?"

"Yeah, that sounds great." I nodded, but something about her question pained me.

There were so many things I wouldn't eat, and I was constantly hungry. It had always been a struggle just to feed me. When I was a baby, I wouldn't even drink breast milk. Which only added more fuel to the idea that I wasn't my mother's child.

Maggie had turned to walk into the kitchen, but I called after her. "Hey, Mags. Thanks for everything. Like . . . making me food and stuff."

"Yeah?" Maggie looked surprised and smiled. "No problem."

Matt came downstairs a minute later, deeply confused by the fact that both Maggie and I were up before him. We ate breakfast together for the first time in years, and Maggie was overly happy, thanks to my small compliment. I was subdued, but I managed to play it off as something resembling happiness.

I didn't know if they were my real family or not. There were so many signs pointing to the contrary. But they had raised me and stood by me the way no one else had. Even my supposed mother had failed me, but not Matt or Maggie. They were unfailing in their love for me, and most of the time they had gotten next to nothing in return.

Maybe that last part was the proof that my mother was right. They only gave, and I only took.

FOUR

changeling

The weekend was turbulent. I kept expecting Finn to appear at my window again, but he didn't, and I wasn't sure if that was good or bad. I wanted to talk to him, but I was terrified. Terrified he might be lying, and terrified he might be telling the truth.

I kept looking for clues in everything. Like, Matt is pretty short and so am I, so he must be my brother. Then a minute later, he would say he prefers winter to summer, and I hate winter, so he must not be my brother.

These weren't clues one way or another, and deep down I knew that. My whole life was now one giant question, and I was desperate for answers.

There was also that burning unanswered question about what exactly Finn wanted with me. Sometimes he treated me like I was nothing more than an irritant. Then there were other times when he looked at me and took my breath away.

I hoped that school would bring some kind of resolution to all of this. When I got up Monday morning, I took extra care to look nice, but I tried to pretend it wasn't for any particular reason. That it wasn't because this was the first time I'd see Finn since he had come into my room, and that I still wanted to talk to him. I still wanted to impress him.

When the first-period bell rang and Finn still hadn't taken his place a few rows behind me, a knot started growing in my stomach. I looked around for him all day, half expecting him to be lurking around some corner. He never was, though.

I barely paid attention to anything all day in school, and I felt incredibly defeated when I walked to Matt's car. I had expected to gain some knowledge today, but in the end I was left with even more questions.

Matt noticed my surly demeanor and tried to ask about it, but I just shrugged him off. He had been growing increasingly concerned since I had come home from the dance, but I had been unable to put his mind at ease.

I already felt the sting of Finn's absence. Why hadn't I gone with him? I was more attracted to him than I had ever been to anyone, and it was more than just physical. In general, people didn't interest me, but he did.

He promised me a life where I fit in, where I was special, and, maybe most important, a life with him. Why was I staying here?

Because I still wasn't convinced that I was evil. I wasn't ready to give up on the good I had worked so hard for in my life.

I knew of one person who had always seen through my

façade and known exactly what I was. She'd be able to tell me if I had any good in me, or if I should just give in, give up, and run off with Finn.

"Hey, Matt?" I stared down at my hands. "Are you busy this afternoon?"

"I don't think so . . ." Matt answered tentatively as he turned on the block toward our house. "Why? What's on your mind?"

"I was thinking . . . I'd like to go visit my mother."

"Absolutely not!" Matt cast me a livid glare. "Why would you even want that? That's so completely out of the question. No way, Wendy. That's just obscene."

He turned to look at me again, and in that moment, staring directly into his eyes, I repeated the same thoughts over and over. *I want to see my mother. Take me to see her. Please. I want to see her.* His expression was hard, but eventually it started to soften around the edges.

"I'll take you to see our mother." Matt sounded like he was talking in his sleep.

I instantly felt guilty for what I was doing. It was manipulative and cruel. But I wasn't just doing it to see if I could. I needed to see my mother, and this was the only way I could do that.

I felt nervous and sick, and I knew Matt would be irate once he realized what he was doing. I didn't know how long this persuasion would last. We might not even make it to the hospital where my mother lived, but I had to try.

It would be the first time I'd see my mother in over eleven years.

There were several times throughout the long car ride when Matt seemed to become aware that he was doing something he would never normally do. He would start ranting about how terrible my mother was and that he couldn't believe he'd let me talk him into this.

Somehow it never occurred to him to turn around, but maybe it *couldn't* occur to him.

"She's a horrible person!" Matt said as we approached the state hospital.

I could see the internal battle waging underneath his grimace and tortured blue eyes. His hand was locked on the steering wheel, but something about the way he gripped it looked like he was trying to let go but couldn't.

Guilt flushed over me again, but I tried to push it away. I didn't want to hurt him, and controlling him like this was reprehensible.

The only real comfort I had was that I wasn't doing anything wrong. I wanted to see my mother, and I had every right to. Matt was just being overzealous about his protective duties once again.

"She can't do anything to hurt me," I reminded him for the hundredth time. "She's locked up and medicated. I'll be fine."

"It's not like she's going to strangle you or anything," Matt allowed, but there was an edge to his voice hinting that he hadn't completely ruled out the possibility. "She's just . . . a bad person. I don't know what you hope to gain from seeing her!"

"I just need to," I said softly and looked out the window.

I had never been to the hospital, but it wasn't exactly as I'd imagined. My entire basis for it was Arkham Asylum, so I had always pictured an imposing brick structure with lightning perpetually flashing just behind it.

It was raining lightly and the skies were overcast as we pulled up, but that was the only thing similar to the psychiatric hospital of my fantasies. Nestled in thick pine forest and rolling grassy hills, it was a sprawling white building that looked more like a resort than a hospital.

After my mother had tried to kill me and Matt tackled her in the kitchen, someone had called 911. She was hauled off in a police car, still screaming things about me being monstrous, while I was taken away in an ambulance.

Charges were brought against my mother, but she pleaded guilty by reason of insanity, and the case never went to trial. They had originally given her a cross-diagnosis of latent postpartum depression and temporary psychosis brought on by the death of my father.

With medication and therapy, there had been the general expectation that she would be out in a relatively short amount of time.

Cut to eleven years later when my brother is talking to the security guard so we can get clearance to get inside the hospital. From what I understood, she refused to admit any remorse for what she'd done.

Matt went to visit her once, five years ago, and what I got out of it was that she didn't know she'd done anything wrong. It was inferred, though never actually spelled out, that if she got out, she'd do it again.

There was a great deal of bustling about once we finally got inside. A nurse had to call a psychiatrist to see if I would even be able to see her. Matt paced anxiously around me, muttering things about everyone being insane.

We waited in a small room filled with plastic chairs and magazines for forty-five minutes until the doctor came to meet with me. We had a brief conversation in which I told him that I only wished to speak with her, and even without persuasion he seemed to think it might be beneficial for me to have some closure.

Matt wanted to go back with me to see her, afraid that she would damage me in some way, but the doctor assured him that orderlies would be present and my mother hadn't had a violent outburst in eleven years. Matt eventually relented, much to my relief, because I had just been about to use persuasion on him again.

He couldn't be there when I talked to her. I wanted an honest conversation.

A nurse led me to an activity room. A couch and a few chairs filled the room, along with a few small tables, some with half-completed puzzles on them. On one wall, a cabinet overflowed with beat-up games and battered puzzle boxes. Plants lined the windows, but otherwise it was devoid of life.

The nurse told me that my mother would be there soon, so I sat down at one of the tables and waited.

A very large, very strong-looking orderly brought her into the room. I stood up when she came in, as some kind of misplaced show of respect. She was older than I had expected her to be. In my mind she had stayed frozen the way I'd seen her last, but she had to be in her mid-forties by now.

Her blond hair had turned into a frizzy mess thanks to the years of neglect, and she had it pulled back in a short ponytail. She was thin, the way she had always been, in a beautifully elegant borderline-anorexic way. A massive blue bathrobe hung on her, frayed and worn, the sleeves draping down over her hands.

Her skin was pale porcelain, and even without any makeup, she was stunningly beautiful. More than that, she carried this regality with her. It was clear that she had come from money, that she had spent her life on top, ruling her school, her social circles, even her family.

"They said you were here, but I didn't believe them," said my mother with a wry smirk.

She stood a few steps away from me, and I wasn't sure what to do. The way she looked at me was the same way people might inspect a particularly heinous-looking bug just before they squashed it under their shoe.

"Hi, Mom," I offered meekly, unable to think of anything better to say.

"Kim," she corrected me coldly. "My name is Kim. Cut the pretense. I'm not your mother, and we both know it." She gestured vaguely to the chair I had pushed out behind me and walked over to the table. "Sit. Take a seat."

"Thanks," I mumbled, sitting down. She sat down across from me, crossing her legs and leaning back in her chair, like I was contagious and she didn't want to get sick.

"That's what this is about it, isn't it?" She waved her hand in front of her face, then laid it delicately on the table. Her nails were long and perfect, recently painted with clear polish. "You've finally figured it out. Or have you always known? I never could tell."

"No, I never knew," I said quietly. "I still don't know."

"Look at you. You're not my daughter." My mother gave me a contentious look and clicked her tongue. "You don't know how to dress or walk or even speak. You mutilate your nails." She pointed a manicured fingertip at my chewed-down nails. "And that hair!"

"Your hair isn't any better," I countered. My dark curls had been pulled up in their usual bun, but I had actually tried styling my hair this morning when I was getting ready. I thought it looked pretty good, but apparently I was wrong.

"Well . . ." She smiled humorlessly. "I have limited resources." She looked away for a moment, then turned back to rest her icy gaze on me. "But what about you? You must have all the styling products in the world. Between Matthew and Maggie, I'm sure you're spoiled rotten."

"I get by," I allowed sourly. She made it sound like I should feel ashamed for the things I had, like I had stolen them. Although I suppose, in her mind, I kinda had.

"Who brought you here anyway?" Clearly the idea had just occurred to her, and she glanced behind her, as if she expected to see Matt or Maggie waiting in the wings.

"Matt," I answered.

"Matthew?" She looked genuinely shocked. "There is no way he would condone this. He doesn't even . . ." Sadness washed across her face and she shook her head. "He's never understood. I did what I did to protect him too. I never wanted you to get your claws into him." She touched her hair, and tears welled in her eyes, but she blinked them back and her stony expression returned.

"He thinks he has to protect me," I informed her, mostly because I knew it would bother her. Disappointingly, she didn't look that upset. She just nodded in understanding.

"For all his sense and maturity, Matthew can be incredibly naive. He always thought of you as some lost, sick puppy he needed to care for." She brushed a frizzy strand of hair from her forehead and stared at a spot on the floor. "He loves you because he's a good man, like his father, and that has always been his weakness." Then she looked up hopefully. "Is he going to visit me today?"

"No." I almost felt bad about telling her that, but she smiled bitterly at me and I remembered why she was here.

"You've turned him against me. I knew you would. But . . ." She shrugged emptily. "It doesn't make things easier, does it?"

"I don't know." I leaned in toward her. "Look, M- . . . Kim. I am here for a reason. I want to know what I am." I backtracked quickly. "I mean, what you think I am."

"You're a changeling," she said matter-of-factly. "I'm surprised you didn't know that by now."

My heart dropped, but I tried to keep my expression

neutral. I pressed my hands flat on the table to keep them from shaking. It was just as I had suspected, and maybe I had always known.

When Finn told me, it had instantly made sense, but I don't know why hearing it from Kim made things feel so different.

"How could you possibly know that?" I asked.

"I knew you weren't mine the second the doctor placed you in my arms." She twisted at her hair and looked away from me. "My husband refused to listen to me. I kept telling him that you weren't ours, but he . . ." She swallowed, pained at the memory of the man she'd loved.

"It wasn't until I was in here, when I had all the time in the world, that I found out what you really were," she went on, her eyes hardening and her voice strengthening with conviction. "I read book after book searching for an explanation for you. In an old book on fairy tales, I found out what kind of parasite you truly are—a *changeling*."

"A changeling?" I fought to keep my voice even. "What does that mean?"

"What do you think it means?" she snapped, looking at me like I was an idiot. "Changeling! You were changed out for another child! My son was taken and you were put in his place!"

Her cheeks reddened with rage, and the orderly took a step closer to her. She held up her hand and fought to keep herself contained.

"Why?" I asked, realizing that I should've asked Finn this question days earlier. "Why would anyone do that? Why would they take your baby? What did they do with him?"

"I don't know what kind of game you're playing." She smiled sadly and fresh tears stood in her eyes. Her hands trembled when she touched her hair, and she all but refused to look at me. "You know what you did with him. You know far better than I do."

"No, I don't!" The orderly gave me a hard look, and I knew I had to at least look like I wasn't freaking out. In a hushed voice I demanded, "What are you talking about?"

"You killed him, Wendy!" My mother snarled. She leaned in toward me, her hand clenched into a fist, and I knew she was using all her willpower to keep from hurting me. "First you killed my son, then you drove my husband insane and killed him. You *killed* them both!"

"Mom . . . Kim, whatever!" I closed my eyes and rubbed my temples. "That doesn't make any sense. I was just a baby! How could I kill anyone?"

"How did you get Matthew to drive you here?" she demanded through gritted teeth, and an icy chill ran down my spine. "He would never drive you here. He would never let you see me. But he did. What did you do to him to make him do it?" I lowered my eyes, unable to even pretend to be innocent. "Maybe that's exactly what you did to Michael!" Her fists were clenched, and she breathed so hard, her delicate nostrils flared.

"I was just a baby," I insisted without any real conviction. "I couldn't have . . . Even if I did, there had to be more people involved. It doesn't explain anything! Why would anybody take him or hurt him and put me in his place?"

She ignored my question. "You were always evil. I knew it

from the moment I held you in my arms." She had calmed herself a bit and leaned back in her chair. "It was in your eyes. They weren't human. They weren't kind or good."

"Then why didn't you just kill me then?" I asked, growing irritated.

"You were a baby!" Her hands shook, and her lips had started to quiver. She was losing the confidence she had come in with. "Well, I thought you were. You know I couldn't be sure." She pressed her lips together tightly, trying to hold back tears.

"What made you so sure?" I asked. "What made you decide that day? On my sixth birthday. Why that day? What happened?"

"You weren't mine. I knew you weren't." She brushed at her eyes to keep the tears from spilling over. "I had known forever. But I just kept thinking about what the day should've been like. With my husband, and my son. Michael should've been six that day, not you. You were a horrible, horrible child, and you were alive. And they were dead. I just . . . it didn't seem right anymore." She took a deep breath and shook her head. "It still isn't right."

"I was six years old." My voice had started quavering. Whenever I'd thought of her or what happened, I'd only ever felt numb. For the first time, I really felt hurt and betrayed.

"*Six years old.* Do you understand that? I was a little kid, and you were supposed to be my mother!" Whether she really was or not was irrelevant. I was a child, and she was in charge of raising me. "I had never done anything to anyone. I never even *met* Michael."

"You're *lying*." My mother gritted her teeth. "You were always a liar, and a monster! And I know you're doing things to Matthew! Just leave him alone! He's a good boy!" She reached across the table and grabbed my wrist painfully. The orderly came up behind her. "Take what you want, take anything. Just leave Matthew alone!"

"Kimberly, come on." The orderly put his strong hand on her arm, and she tried to pull away from him. "Kimberly!"

"Leave him alone," she shouted again, and the orderly started pulling her up. She fought against him, screaming at me. "Do you hear me, Wendy? I will get out of here someday! And if you've hurt that boy, I will finish the job I started!"

"That's enough," the orderly bellowed, dragging her out of the room.

"You're not human, Wendy! And I know it!" That was the last thing she yelled before he carried her out of my sight.

The staff let me sit there for a minute, trying to catch my breath and get myself under control. Matt couldn't see me like this. I really, really thought I was going to throw up, but I managed to keep it down.

Everything was true. I was a changeling. I wasn't human. She wasn't my mother. She was just Kim, a woman who had lost her grasp on reality when she realized I wasn't her child. I had been switched for her son, Michael, and I had no idea what happened to him.

Maybe he was dead. Maybe I really had killed him, or someone else had. Maybe someone like Finn.

She was convinced that I was a monster, and I couldn't argue that I wasn't. In my life, I had caused nothing but pain. I had ruined Matt's life, and I still was doing that.

Not only did he constantly have to uproot himself for me and spend every minute worrying about me, but I was manipulating and controlling him, and I couldn't say for sure how long that had been going on. I didn't know the long-term effects of it either.

Maybe it would've been better if she had killed me when I was six. Or better yet, when I was still a baby. Then I wouldn't have been able to hurt anybody.

When the staff finally led me back to the waiting room, Matt rushed over to hug me. I stood there, but I didn't hug him back. He inspected me to make sure I was all right. He had heard there was some kind of scuffle and was petrified that something had happened to me. I just nodded and got out of there as fast as I could.

FIVE

insanity

"So . . ." Matt began on the drive home. I rested my forehead against the cold glass of the car window and refused to look at him. I had barely spoken since we'd left. "What did you say to her?"

"Things," I replied vaguely.

"No, really," he pressed. "What happened?"

"I tried talking to her, she got upset." I sighed. "She said I was a monster. You know, the usual."

"I don't know why you even wanted to see her. She's a terrible person."

"Oh, she's not that bad." My breath fogged up the window, and I started drawing stars in the mist. "She's really worried about you. She's afraid I'm going to hurt you."

"That woman is insane," Matt scoffed. "Literally, since she lives there, but . . . you can't listen to her, Wendy. You aren't letting anything she said get to you, are you?"

"No," I lied. Pulling my sleeve up over my hand, I erased my drawings on the window and sat up straighter. "How do you know?"

"What?"

"That she's insane. That . . . I'm not a monster." I twisted my thumb ring nervously and stared at Matt, who just shook his head. "I'm being serious. What if I am bad?"

Matt suddenly put on his turn signal and pulled the car over to the shoulder. Rain pounded down on the windows as other cars sped by us on the freeway. He turned to face me completely, putting an arm across the back of my seat.

"Wendy Luella Everly, there is nothing bad about you. *Nothing*," Matt emphasized solemnly. "That woman is completely insane. I don't know why, but she was never a mother to you. You can't listen to her. She doesn't know what she's talking about."

"Be serious, Matt." I shook my head. "I've gotten expelled from every school I've ever gone to. I'm unruly and whiny and stubborn and so picky. I know that you and Maggie struggle with me all the time."

"That doesn't mean you're bad. You've had a *really* traumatic childhood, and yeah, you're still working through some things, but you are not bad," Matt insisted. "You are a strong-willed teenager who isn't afraid of anything. That's all."

"At some point that has to stop being an excuse. Sure she tried to kill me, but I have to take responsibility for who I am as a person."

"You are!" Matt said with a smile. "Since we've moved

here, you have shown so much promise. Your grades are going up, and you're making friends. And even if that makes me a little uncomfortable, I know it's a good thing for you. You're growing up, Wendy, and you're going to be okay."

I nodded, unable to think of an argument for that.

"I know I don't say it enough, but I'm proud of you, and I love you." Matt bent over so he could kiss the top of my head. He hadn't done that since I was little, and it stirred something inside me. I closed my eyes and refused to cry. He straightened back up in his seat and looked at me seriously. "Okay? Are you okay now?"

"Yeah, I'm fine." I forced a smile.

"Good." He pulled back into traffic, continuing the drive home.

As much as I inconvenienced Matt and Maggie, it would break their hearts if I left. Even if going with Finn would be more promising, it would hurt them too much. Leaving would put my needs in front of theirs. So if I stayed, I put them before me.

Staying would be my only proof that I wasn't evil.

When we got home, I went up to my room before Maggie could try to talk to me. My room felt too quiet, so I went over to my iPod and started scrolling through songs. A light tapping sound startled me from my search, and my heart skipped a beat.

I walked over to my window, and when I pulled back the curtain, the rain had stopped, and there was Finn, crouched on the roof outside. I considered closing the curtain and ignoring him, but his dark eyes were too much. Besides, this would give me a chance to say a proper good-bye.

"What are you doing?" Finn asked as soon as I opened the window. He stayed out on the roof, but I hadn't moved back so he could come in.

"What are *you* doing?" I countered, crossing my arms.

"I came to make sure you're all right," he said, concern in his eyes.

"Why wouldn't I be all right?" I asked.

"It was just a feeling I had." He avoided my gaze, glancing behind him at a man walking his dog on the sidewalk before turning back to me. "Mind if I come in so we can finish this conversation?"

"Whatever."

I took a step back and tried to seem as indifferent as possible, but when he slid through the window past me, my heartbeat sped up. He stood in front of me, his dark eyes burning into mine, and he made the rest of the world disappear. I shook my head and stepped away from him, so I wouldn't let myself get mesmerized by him anymore.

"Why did you come in the window?" I asked.

"I couldn't very well come to the door. That guy would never let me in here to see you." Finn was probably right. Matt had hated him ever since the dance.

"That *guy* is my brother, and his name is Matt." I felt incredibly defensive and protective of him, especially after the way he supported me after we saw Kim.

"He's not your brother. You need to stop thinking of him

like that." Finn cast a disparaging look around my room. "Is that what this is all about? This is why you won't leave?"

"You couldn't possibly understand my reasons." I went over and sat on my bed, making a point of laying physical claim to this space.

"What happened tonight?" Finn asked, ignoring my attempts at defiance.

"How are you so certain something happened?"

"You were gone," he said, without any fear that I might find it disturbing that he knew about my comings and goings.

"I saw my mother. Er, well . . . the woman who is supposed to be my mother." I shook my head, hating the way this all sounded. I considered lying to him, but he already knew more about all of this than anyone. "What do you call her? Is there a name for her?"

"Usually her name will suffice," Finn replied, and I felt like an idiot.

"Yeah. Of course." I took a deep breath. "Anyway, I went and saw Kim." I looked up at him. "Do you know about her? I mean . . . how much do you really know about me?"

"Honestly, not that much." Finn seemed to disapprove of his own lack of knowledge. "You were incredibly elusive. It was rather disconcerting."

"So you don't . . ." I realized with dismay that I was on the verge of tears. "She knew I wasn't her daughter. When I was six, she tried to kill me. She had always told me that I was a monster, that I was evil. And I guess I had always believed her."

"You're not evil," Finn insisted earnestly, and I smiled thinly at him, swallowing back my sadness. "You can't possibly stay here, Wendy."

"It's not like that anymore." I shook my head, looking away from him. "She doesn't live here, and my brother and my aunt would do anything for me. I can't just leave them. I won't."

Finn eyed me carefully, trying to decide if I was serious. I hated how attractive he was and whatever power it was he held over me. Even now, with my life in complete shambles, the way he looked at me made it hard to focus on anything besides my racing heart.

"Do you realize what you're giving up?" Finn asked softly. "There is so much that life has to offer you. More than anything they can give you here. If Matt understood what was in store for you, he would send you with me himself."

"You're right. He would, if he thought it was what's best for me," I admitted. "Which is why I have to stay."

"Well, I want what's best for you too. That's why I found you, and why I've been trying to bring you home." The underlying affection in his voice shivered through me. "Do you really believe I would encourage you to return home if it would adversely affect you?"

"I don't think you know what's best for me," I replied as evenly as I could.

He had thrown me off guard by hinting at caring about me, and I had to remind myself that that was part of his job. All of this was. He needed to make sure I was safe and convince me to return home. That wasn't the same as actually caring about *me.*

"You're sure this is what you want?" Finn asked gently.

"Absolutely." But I sounded more confident than I really was.

"I'd like to say that I understand, but I don't." Finn sighed resignedly. "I can say that I'm disappointed."

"I'm sorry," I said meekly.

"You shouldn't be sorry." He ran a hand through his black hair and looked at me again. "I won't be going to school anymore. It seems unnecessary, and I don't want to disturb your studies. You should at least get an education."

"What? Don't you need one?" My heart dropped to the pit of my stomach as I realized that this might be the last time I saw Finn.

"Wendy." Finn gave a small humorless laugh. "I thought you knew. I'm twenty years old. I'm done with my education."

"Why were you . . ." I said, already figuring out the answer to my question.

"I was only there to keep track of you, and I have." Finn dropped his eyes and sighed. "When you change your mind . . ." He hesitated for a moment. "I'll find you."

"You're leaving?" I asked, trying to keep the disappointment from my voice.

"You're still here, so I am too. At least for a while," Finn explained.

"How long?"

"It depends on . . . things." Finn shook his head. "Everything about your situation is so different. It's hard to say anything with certainty."

"You keep saying that I'm different. What does that mean? What are you talking about?"

"We usually wait until changelings are a few years older, and by then you've already figured out that you're not human," Finn explained. "When the tracker comes to find you, you're relieved and eager to go."

"So why did you come for me now?" I asked.

"You moved so much." Finn gestured to the house. "We were afraid that something might be the matter. So I was here monitoring you until you were ready, and I thought you might be." He exhaled deeply. "I guess I was wrong."

"Can't you just 'persuade' me to go along?" I asked, and some part of me that wanted to go with him hoped he could.

"I can't." Finn shook his head. "I can't force you to come with me. If this is your decision, then I'll have to respect it."

I nodded, knowing full well that I was turning down any chance of getting to know my real parents, my family history, and spending more time with Finn. Not to mention my abilities, like persuasion, which Finn had promised there would be more of as I got older. On my own, I'm sure I'd never be able to master or understand them.

We looked at each other, and I wished he wasn't so far away from me. I was wondering if it would be appropriate if we hugged when the door to my bedroom opened.

Matt had come in to check on me. As soon as he saw Finn, his eyes burned. Quickly I jumped up, moving in front of Finn to block any attempts by Matt to kill him.

"Matt! It's okay!" I held up my hands.

"It is not okay!" Matt growled. "Who the hell is this?"

"Matt, please!" I put my hands on his chest, trying to push him away from Finn, but it was like trying to push a brick wall. I glanced back at Finn, and he just stared blankly at my brother.

"You have some nerve!" Matt reached over my shoulder, pointing at Finn as he yelled. "She is seventeen years old! I don't know what the hell you think you're doing in her room, but you're never doing anything with her again!"

"Matt, please, stop," I begged. "He was just saying goodbye! *Please!*"

"Perhaps you should listen to her," Finn offered calmly.

I knew his composure must be pissing off Matt even more. Matt's day had been horrible too, and the last thing he needed was some kid in here defiling me. Finn's only reaction was to stand there, cool and collected, and Matt would want him too scared to ever come near me again.

Matt actually knocked me out of the way, and I fell backward onto the floor. Finn's eyes flashed darkly at that, and when Matt pushed him, Finn didn't move an inch. He just glared down at my brother, and I knew that if they fought, Matt would be the one with a serious injury.

"Matt!" I jumped to my feet.

Already I had started chanting, *Leave my room. Leave my room. You need to calm down and get out of my room. Please.* I wasn't sure how effective it was without eye contact, so I grabbed his arm and forced him to turn to me.

He tried to look away instantly, but I caught him. I kept my eyes focused and just kept repeating it over and over in my head. Finally, his expression softened and his eyes glazed.

"I'm going to leave your room now," Matt said robotically.

Much to my relief, he actually turned and walked out into the hall, closing the door behind him. I'm not sure if he walked any farther than that, or how much time I had, so I turned to Finn.

"You have to leave," I insisted breathlessly, but his expression had changed to one of concern.

"Does he do that often?" Finn asked.

"Do what?"

"He pushed you. He clearly has an anger problem." Finn glared at the door Matt had left through. "He's unstable. You shouldn't stay here with him."

"Yeah, well, you guys should be more careful who you leave babies with," I muttered and went to the window. "I don't know how much time we have, so you need to go."

"He probably shouldn't ever be able to come into your room again," Finn said absently. "I'm serious, Wendy. I don't want to leave you with him."

"You don't have much of a choice!" I said, exasperated. "Matt's not usually like that, and he would never hurt me. He's just had a *really* hard day, and he blames you for upsetting me, and he's not wrong." The panic was wearing away, and I realized that I had just used persuasion on Matt again. I felt nauseous. "I *hate* doing that to him. It's not fair and it's not right."

"I am sorry." Finn looked at me sincerely. "I know you did

that to protect him, and it's my fault. I should've just backed down, but when he pushed you . . ." He shook his head. "My instincts kicked in."

"He's not going to hurt me," I promised.

"I'm sorry for the trouble I've caused you."

Finn glanced back at the door, and I could tell he really didn't want to leave. When he looked back at me, he sighed heavily. He was probably fighting the urge to throw me over his shoulder and take me with him. Instead, he climbed out the window and swung back down to the ground.

With that, he turned past the neighbors' hedges and I couldn't see him anymore. I kept looking after him, wishing that this didn't mean we had to say good-bye.

The awful truth was that I was more than a little sad to see Finn go. Eventually, I shut the window and closed my curtains.

After Finn left, I found Matt sitting on the steps, looking bewildered and pissed off. He wanted to yell at me about Finn, but he couldn't seem to understand exactly what had happened. The best I could get out of it was that he vowed to kill Finn if he ever came near me, and I pretended like I thought that was a reasonable thing to do.

The next few days, school dragged on and on. It didn't help that I found myself constantly looking around for Finn. Part of me kept insisting that the last week had been a bad dream, and that Finn should still be here, staring at me like he always had.

On top of that, I kept feeling like I was being watched. My neck got that scratchy feeling it did when Finn stared at me for too long, but whenever I turned around, nobody was there. At least nobody worth noting.

At home, I felt distracted and ill at ease. I excused myself from supper early on Thursday night and went up to my room. I peered out my curtains, hoping to find Finn lurking around somewhere nearby, but no such luck. Every time I looked for him and didn't find him, my heart hurt a little more.

I tossed and turned all night, trying not to wonder if Finn was still hanging around. He'd made it painfully clear that he'd soon have to move on and end this assignment.

I wasn't ready for that. I didn't like the idea of him moving on when I hadn't.

Around five in the morning I gave up entirely on sleep. I looked out the window again, and this time I thought I saw something. Nothing more than a shadowy blur of movement in the corner of my eye, but it was enough to indicate that he was out there, hiding nearby.

I just needed to go out and talk to Finn, to make sure he was still there. I didn't even bother changing out of my pajamas or fixing my hair.

Hastily, I climbed out onto the roof. I tried to grab on to the branch and swing to the ground like Finn had. As soon as my fingers grabbed the branch, they slipped off and I fell to the ground, landing heavily on my back. All the wind had been knocked out of me, and I coughed painfully.

I would've loved to lie on the lawn for ten minutes while the pain subsided, but I was afraid that Matt or Maggie might have heard my fall. I gingerly got to my feet and rounded the hedges toward the neighbors' house.

The street was completely deserted. I wrapped my arms tightly around myself to ward off the cold that seeped in and looked around. I *knew* he had been out here. Who else would be moving around out here just before dawn? Maybe my fall had scared him away; he might have thought it was Matt.

I decided to walk a little farther down the street, investigating everyone's lawn for a hidden tracker. My back ached from the fall, and my knee felt a little twisted and weird. That left me hobbling down the street in my pajamas at five in the morning. I had truly lost my mind.

Then I heard something. Footsteps? Somebody was definitely following me, and based on the dark chill running down my spine, it wasn't Finn. It was hard to explain how I knew it wasn't him, but I knew it just the same. Slowly, I turned around.

SIX

monsters

A girl stood a few feet behind me. In the glow from the streetlamp, she looked ravishing. Her short brown pixie cut spiked up all over. Her skirt was short and her black leather jacket went down to her calves. A wind came up, blowing back her coat a bit, and she reminded me of some kind of action star, like she should be in *The Matrix*.

But the thing that caught my attention the most was that she was barefoot.

She just stared at me, so I felt like I had to say something.

"Okay . . . um, I'm going to go home now," I announced.

"Wendy Everly, I think you should come with us," she said with a sly smile.

"Us?" I asked, but then I felt him behind me.

I don't know where he had been before that, but suddenly I felt his presence behind me. I looked over my shoulder, where a tall man with dark, slicked-backed hair stared down at me. He wore the same kind of jacket as the girl, and I thought it was neat that they had matching outfits, like a crime-fighting duo.

He smiled at me, and that's when I decided that I was in trouble.

"That's a really nice invitation, but my house is like three houses down." I pointed toward it, as if I didn't think they already knew exactly where I lived. "So I think that I should probably just get home before my brother starts looking for me."

"You should've thought of that before you left the house," the guy behind me suggested.

I wanted to take a step forward to get away from him, but I thought that would only encourage him to pounce on me. I could probably take the girl, but I wasn't so sure about him. He was like a foot taller than me.

"You guys are trackers?" I asked. Something in the way they stared at me reminded me of Finn, especially when I'd first met him.

"You're a quick one, aren't you?" The girl smiled wider, and it didn't sit right with me.

They might be trackers, but not the same kind as Finn. Maybe they were bounty hunters or kidnappers or just big fans of chopping up girls into little pieces and disposing of them in a ditch. Fear crept through me, but I tried not to let on.

"Well, this has been a blast, but I have to get ready for school. Big test and all that." I started taking a step away, but the guy's hand clamped painfully on my arm.

"Don't damage her," the girl insisted, her eyes flashing wide. "She's not to be hurt."

"Yeah, ease up." I tried to pull my arm from him, but he refused to let go.

I had already decided that I wasn't going wherever they wanted to take me. Since they were under some kind of instruction not to hurt me, it would give me the advantage in a fight. I only had to get a few houses down, then I'd be at home, where Matt kept a gun under his bed.

I elbowed the guy in the stomach as hard as I could. He made a coughing sound and doubled over but didn't let go of my arm. I kicked him in the shin and moved to bite the hand that was gripping me.

He yowled in pain, and then the girl was in front of me. He had let go of me, and she tried to grab me, so I punched her. She dodged, so my fist just connected with her shoulder.

Then I was off balance, and the guy grabbed me around the waist. I screamed and kicked at him as hard as I could. Apparently he got tired of that, so he dropped me on the ground.

I was on my feet instantly, but he grabbed my arm again and turned me so I was facing him. He raised his hand and slapped me harder than I had ever been hit before. Everything went white, and my ear started ringing. Then he let go of me, and I collapsed backward on the grass behind me.

"I said not to hurt her," the girl hissed.

"I didn't. I was subduing her," the guy growled and looked down at me. "And if she doesn't knock it off, I'll subdue her again, but harder this time."

My neck ached from the force of his hit, and my jaw screamed painfully. A throbbing spread behind my left eye, but I still tried to stagger to my feet. She kicked me then, not hard enough to really hurt, but enough so I'd fall back down.

I lay on my back, staring up at the sky. From the corner of my eye, I could see a light flick on in the window of a house behind me. We were making enough of a ruckus to wake the neighbors, even if we weren't close enough for Matt to hear us.

I opened my mouth to scream and yell for help, but the male tracker must've realized what I meant to do. Little more than a yelp had escaped my lips when I felt his foot press down hard on my throat.

"If you make a sound, I'll make this much harder for you," the guy warned me. "I might not be allowed to snap your neck, but I can make you wish you were dead."

I couldn't breathe, and I clawed at his foot, trying to get it off me. When he asked if I promised to be good, I nodded frantically. I would've agreed to anything that let me breathe again.

He stepped back and I gasped for breath, taking in big gulps of air that burned my throat.

"Let's just get her to the car," the girl said, exasperated.

He bent down to try to pick me up, but I hit away his hands. I was lying on my back, and I lifted up my legs. I wasn't really trying to kick him, but I was going to use my legs to push him back if he came near me.

In response, he hit my calf hard enough to give me a charley horse, which I gritted my teeth through. He put his knee on my stomach, holding me down so I couldn't fight as much.

When he tried to grab me, I pushed him back with my hands, so he grabbed my wrists, pressing them tightly together with one hand.

"Stop," he commanded. I tried to pull my hands free, but he just squeezed tighter and my bones felt like they were about to snap. "Just stop. We're going to take you no matter what."

"Like hell you are!" Finn barked, his voice coming from out of nowhere.

I swiveled my head so I could see Finn. I had never been so happy to see anyone in my life.

"Oh, dammit," the girl said with a sigh. "If you hadn't spent so much time fighting with her, we'd be out of here by now."

"She was the one fighting with me," the guy insisted.

"Now I'm the one fighting with you!" Finn growled, glaring at him. "Get off her! *Now!*"

"Finn, can't we just talk about this?" The girl tried to sound sultry and flirty as she took a step closer to Finn, but he didn't even look at her. "I know how you feel about duty, but there's got to be some kind of agreement we can come to."

She took another step closer to him, and he pushed her back, so hard she stumbled and fell backward.

"I hate fighting with you, Finn." The guy let go of my hands and took his knee off my stomach. I took the opportunity to try to kick him in the nuts, and reflexively he whirled on me and smacked me hard again.

Before I could even curse him for hitting me, Finn was on

him. I had rolled onto my side, cradling my injured face, so I could only see part of what was going on.

My attacker had managed to get to his feet, but I could hear the sounds of Finn punching him. The girl leaped on his back to stop him, but Finn elbowed her in the face. She collapsed to the ground, holding her bleeding nose.

"Enough!" The guy had cowered down, his arms shielding his face against any more blows. "We're done! We'll get out of here!"

"You better fucking get out of here," Finn shouted. "If I see you anywhere near her again, I will kill you!"

The guy walked over to the girl and helped her to her feet, then they both headed down the street to a black SUV parked at the end of the block. Finn stood on the sidewalk in front of me, watching them until they got in and sped off.

A moment later, he knelt down next to me where I was lying on the ground. He placed his hand on my cheek where I had been slapped. The skin was tender, so it stung a little, but I refused to show it. His hand felt too good to push away.

His dark eyes were pained when he looked me over, and as terrible as everything had been up until this moment, I wouldn't have traded it for anything because it led to this, to him touching me and looking at me like that.

"I'm sorry it took me so long." He pursed his lips, clearly blaming himself for not getting here sooner. "I was sleeping, and I didn't wake up until you were completely panicked."

"You sleep in your clothes?" I asked, looking at his usual dark jeans and button-down shirt combo.

"Sometimes." Finn pulled his hand from my face. "I knew something was up today. I could feel it, but I couldn't pinpoint it because I couldn't stay as close to you as I would've liked. I never should've slept at all."

"No, you can't blame yourself. It was my fault for coming out of my room."

"What were you doing out here?" Finn looked at me curiously, and I looked away, feeling embarrassed.

"I thought I saw you," I admitted quietly, and his face went dark.

"I should've been here," he said, almost under his breath, and then he got to his feet. He held out his hand and pulled me to my feet. I grimaced a little but tried not to show it. "Are you all right?"

"Yeah, I'm fine." I forced a smile. "A little sore, but fine."

He touched my cheek again, just with his fingertips, sending flutters through me. He studied my injury intently, and then his eyes met mine, dark and wonderful. It was at that moment that I knew I had officially fallen for him.

"You're going to have a bruise," Finn murmured, dropping his hand. "I'm sorry."

"It's not your fault," I insisted. "It's mine. I was being an idiot. I should've known . . ." I trailed off. I had been about to say that I should've known it was dangerous, but how could I have possibly known that? I had no idea who those people were. "Who were they? What did they want?"

"Vittra," Finn growled, glaring down the road as if they would appear at the sound of their name. He tensed up as he scanned the horizon, then put his hand on the small of my back to usher me away. "Come on. I'll explain more in the car."

"The car?" I stopped where I was, making him press his palm harder on my back until he realized I wasn't going anywhere. His hand stayed there, and I had to ignore the small pleasure of it so I could argue with him. "I'm not going in the car. I have to go home before Matt realizes I'm gone."

"You can't go back there," Finn said, apologetic but firm. "I'm sorry. I know this is directly against your wishes, but it's not safe for you there anymore. The Vittra have found you. I will not leave you here."

"I don't even understand what this Vittra is, and Matt is . . ." I shifted uncomfortably and looked backed toward my house.

Matt was tough, as far as people went, but I wasn't sure what kind of match he would be for the guy who attacked me. And even if he could take him, I didn't want to bring that element into the house. If something happened to Matt or Maggie because of me, I could never forgive myself.

Red and blue lights lit up the neighborhood as a police car drew near. The neighbors must've called the cops when they heard me fighting with the trackers. It apparently hadn't sounded dangerous enough to warrant sirens, but the lights were flashing a block away.

"Wendy, we must hurry," Finn insisted. The police expedited his urgency, so I nodded and let him take me away.

Apparently he'd run to my rescue this morning, because his car was still parked at his house two blocks away. We jogged toward it, but when the cop car got closer, we ducked behind a shed to hide.

"This is going to break Matt's heart," I whispered as we waited for the police to pass us.

"He'd want you to be safe," Finn assured me, and he was right. But Matt wouldn't know I was safe. He wouldn't know anything about me.

Once Finn was certain we were in the clear, we stepped out from behind the shed and hurried on to his car.

"Do you have a cell phone?" I asked.

"Why?" Finn kept glancing around as we approached his car. He pulled his keys from his pocket and used the remote to unlock it.

"I need to call Matt and let him know that I'm okay," I said. Finn held the passenger door open while I got inside. As soon as he got in the driver's seat, I turned to him. "Well? Can I call him?"

"You really want to?" Finn asked as he started the car.

"Yes, of course I do! Why is that so surprising?"

Finn threw the car in gear and sped off down the road. The whole town was still asleep, except for us and the neighbors we'd awoken. He glanced over at me, debating. Finally, he dug in his pocket and pulled out his cell phone.

"Thank you." I smiled gratefully at him.

When I started dialing the phone, my hands shook, and I felt sick. This was going to be the hardest conversation of my life. I held the phone to my ear, listening to it ring, and I tried to slow my breathing.

"Hello?" Matt answered the phone groggily. He clearly hadn't woken up yet, so he must not know I was gone. I wasn't sure if that was a good thing or not. "Hello? Who's there?"

I closed my eyes and took a deep breath. "Matt?"

"Wendy?" Matt instantly sounded alert, panic in his voice. "Where are you? What's going on? Are you all right?"

"Yeah, I'm fine." My cheek still hurt, but I was fine. Even if I wasn't, I couldn't tell him that. "Um, I'm calling because . . . I'm leaving, and I wanted you to know that I'm safe."

"What do you mean, you're leaving?" Matt asked. I could hear him open his door, and then the bang of my bedroom door being thrown open. "Where are you, Wendy? You need to come home right now!"

"I can't, Matt." I rubbed my forehead and let out a shaky breath.

"Why? Does somebody have you? Did Finn take you?" Matt demanded. In the background, I could hear Maggie asking questions. He must have woken her up with all the commotion. "I'll kill that little bastard if he lays one hand on you."

"Yeah, I'm with Finn, but it's not like you think," I said thickly. "I wish I could explain everything to you, but I can't. He's taking care of me, though. He's making sure I'm safe."

"Safe from what?" Matt snapped. "I take care of you! Why are you doing this?" He took a deep breath and tried to calm down. "If we're doing something wrong, we can change it, Wendy. You just need to come home, right now." His voice was cracking, and it broke my heart. "Please, Wendy."

"You're not doing anything wrong." Silent tears slid down

my face, and I tried to swallow the lump in my throat. "You didn't do anything. This isn't about you or Maggie, honest. I love you guys, and I would take you with me if I could. But I can't."

"Why do you keep saying 'can't'? Is he forcing you? Tell me where you are so I can call the police."

"He's not forcing me, Matt." I sighed and wondered if this phone call had been a bad idea. Maybe I just made it worse for him. "Please don't try and find me. You won't be able to, and I don't want you to. I just wanted you to know that I'm safe and that I love you and you never did anything wrong. Okay? I just want you to be happy."

"Wendy, why are you talking like that?" Matt sounded more afraid than I had ever heard him before, and I couldn't be certain, but I think he'd started to cry. "You sound like you're never coming back. You can't leave forever. You . . . Whatever is going on, I can take care of it. I'll do whatever I have to do. Just come back, Wendy."

"I'm so sorry, Matt, but I can't." I wiped at my eyes and shook my head. "I'll call you again if I can. But if you don't hear from me, don't worry. I'm okay."

"Wendy! Stop talking like that!" Matt shouted. "You need to come back here! Wendy!"

"Good-bye, Matt." I hung up to the sound of him yelling my name.

I took a deep breath and reminded myself that this was the only thing I could do. It was the only way that I could keep them safe, and it was the safest thing for me, which was exactly what Matt would want.

If he knew what was going on, he would agree with this completely. It didn't change the fact that it was absolute torture to say good-bye to him like that. Hearing his pain and frustration so evident over the phone . . .

"Hey, Wendy. You did the right thing," Finn assured me, but I just sniffled.

He reached over and took my hand, squeezing it lightly. Ordinarily I would've been delighted by that, but right now it took everything I had to keep from sobbing or throwing up. I wiped at my tears, but I couldn't seem to stop crying.

Finn pulled over to the side of the road. "Come here," he said gently. He put his arm around my shoulders and pulled me closer to him. I rested my head against his shoulder, and he held me tightly to him.

SEVEN

förening

Taking a deep breath, I finally managed to stop crying. Even though Finn no longer had his arm around me, we still sat so close we were practically touching. When I looked at him, he seemed to become aware of this and moved his arm farther away.

"What's going on?" I asked. "Who were those people? Why did we have to run away?"

Finn looked at me for a moment, then pulled back on the road and took a breath. "That is a very long answer, one that is best explained by your mother."

"My mother?" I didn't understand what more Kim would know about this, then I realized he meant my *real* mother. "We're going to see her? Where is she? Where are we going?"

"Förening," Finn explained. "It's where I live—where you'll live." He gave a small smile, meant to ease my concerns, and it did, a little. "Unfortunately, it's about a seven-hour drive."

"Where is it?"

"It's in Minnesota, along the Mississippi River in a very secluded area," Finn said.

"So what is this Förening place we're going to?" I asked, watching him.

"It's a town, sort of," Finn said. "They consider it to be more of a compound, but in the way the Kennedys have a compound. It's just a glorified gated community, really."

"So do people live there too? Humans, I mean." I was already wondering if I could bring Matt along with me.

"Not in the sense you're talking about." He hesitated before he continued, and glanced at me out of the corner of his eye. "It's entirely Trylle, trackers, and mänsklig. There are about five thousand who live there in total, and we have gas stations, a small grocery store, and a school. It's just a very small, quiet community."

"Holy hell." My eyes widened. "You mean there's just a whole town of . . . trolls? In Minnesota? And nobody ever noticed?"

"We live very quietly," Finn reiterated. "And there are ways to make people not notice."

"You sound like you're in the Mafia," I commented, and Finn smiled crookedly. "Do you guys make people sleep with the fishes or something?"

"Persuasion is a very powerful ability," he said, and his smile disappeared.

"So you have persuasion?" I asked carefully. Something seemed to upset him, and as I expected, he shook his head. "Why not?"

"I'm a tracker. Our abilities are different." He glanced over at me, and, sensing that I would just ask more questions, he went on. "They're more suited for tracking, obviously. Persuasion isn't particularly useful in that arena."

"What is useful?" I pressed, and he sighed wearily.

"It's hard to explain. They're not even real abilities in the sense of the word." His jaw ticked, and he shifted in his seat. "It's more instinct and intuition. Like the way a bloodhound follows a scent, except it's not actually something I can smell. It's just something I know." He looked over to see if I was getting it, but I just stared at him blankly.

"For example, when you went to visit that woman the other night"—that woman being someone who I had thought was my mother my entire life—"I knew you were far away, and I knew something was distressing you."

"You can tell when I'm upset? Even when you're not around me?" I asked.

Finn nodded. "As long as I'm tracking you, yes."

"I thought you said you weren't psychic," I muttered. "Being able to know my feelings sounds awfully psychic to me."

"No, I said I couldn't read minds, and I can't." Then, with an exasperated sigh, he added, "I never have any idea what you're thinking.

"I can't even tell everything you're feeling," he went on. "Just distress and fear. I need to be alert to situations when you're in danger so I can help you. My job is to keep you safe and bring you home."

"How do you know how to track people like me? Before you find us, I mean."

"Your mother has things from when you were a baby. A lock of hair usually," Finn elaborated. "I get a vibe from that, and the parents usually have a general idea where you are. Once I'm around you, I start to get a real scent of you, and that's it."

An odd warmth filled my chest. My mother had things from me. Kim had never treasured anything about me, but someone out there had. She had taken a lock of hair when I was born and kept it safe all these years

"Is that why you stared at me all the time? Because you were feeling this . . . this vibe?" I thought of the way his eyes were always on me, and the way I could never make sense of his expression.

"Yes." There was something about his answer—he wasn't lying exactly, but he was holding something back. I thought about pressing him further but there were so many other things I wanted to know.

"So . . . how often do you do this?"

"You are my eleventh." He looked at me to gauge my response, so I kept my face as expressionless as possible.

I was a little surprised by his answer. It seemed like an incredibly time-consuming process, for one thing. And he seemed fairly young to have done it eleven times. Plus, it was unnerving to think there were that many changelings out there.

"How long have you been doing this?"

"Since I was fifteen," Finn answered.

"Fifteen? No way." I shook my head. "So you're trying to tell me that at fifteen years old, your parents sent you out into the world to track and find kids? And these kids, they trusted you and believed you?"

"I'm very good at what I do," Finn replied matter-of-factly.

"Still. That just seems . . . unreal." I couldn't wrap my mind around it. "Did they all come back with you?"

"Yes, of course," he said simply.

"Do they always? With all the trackers, I mean?"

"No, they don't. They usually do, but not always."

"But they always do with you?" I persisted.

"Yes." Finn looked over at me again. "Why do you find it so hard to believe?"

"I find this all hard to believe." I tried to pinpoint what was bothering me. "Wait. You were fifteen? That means that you were never . . . you weren't a changeling. So not all Trylle begin life as changelings? How does this work?"

"Trackers are never changelings." He rubbed the back of his neck and pursed his lips. "I think it's best if your mother explains the changelings to you."

"How come trackers aren't ever changelings?" I questioned.

"We need to spend our lives being trained to be a tracker," Finn said. "And our youth is an asset. It's much easier to get close to a teenager when you are a teenager than it is when you're forty."

"A big part of what you do is building trust." I eyed him with renewed suspicion.

"Yes, it is," Finn admitted.

"So at the dance, when you were being a total dick to me. That was you building trust?"

For a split second he looked pained, then his normal emotionless expression returned. "No. That was me putting a distance between us. I shouldn't have asked you to dance. I was trying to correct the error. I needed you to trust me, but anything more would be misleading."

Everything that had transpired between us had just been because he was trying to get me to the compound. He had been keeping me safe, getting me to like him, and when he noticed my crush developing, he had tried to put me in my place. It stung painfully, so I just swallowed hard and stared out the window.

"I'm sorry if I've hurt you," Finn said quietly.

"Don't worry about it," I replied icily. "You were just doing your job."

"I know that you're being facetious, but I was." He paused. "I still am."

"Well, you're very good at it." I crossed my arms and continued to stare out the window.

I didn't feel much like talking anymore. There were still a million questions I had about everything, but I'd rather wait and talk to somebody else, anybody else. I thought I would be too anxious and excited to sleep, but after about an hour into the drive, I started nodding off. I fought to stay awake until I realized the ride would go quicker if I just slept.

When I opened my eyes, the sun was shining brightly above us. I had curled up on the seat with my knees pressed against my chest, so my whole body felt sore and achy. I looked around, then I sat up and stretched, trying to work the kinks out of my neck.

"I thought you were going to sleep the whole ride," Finn said.

"How far away are we?" I yawned and slouched low in the seat, resting my knees against the dashboard.

"Not far."

The scenery had started giving way to tall tree-lined bluffs. The car rolled up and down through the hills and valleys, and it really was stunningly beautiful. Eventually Finn slowed and we turned, driving to the top of a bluff. Soon the road curved down again, winding among the trees. Through them I could see the Mississippi River cutting through the bluffs.

A large metal gate blocked our path, but when we reached it, a guard nodded at Finn and waved us on. Once we were through, I saw beautiful houses dotting the bluffs.

They were all heavily obscured by trees, which gave me an odd sensation that there were more homes than I could actually see. But every one of them appeared luxurious and perfectly positioned to make the best of the view.

We pulled up in front of an opulent mansion perched precariously on the edge of a bluff. It was pure white, with long vines growing up over it beautifully. The back, which faced the river, was made entirely of windows, but it seemed to be held up by weak supports. While stunningly gorgeous, the house looked as if it could fall off the edge at any moment.

"What's this?" I took a break from gaping at the house to look back at Finn.

He smiled in the way that sent shivers through me. "This is it. Welcome home, Wendy."

I had come from money, but it had never been anything like this. This was aristocratic. Finn walked me to the house, and I couldn't believe that I'd truly come from this. I had never felt so small or ordinary in my entire life.

With a house like this, I had expected a butler to answer the door. Instead, it was just a kid. He looked about my age, with sandy hair cascading across his forehead. He was very attractive, but that made sense, because I couldn't believe that anything ugly ever came from a house like this. It was too perfect.

He seemed confused and surprised at first, but when he saw Finn, an understanding came to him and he smiled broadly.

"Oh, my God. You must be Wendy." He opened the massive front door so we could come in.

Finn let me go in first, which made me nervous, and I felt embarrassed with the way this kid smiled at me, especially considering my pajamas and bruised cheek. He was dressed like any other normal kid I had gone to school with, at least in the private schools, and I found that weird. As if it would be more natural for him to run around in a tuxedo first thing in the morning.

"Um, yeah," I mumbled awkwardly.

"Oh, sorry, I'm Rhys." He touched his chest, gesturing to himself, and turned back to Finn. "We weren't expecting you this soon."

"Things happen," Finn explained noncommittally.

"I'd really love to stay and talk, but I just came home for lunch, and I'm already running late on getting back to school." Rhys glanced around and looked at us apologetically. "Elora is down in the drawing room. You can get yourself there, right?"

Finn nodded. "I can."

"All right. Sorry to rush out like this." Rhys smiled sheepishly and picked up the messenger bag lying by the front door. "It was really nice meeting you, Wendy. I'm sure I'll be seeing a lot more of you."

Once he hurried out the door, I took a moment to take in my surroundings. The floors were marble, and a giant crystal chandelier hung above us. From where I stood, I could see the breathtaking view through the windowed back wall of the house. It was floor-to-ceiling glass, and all I could see were the tops of trees and the river plummeting below us. It was enough to give me vertigo, and I was on the other side of the house.

"Come on." Finn walked ahead of me, turning down a decadently furnished hall, and I scampered after him.

"Who was that?" I whispered, as if the walls could hear me. They were lined with pictures, a few of which I recognized as being painted by master painters.

"Rhys."

"Yeah, I know, but . . . is he my brother?" I asked.

"No," Finn replied. I waited for more, but apparently that was all he would say on the subjet.

Abruptly he turned and entered a room. It was the corner of the house, so two of the walls were entirely glass. One interior wall had a fireplace, and hanging above it was the portrait of an attractive older gentleman. Books lined the other interior wall. Elegant antique furniture filled the room, and a velvet chaise lounge sat poised in front of the fireplace.

A woman sat on a stool in the corner, her back to us. Her dress was dark and flowing, just like the hair that hung down her back. A large canvas was set on the easel before her. The painting was only partially finished, but it appeared to be some kind of fire, with dark smoke filtering over broken chandeliers.

She continued painting for several minutes while we stood there. I glanced over at Finn, but he just shook his head, trying to quiet me before I voiced a complaint. His hands were clasped behind his back, and he stood rigidly straight, reminding me of a soldier.

"Elora?" Finn said cautiously, and I got the sense that she intimidated him. This was as unnerving as it was surprising. He didn't seem like he could be intimidated by anyone.

When she turned to look at us, I forgot to breathe. She was much older than I had expected, in her fifties probably, but there was something stunningly elegant and beautiful about her, particularly her large dark eyes. In her youth she had probably been unbearably attractive. As it was, I could hardly believe that she was real.

"Finn!" Her voice was angelic and clear, and her surprise was endearing. With a graceful move, she swiftly stood up, and Finn did a small bow to her. It confused me, but I clumsily tried to copy it, and this caused her to laugh. She looked at Finn, but gestured to me. "This is her?"

"Yes. It is." There was a hint of pride in his voice. He had brought me here, and I was starting to realize that I must have been a very special request.

When she moved, she looked even more poised and regal. The length of her skirt swirled around her feet, making it seem as if she floated rather than walked.

Once in front of me, she inspected me carefully. She seemed to disapprove of my pajamas, especially the dirt stains on my knees I had sustained during the fight, but it was the bruise on my face that caused her to purse her lips.

"Oh, my." Her eyes widened with surprise, but her expression lacked anything resembling concern. "What happened?"

"Vittra," Finn answered with the same contempt he had used when speaking that term before.

"Oh?" Elora raised an eyebrow. "Which ones?"

"Jen and Kyra," Finn said.

"I see." Elora stared off for a minute, smoothing out the nonexistent wrinkles in her dress. Sighing tiredly, she looked to Finn. "You're sure it was only Jen and Kyra?"

"I believe so," Finn said, thinking hard. "I didn't see any signs of others, and they would've called for backup, had there been any to call. They were quite insistent on taking Wendy. Jen got violent with her."

"I can see that." Elora looked back at me. "Just the same, you are lovely." She sounded almost awed by me, and I felt a blush redden my cheeks. "It's Wendy, isn't it?"

"Yes, ma'am." I smiled nervously at her.

"What an ordinary name for such an extraordinary girl."

She looked displeased for a moment, and then turned to Finn. "Excellent work. You may be excused while I talk to her. Stay close by, though. I'll call when I need you."

Finn did another small bow before leaving the room. His level of reverence made me uncomfortable. I wasn't sure how to act around her.

"I'm Elora, and I won't expect you to call me any different. I know you still have so much to get accustomed to. I remember when I first came back." She smiled and gave a light shake of her head. "It was a very confusing time." I nodded, unsure what else to do as she gestured expansively to the room. "Sit. We have much to talk about."

"Thanks." Uncertainly, I took a seat on the edge of the sofa, afraid that if I really sat down on it I would break it or something.

Elora went to the chaise lounge, where she lay on her side, letting her dress flow around her. She propped her head up with her hand and watched me with intense fascination. Her eyes were dark and beautiful, but there was something familiar about them. They reminded me of a wild animal trapped in a cage.

"I'm not sure if Finn has explained it to you, but I am your mother," Elora said.

EIGHT

family

It was impossible. I wanted to correct her. There must be some mistake. Nothing as stunning and elegant as that could spawn me. I was awkward and impulsive. Her hair was like silk, and as it had been pointed out to me before, my hair was like a Brillo pad. I couldn't be related to her.

"Ah. I see he did not," Elora said. "From your bewildered expression, I take it you don't believe me. But let me assure you, there is no mistaking who you are. I personally chose the Everly family for you and delivered you to them myself. Finn is the best tracker we have, so there is no way you could be anyone else but my daughter."

"I'm sorry." I shifted uncomfortably in my seat. "I didn't mean to question you. I just . . ."

"I understand. You're still used to your normal human way of being. That will all change soon. Did Finn explain anything to you about Trylle?"

"Not really," I admitted carefully, afraid that I might get him in trouble.

"I'm certain you have many questions, but let me explain everything to you, and if you still have questions, you can ask me when I'm done." Elora had a coldness to her voice, and I doubted I'd ever be able to question her on anything.

"Trylle are, to the layman, trolls, but that term is antiquated and demeaning, and as you can tell, it doesn't do us justice at all." Elora gestured to the expanse of the room, with all its grace and luxury, and I nodded. "We are beings closely related to humans, but more in tune with ourselves. We have abilities, intelligence, and beauty that far surpass that of humans.

"There are two important distinctions to our lifestyle as Trylle that separate us from the humans," Elora continued. "We want to live a quiet life communing with the earth and ourselves. We work to strengthen our abilities and use them to better our lives, to protect ourselves and the things around us. We devote our entire lives to this. Förening exists only to preserve and enhance the Trylle way of life.

"The other distinction is how we maintain this lifestyle, although it isn't that different, really." She looked thoughtfully out the window. "Human children have their schools, but these places prepare them for a life of servitude. That's not what we want. We want a life of complete and total freedom. That is why we have changelings.

"The changeling practice dates back hundreds, maybe thousands of years." Elora looked at me gravely, and I gulped back the growing nausea in my belly. "Originally we were forest dwellers, far less . . . industrialized than you see now. Our children were prone to starvation and medical problems, and we did not have an adequate educational system. So we'd leave our babies in place of human children so they would have the benefits that only a human childhood could offer, then when they were old enough they would come back to us.

"That practice evolved because we evolved. Changelings were healthier, more educated, and wealthier than the Trylle counterparts that stayed behind. Eventually, every child born became a changeling. Of course, now we could easily match the benefits of the human population, but to what end? In order to maintain our current level of existence, we'd have to leave the solace of the compound and spend our lives doing menial jobs. That simply would not do.

"And so we leave our children with the most sophisticated, wealthiest human families. The changelings live a childhood that is the best this world has to offer, and then return with an inheritance from their host families that infuses our society with wealth. That, of course, isn't the only goal, but it is a large part of how we can live like this. The money you obtain from your host family will support you for the rest of your life."

"Wait. I'm sorry. I know I'm not supposed to interrupt, but . . ." I licked my lips and shook my head. "I just need to clarify a few points."

"By all means," Elora said, but venom tinged her voice.

"When I was a baby, you gave me to strangers to raise me so I could have a good education, a good childhood, and I would bring money back. Is that right?"

"Yes." Elora raised an eyebrow, daring me to question this.

I wanted to yell so badly I was shaking. But I was still afraid of her. She looked like she could snap me in half with her mind, so I just twisted my thumb ring and nodded. She had dumped me off on a crazy woman who tried to murder me, just because Elora never wanted to work and needed cash.

"Shall I continue?" Elora asked without even trying to mask the condescending tone in her voice. I nodded meekly. "I don't even remember what I was saying." She waved her hand in irritation. "If you have any other questions, I suppose you can ask them now."

"What are the Vittra?" I asked, trying to distract myself from how angry I was with her. "I don't understand who they are or what they wanted with me."

"Förening is populated with Trylle." Elora extended her arm in a wide gesture. "The term Trylle is a distinction similar to a tribe. We are trolls, and over the years, the troll population has been dwindling. Our numbers used to be great, but now there are less than a million of us on the entire planet.

"We are one of the largest tribes left, but we are not the only one," Elora continued. "The Vittra are a warring faction, and they are forever looking to pick off some of us. Either by turning us to their side, or simply by getting rid of us."

"So the Vittra want me to live with them?" I wrinkled my nose. "Why? What could I do for them?"

"I am the Queen." She paused, letting me take this in. "You are the Princess. You are my only child, the last of my legacy."

"What?" I felt my jaw drop.

"You are the Princess," Elora explained with a condescending smile. "You will one day be Queen, and being the leader of Trylle carries great weight."

"But if I'm not here, won't you just find a replacement? I mean, there's going to be a Queen here even if I'm not," I said, scrambling to make sense of this all.

"There is more to it than that. We are not all created equal," Elora went on. "Trylle are far more gifted than the others. You have already tapped into persuasion, and you have the potential for much more. Vittra are lucky to have any abilities. Adding you to their ranks would greatly add to their power and influence."

"You're saying I'm powerful?" I raised a sardonic eyebrow.

"You will be," Elora amended. "That is why you need to live here, to learn our ways so you can take your rightful place."

"Okay." I took a deep breath and ran my hand along my pajama pants.

None of this seemed real or made sense. The idea of myself as a Queen was completely absurd. I barely managed to pass for an awkward teenager.

"Finn will be staying to watch over you. Since they're looking for you, added protection would be prudent." Elora ran her hand over her skirt, not looking at me. "I'm sure you have many more questions, but you'll get the answers over time. Why don't you go get yourself cleaned up?"

"Wait," I said, my voice small and uncertain. She raised her head, looking at me with disdain. "Just . . . um . . . where's my father?"

"Oh." Elora looked away from me and stared out the window. "Dead. I'm sorry. It happened shortly after you were born."

Finn had promised me a different life where I belonged, but really, it seemed to be the exact same life with different trappings. My mother here seemed almost as cold as my fake mom, and in either life, my dad was dead.

"Also, I don't have any money." I shifted uneasily.

"Of course you don't. You probably won't have access to your trust fund until you're twenty-one, but with persuasion, you can get it sooner. Finn tells me you're very advanced with that."

"What?" I shook my head. "No. I don't even have a trust fund."

"I specifically chose the Everlys because of their wealth," Elora said matter-of-factly.

"Yeah, I know you chose them for their money, because it certainly wasn't for their mental health." I lowered my eyes, realizing I had been smart with her, but quickly plowed through it.

"My dad killed himself when I was five, so none of his insurance paid out. My mom never worked a day in her life, and she's been in a mental institution for the past eleven years, which has eaten a lot of her funds. Not only that, we've moved around a lot and wasted tons of money on houses and tuition. We're not poor by any means, but I don't think we're anywhere near the kind of rich you think we are."

"Stop saying 'we.' They're not part of you," Elora snapped

and sat up. "What are you talking about? The Everlys were one of the wealthiest families in the country. You couldn't have bled them completely dry."

"I don't know how much money we—*they*—have, but we don't . . . er . . . I didn't live like they were that rich." I was almost shouting in frustration. "And you weren't listening, I had a *terrible* childhood. My fake mother tried to kill me!"

Elora seemed more shaken by my confession that my family wasn't loaded than she was about Kim trying to kill me. She sat very still for a moment, then took a deep breath.

"Oh. So she was one of those."

"What do you mean by that?" I pressed, and by now I was livid. I couldn't believe the casual, callous air that she had about my attempted murder. " 'One of those'?"

"Oh, well." Elora shook her head as if she hadn't meant to say that. "Every now and again, a mother knows. Sometimes they hurt the child or kill them."

"Whoa, whoa, whoa. You knew there was a chance that she might kill me?" I snapped and stood up. "You knew that I could die but you just left me? You didn't care what happened to me at all!"

"Don't be so melodramatic." Elora rolled her eyes. "This is the way we live. It's a very small risk, and it rarely happens. And you lived. No harm done."

"No harm done?" I pulled up my shirt, showing her the scar that stretched across my belly. "I was six years old, and I had sixty stitches. You call that no harm done?"

"You're being disgusting." Elora stood up and waved me off. "That's not at all how a Princess should behave."

I wanted to protest, but nothing came out of my mouth. Her reaction left me feeling dazed and strange. I let my shirt fall back down over my belly, as Elora glided over to the window. She clasped her hands in front of her and stared outside. She never said a single word, but a minute later Finn appeared in the doorway.

"You need something, Elora?" Finn did a small bow to her back, making me think she probably had ways of seeing him even when she wasn't looking.

"Wendy is tired. Set her up in her room," Elora commanded diffidently. "See that she has everything she needs."

"Of course." Finn looked at me. His dark eyes were comforting, and even though I knew this was just his job, I felt relieved knowing he was there.

He left hastily, and I hurried after him. I wrapped my arms tightly around myself, trying to steady my nerves. I was still reeling from everything, trying to make sense of how I fit into all this.

Elora was right, though. I probably did need to get cleaned up, and maybe if I slept on it, everything would seem better somehow. But I doubted it.

Finn led me up a winding staircase and down another elaborate hall. At the end, he opened a heavy wooden door, revealing what I assumed was my room. It was massive, with high-vaulted ceilings, and one entirely windowed wall that made it seem even larger.

A gigantic four-poster bed sat in the center, and an array of gleaming modern furnishings surrounded it. The room boasted a laptop, flat-screen, gaming systems, iPod, and every other gadget I could possibly want. Finn opened the closet door, which was already stocked with clothing. He opened another door and flicked on the light, revealing my own private bathroom, which more closely resembled a spa.

"How do you know where everything is?" I asked. He seemed to know this house very well, and having him there beside me helped calm me some.

"I stay here from time to time," Finn replied nonchalantly.

"What? Why?" I felt a horrible pang of jealousy, terrified that he was somehow involved with Elora in a perverse fashion. He did seem to revere her more than I thought he should.

"Protection. Your mother is a very powerful woman, but she's not all-powerful," Finn explained vaguely. "Since I'm a tracker, I can tune in to her. I can sense danger and aid her if it's required."

"Is it required?" At that moment I didn't particularly care if a band of raging marauders tried to do her in, but if there were frequent attacks on her "castle," I thought I should know.

"I'll help you get acclimated. Everybody knows this isn't a perfect system. Rhys's room is down the hall. My room, along with Elora's, is on the other wing."

It didn't escape me that Finn had ignored my question entirely, but it had been a long day, so I let it pass. I definitely felt better knowing he would be around. I didn't think I could handle it all if I was left alone in this house with that woman.

While she was clearly stunning and powerful, there wasn't any warmth to her.

I hadn't realized that I even wanted that until now. After all the years of rejecting Maggie's and even Matt's attempts at bonding, I hadn't known how much I'd crave basic human warmth once it was gone.

"So . . . did you do this?" I gestured to my high-tech room.

"No. Rhys decorated it." Finn didn't look that interested in any of the expensive gear I had lying about, so that made sense. "The clothes were all Willa, I believe. You'll meet her later on."

"Rhys isn't my brother?" I asked again. I couldn't figure out how he fit into all of this. We had only met briefly, but he seemed nice and normal.

"No. He's mänsklig," Finn answered, as if I would understand.

"What does that mean?" I furrowed my brow at him.

"It means he's not your brother," Finn replied glibly and made a step toward the door. "Is there anything you need before I go?"

His abrupt decision to leave disappointed me, especially when I felt so isolated and confused, but I had no reason to keep him. Still hugging myself tightly, I shook my head and sat on the bed. Instead of leaving, Finn paused and looked back at me.

"Are you going to be all right with all of this?" Finn asked, eyeing me intently.

"I don't know," I admitted. "This wasn't at all what I had expected." It was far grander and far worse than anything I had envisioned. "I just . . . I feel like I'm in *The Princess Diaries*, if Julie Andrews had been a thief."

"Mmm," Finn murmured knowingly and walked back over to me. He sat on the bed and crossed his arms over his chest. "I know this way of life is a hard concept for some."

"They're grifters, Finn." I swallowed hard. "That's all they are. I'm just a means of swindling money out of rich people. Joke's on her, though. My family's not that rich."

"I can assure you that you are much more than that to her, much more. Elora is a complicated woman, and showing emotion doesn't come easy for her. But she is a good woman. Regardless of whether you have money or not, you will have a place here."

"Do you know how much money they have? The Everlys?" I asked.

"Yes," Finn said almost hesitantly. "Elora had me checking your finances while I tracked you."

"How much?" I asked.

"Do you want to know your trust and what you stand to inherit, or your guardian and brother's total wealth?" Finn's face had gone expressionless. "Do you want net worth? Liquid assets? Are you including real estate, like the house they still own in the Hamptons? Dollar amount?"

"I don't really care." I shook my head. "I was just . . . Elora was convinced that we really did have a lot of money, and I was just curious. I didn't even know I had a trust fund until today."

"Yes. You really do have a lot of money," Finn said. "More

than even Elora had originally thought." I nodded and looked at my feet. "You lived well below your means."

"I think Maggie thought it would be better for me and Matt, and I never really cared that much about money." I kept staring at my feet, and then finally I looked up at Finn. "They would give me anything. They would give me all of it if I asked. But I'm never taking any money from them, not for myself and certainly not for Elora. Make sure you tell her that when you go back to her."

I had expected him to protest in some way, but Finn surprised me. His lips curled into the hint of a smile, and if anything, he looked almost proud of me.

"I will," he promised, amusement tinging his voice. "But right now you should shower. You'll feel better after."

Finn helped me settle into my room. My closet was massive and overstocked, but he knew exactly where my new pajamas were. He taught me how to close the blinds for my windows, which were run by remote control, and how to turn on my overly complicated shower.

Once he left, I sat on the edge of the tub and tried not to let this all get to me. I was starting to think that Matt and Maggie might have been the only people who loved me for me, and now I was supposed to steal from them. Even if it wasn't really stealing. I knew they would freely give me anything I asked for, and that only made it hurt worse.

NINE

homesick

When I came out of my shower, wrapped in a fluffy bathrobe, I was surprised to find Rhys sitting on my bed. He had my iPod, the one that had come with the room, and he was scrolling through it. I cleared my throat loudly, since he apparently hadn't heard me exit the bathroom.

"Oh, hey!" Rhys set aside the iPod and got to his feet, grinning at me in a way that made his eyes sparkle. "Sorry. I didn't mean to interrupt you. I just wanted to see how you were doing, how you liked it here."

"I don't know." My hair had to be terrible mess, and I pulled a hand through the wet tangles. "It's too soon to tell yet."

"You like the stuff?" Rhys asked, gesturing around the room. "I picked out everything that I liked, which I know sounds kind of vain. I asked for some input from Rhiannon, because she's a girl, but it's still so hard to pick out stuff for someone you've never met."

"No, it all looks really good. You did a great job." I rubbed my eyes and yawned.

"Oh, sorry. You're probably exhausted." Rhys stood up. "I just got done with school, and I didn't have a chance to talk to you earlier. But . . . yeah. I'll leave you be."

"Wait. You just got done with school?" I furrowed my brow, trying to understand. "Does that mean you're a tracker?"

"No." It was his turn to look confused. "I'm mänks." When he saw the perplexed look on my face, he corrected himself. "Sorry. It's just short for mänsklig."

"What the hell does that mean?" I demanded. My low energy made it hard to conceal my exasperation.

"They'll explain it to you later." Rhys shrugged. "Anyway, I should let you freshen up. If I'm not in my room, I'll be downstairs, getting some food."

"Are you happy here?" I blurted out before I could think about how rude that sounded. His eyes met mine just for a second, revealing something intense I couldn't quite decipher, but then he quickly dropped them.

"Why wouldn't I be happy?" Rhys asked wryly. He ran his fingers along my silk sheets, staring at the bedspread intently. "I have everything a kid could want. Video games, cars, toys, money, clothes, servants . . ." He trailed off, but then a slow smile returned to his face and he looked up at me. "And now I have a Princess living across the hall from me. I'm ecstatic."

"I'm not really a Princess." I shook my head and tucked my hair behind my ears. "Not in the real sense of the word. I mean . . . I just got here."

"You look like a Princess to me." The way he smiled at me made me want to blush, so I looked down, unsure of what else to do.

"So what about you?" I kept my head down, but I raised my eyes to meet his. The smile playing on my lips felt oddly flirtatious, but I didn't mind. "Are you some kind of Prince?"

"Hardly." Rhys laughed. He plucked at his sandy hair, looking rather sheepish. "I should probably let you finish getting dressed. The chef is off tonight, so supper is on me."

Rhys turned and walked down the hall, whistling a song I didn't recognize. I shut my door, wishing I could understand this all better. I was a Trylle Princess to a grifter empire, and I had a mänsklig living across the hall from me, whatever the hell that meant.

I lived in this amazingly stunning house with these cold, indifferent people, and the price of admission was stealing from the only people who cared about me. Sure, Finn was here, but he had made it perfectly clear that his only interest in me was business.

I went through my closet, looking for something to wear. Most of the clothes seemed too fancy for me. Not that I had grown up wearing rags or anything. In fact, if my mother . . . er, Kim . . . hadn't gone crazy and left, these would be exactly the kind of clothes I'd be expected to wear now. All high-class fashion pieces. Eventually I managed to dig up a simple skirt and shirt that resembled something I'd actually wear.

I was starving, so I headed off to find the kitchen to take Rhys up on his offer. The tile floors were cold under my feet, and strangely, I had yet to see any rugs or carpet in the entire house.

I had never been fond of the feel of carpet on my feet, or really the feel of anything on them. When I thought back to my glimpse of the closet here, as large and full as it had been, there hadn't been any shoes. It must be a Trylle thing, and that thought was oddly comforting. I was part of something.

I passed through the living room, where a fireplace filled the partial wall separating it from an elegant dining room. The furniture appeared to be handcrafted wood and was upholstered in white. The floors were all smooth golden wood, and everything was aimed toward the glass wall, forcing you to admire the view.

"Nice digs, right?" Rhys said, and I whirled around to find him standing behind me, smiling.

"Yeah." I looked around the room appreciatively. "Elora definitely has good taste."

"Yeah." Rhys shrugged. "You gotta be hungry, though. Come on. I'll whip you up something in the kitchen." He started walking out of the room, and I followed him. "You'll probably hate what I make, though. You're into all that health food junk like everybody else, right?"

"I don't know." I had never thought of myself as a health nut, but the things I preferred tended to be organic and vegan. "I like natural things, I guess."

He nodded knowingly as he led me past the ornate dining room into a massive kitchen. There were two professional-grade stoves, two massive stainless-steel fridges, a gigantic island in the center, and more cupboards than the residents in this house could possibly use. Rhys went over to the fridge and pulled out a bottle of Mountain Dew and a bottle of water.

"Water, right?" Rhys held it out to me, and I took it from him. "I'm really not the best cook, but you'll have to settle for my cooking."

"How often do you have a chef?" I asked. In a place like this, they definitely had some kind of staff.

"Part-time." Rhys took a sip from his Mountain Dew, then set it on the island and went to the other fridge to start rooting around. "Just weekends, but that's because it's usually when we entertain. I don't know what Elora eats during the week, but I'm on a fend-for-yourself basis."

I leaned on the island, drinking my water. This kitchen reminded me of the one in our house in the Hamptons, the one Kim had attempted filicide in, but that one had been smaller. If she hadn't left, this was probably how I would've been raised. In fact, I'm sure this was how she had been brought up.

Maggie easily could've lived like this. I thought back to what Finn had told me about Matt and Maggie living well below their means. I wondered why it was so important to them to preserve the family nest egg.

The only explanation that made sense was that they were saving it for me—to make sure I was taken care of for the rest of my life. Which probably seemed all the more necessary given my problems at school.

Funny that the very thing Elora planned to steal from them was precisely what they planned to give.

And Maggie had made it clear through her choices that taking care of me herself was more important than spending money. She had made a choice that my own mother never would have.

"So you like shitake mushrooms, right?" Rhys was saying. He had been pulling things out of the fridge, but I had been too lost in thought to notice. His arms were overflowing with vegetables.

"Uh, yeah, I love mushrooms." I straightened up and tried to see what all he had, and for the most part it looked like things I enjoyed.

"Excellent." Rhys grinned at me and dropped his armload of food into the kitchen sink. "I'm going to make you the best stir-fry you've ever tasted."

He went about chopping things up, and I offered to help him, but he insisted that he could handle it. The whole time, he talked amicably about the new motorcycle he'd gotten last week. I tried to keep up with the conversation, but all I knew about motorcycles were that they went fast and I liked them.

"What are you making in here?" Finn came into the kitchen, his expression vaguely disgusted.

His hair was damp from a recent shower, and he smelled like the grass after a rain, only sweeter. He walked past me without even a glance in my direction and went over to where Rhys had thrown everything into a wok on the stove.

"Stir-fry!" Rhys proclaimed.

"Really?" Finn leaned over his shoulder and peered down at the ingredients in the pan. Rhys moved to the side a little so

Finn could reach in and grab something out of it. He sniffed it, then popped it into his mouth. "Well, it's not terrible."

"Stop my beating heart!" Rhys put his hand over his heart and feigned astonishment. "Has my food passed the test of the hardest food critic in the land?"

"No. I just said it wasn't terrible." Finn shook his head at Rhys's dramatics and went to the fridge to get a bottle of water. "And I'm certain that Elora is a much harsher food critic than I'll ever be."

"That's probably true, but she's never let me cook for her," Rhys admitted, shaking the wok to stir up the vegetables more.

"You really shouldn't let him cook for you," Finn advised, looking at me for the first time. "He gave me food poisoning once."

"You cannot get food poisoning from an orange!" Rhys protested and looked back at him. "It's just not possible! And even if you can, I *handed* you the orange. I didn't even have a chance to contaminate it!"

"I don't know." Finn shrugged. A smile was creeping onto his face, and I could tell he was amused by how much Rhys was getting worked up.

"You didn't even eat the part I touched! You peeled it and threw the skin away!" Rhys sounded exasperated. He wasn't paying attention to the wok as he struggled to convince us of his innocence, and a flame licked up from the food.

"Food's on fire." Finn nodded to the stove.

"Dammit!" Rhys got a glass of water and splashed it in the

stir-fry, and I started to question how good this was going to taste when he was done with it.

"If being picky is a Trylle trait—and it sounds like it is—how come Rhys isn't picky?" I asked. "Is it because he's mänks?"

In a flash, Finn's face changed to a mask of stone. "Where did you hear that word? From Elora?"

"No, from Rhys," I said. Rhys was still bustling around the stove but something about his posture had changed. He appeared almost sheepish. "And I wish one of you would tell me what that means. What's the big mystery?"

Rhys turned around, a nervous glint in his eye, and exchanged a look with Finn that I couldn't read.

"Elora will explain everything in time," Finn said. "But until then, it's not our place to discuss it."

Rhys turned around again, but I knew that the icy edge in Finn's voice hadn't escaped him.

On that note, Finn turned and walked out of the kitchen.

"Well, that was weird," I said to no one in particular.

When Rhys finished cooking, he pulled stools up to the island. Fortunately, the awkward moment had passed and our mood lightened again.

"So what do you think?" Rhys nodded at the plate of food I was trying to eat.

"It's pretty good," I lied. He had obviously worked hard on it, and his blue eyes showed how proud he was of it, so I couldn't let him down. To prove my point, I took a bite and smiled.

"Good. You guys are hard to cook for." When Rhys took a

mouthful of his own food, his sandy hair fell into his eyes, and he brushed it away.

"So . . . you know Finn pretty well?" I asked carefully, stabbing my fork into a mushroom.

Their banter earlier had left me curious. Before things got weird, Finn seemed to genuinely enjoy Rhys, and I had never seen Finn enjoy anybody. The closest he came was respect and obedience for Elora, but I couldn't tell what his true feelings were for her.

"I guess." Rhys shrugged like he hadn't really thought about it. "He's just around a lot."

"Like how often?" I pressed as casually as I could.

"I don't know." He took a bite and thought for a minute. "It's hard to say. Storks move around a lot."

"Storks?"

"Yeah, trackers." Rhys smiled sheepishly. "You know how you tell little kids that a stork brings the babies? Well, trackers bring the babies here. So we call them storks. Not to their faces, though."

"I see." I wondered what kind of nickname they had for people like me, but I didn't think that now was the best time to ask. "So they move around a lot?"

"Well, yeah. They're gone tracking a lot, and Finn is in pretty high demand because he's so good at it," Rhys explained. "And then when they come back, a lot of them stay with some of the more prestigious families. Finn's been here off and on for the past five years or so. But when he's not here, somebody else usually is."

"So he's a bodyguard?"

"Yeah, something like that." Rhys nodded.

"But what do they need bodyguards for?" I thought back to the iron gate and the security guard who had allowed our entrance into Förening in the first place.

When I had looked around the entryway, I remembered seeing a fancy alarm system by the front door. This all seemed like an awful lot of trouble to go to for a small community hidden in the bluffs. I wondered if this was all for the Vittra, but I didn't want to ask.

"She's the Queen. It's just standard procedure," Rhys answered evasively, and he purposely stared down at his plate. He tried to erase his anxiety before I noticed, and forced a smile. "So how does it feel being a Princess?"

"Honestly? Not as awesome as I thought it would be," I said, and he laughed heartily at that.

Rhys kind of straightened up the kitchen after we finished eating, explaining the maid would be in tomorrow to take care of the rest of it. He gave me a brief tour of the house, showing me all the ridiculous antiquities that had been passed down from generation to generation.

One room only held pictures of previous Kings and Queens. When I asked where a picture of my father was, Rhys just shook his head and said he didn't know anything about it.

Eventually we parted ways. He cited some homework he had to get done and having to get to bed because he had school in the morning.

I wandered around the house a bit more, but I never saw

either Finn or Elora. I played around with the stuff in my room, but I quickly tired of it. Feeling restless and bored, I tried to get some rest, but sleep eluded me.

I felt incredibly homesick. I longed for the familiar comfort of my regular-sized house with all my ordinary things. If I were at home, Matt would be sitting in the living room, reading a book under the glow of the lamplight.

Right now he was probably staring at the phone, or driving around to look for me. And Maggie was probably crying her eyes out, which would only make Matt blame himself more.

My actual mother was somewhere in this house, or I assumed she was, anyway. She had abandoned me with a family that she knew nothing about except that they were rich, and she knew there was a risk that I could be killed. It happens sometimes. That's what she said. When I came back, after all these years away from me, she hadn't hugged me, or even been that happy to see me.

Everything felt way too big in this house. With all this vast space between everything, it felt like I was trapped on an island. I had always thought that's what I wanted, to be my very own island. But here I was, and I felt nothing but isolated and confused.

It didn't help that people weren't telling me things. Every time I asked something, there were only half answers and vague responses before the person I'd asked quickly changed the subject. For being set to inherit a kingdom of sorts, I was pretty low on the information ladder.

TEN

precognition

After sleeping fitfully, I got up and got ready for the day. I wandered around the house, but not intentionally. I had been trying to get to the kitchen, but I took a wrong turn somewhere and got lost. Rhys had given me an explanation of the palace layout the day before, but not enough, apparently.

The palace was divided into two massive wings, separated by the grand entryway. All official business took place in the south wing, which housed the meeting rooms, ballroom, a massive dining hall, offices, the throne room, as well as staff quarters and the Queen's bedroom.

The north wing was more casual and contained my room, guest bedrooms, a living room, the kitchen, and the sitting parlor.

I was wandering around the north wing, opening doors and investigating. As far as I could tell, this place had almost as many guest rooms as a Holiday Inn, only they were a whole lot fancier. I eventually found Elora's parlor, but she wasn't there, so it didn't help me any.

I moved on and tried to open the door across the hall from Elora's space, but it wouldn't budge. So far, this was the only door I'd found that had been locked, and I found that strange. Especially in this wing. I suppose in the south wing, locking up official business would make sense.

Fortunately, I knew a thing or two about lock-picking. In attempts to keep from being expelled, I had broken into a few school offices and stolen papers. I don't recommend it, and in the end, it was usually ineffective.

I pulled a bobby pin from my hair and looked around. I didn't see anyone, and hadn't so far this morning, so I set about breaking in. After a few unsuccessful twists in the lock, I felt something give, and I turned the knob.

Pushing the door open slowly, I peeked in, half expecting to find the royal bathroom or something. When nobody screamed at me to go away, I pushed the door open wider and stepped inside. Unlike the other rooms, this one was completely dark.

Feeling along the wall, I finally found the light switch and flicked it on. The room reminded me of a large storeroom. It had no windows, and the walls were dark brown. With a bare lightbulb in the ceiling, it held none of the grandeur of the rest of the house, and it had no furniture.

But it was filled to the brim with paintings. Not hanging on the wall. Just stacked and piled around in every available space. At first I assumed they must be leftovers from the King and Queen room, but from what I could see, none of them were portraits.

I picked up the one nearest to me, and it was a lovely picture of a newborn baby wrapped in a blue blanket. I set it aside and picked up another, which appeared to be Elora, looking much younger and even more beautiful, dressed in a gorgeous white gown. Despite the beauty of the picture, her eyes looked sad and remorseful.

Holding the picture at arm's length so I could get a better look at it, I realized something. It had the same brushstrokes, the same technique as the painting of the baby. I picked up another picture to compare, and it was the same too.

These were all painted by the same artist.

I thought back to the drawing room and the painting I had seen Elora working on. Something with dark smoke and chandeliers. I couldn't be certain, but I would guess these were hers.

I sifted through a few more of the paintings, growing even more bewildered, and then I saw one that stopped my heart cold. When I picked it up, I wasn't surprised to see my hands were shaking.

It showed me, looking about the same as I did now, except dressed nicer. I wore a beautiful flowing white gown, but there was a tear in the side of the dress, revealing a thin line of red blood. My hair had been pulled back, but it was starting to come loose, wild strands falling free.

In the painting, I lay on my belly on a marble balcony. The floor around me was covered in pieces of glass that shimmered like diamonds, but I didn't seem to notice. My outstretched hand extended past the balcony, reaching into a dark oblivion.

But my face was what struck me the most. I looked absolutely horrified.

Once I got past that, I realized something even more disturbing. This picture looked *exactly* like me. And I'd only been here for a day. There was no way Elora could've painted something this detailed within twenty-four hours of meeting me.

But how could she paint me with such accuracy if we'd never met?

"I should've known you'd be snooping," Finn said from behind me, startling me so much I dropped the painting.

"I—I got lost." I turned to look at him standing in the doorway.

"In a locked room?" He raised an eyebrow and crossed his arms.

"No, I—" I started to formulate some kind of lame excuse, but decided against it. I picked up the picture, the one of me reaching for nothing, and held it up for him to see. "What's this?"

"It appears to be a painting, and if you hadn't gathered from the locked door, it's also none of your business." It came as a relief that Finn didn't sound very upset. At least not as upset as Elora would be if she found out I was in here, I'm sure.

"This is me." I tapped the picture.

"Maybe." He shrugged, as if he wasn't convinced.

"No, I wasn't asking. This is me," I insisted. "What am I doing?"

"I haven't the faintest idea," Finn sighed. "I didn't paint it."

"Did Elora?" I asked, and when he didn't say anything, I took that as my answer. "Why would she paint this? *How* did she paint this? We'd never met before yesterday."

"She gave birth to you. You'd met before," Finn replied dryly.

"Yeah, when I was a baby. That doesn't count." I raised the picture higher so he couldn't help but look at it. "Why would she paint this? Or any of these?"

"In all your myriad questions about this room, did you ever stop to ask yourself *why* this room is locked?" Finn gave me a hard look. "That Elora might not want people looking at these?"

"Yeah, it did occur to me." I looked back down at the painting, ignoring him. "But this is me. I have a right to know."

"That's not how it works. You don't have the right to know other people's thoughts just because they include you," he said. "Just the same as I don't have the right to yours just because they're about me."

"You presume that I think of you?" I fought the growing blush on my cheeks and shook my head, trying to get back to the point. "Just tell me what's going on. And don't just tell me to wait for Elora to tell me, because that's not good enough. Not after seeing this."

I put the painting down and returned my gaze to Finn.

"Fine. But get out of there before Elora finds you." He moved back from the doorway, making room for me to step out.

I had to climb over all the paintings I had disturbed, but he didn't tell me to put them back in order, which was good because I didn't think I could. The room had no organization, and all the paintings were placed haphazardly.

Once I made my escape, Finn shut the door, making certain it was locked properly.

"So?" I asked, looking at him expectantly. He had his back to me, testing the door again to be sure it wouldn't budge.

"So, that's Elora's private room." He turned to look at me and pointed at the door. "Do not go in there. Do not touch her private things."

"I don't know what's so bad about them. Why does she paint them if she's gonna hide them away?"

He started walking down the hall, so I went after him. "She paints them because she has to."

"What do you mean?" I crinkled my brow. "Like an artist's urge takes hold of her?" I thought about it more, and it made even less sense. "Elora doesn't seem like an artist type."

"She's not, really." Finn sighed. "She has precognition."

"What? Like she can see the future?" I asked dubiously.

"Kind of." He wagged his head, like that wasn't quite right. "She can't see it. She can only *paint* it."

"Wait." I stopped short, and he walked a few more steps before stopping to look back at me. "You're telling me all those paintings were of the future?"

Finn nodded. "At the time they were painted, yes. Some of them are old, and they've already happened."

"But that means the picture of me, that's in the future!" I pointed back at the room. "What does that mean? What am I doing?"

"I don't know." He shrugged, as if he hadn't thought of it. "Elora doesn't know."

"How can she not know? That makes no sense—she painted it."

"Yes, and all she knows is what she paints," Finn explained slowly. "She doesn't see anything. She picks up the brush, and it just . . . comes out. Or at least that's my understanding of the process."

"But why would she just randomly paint me looking so scared?"

"It's just how it is," he said, a note of sadness in his voice. Breathing deeply, he started walking away again. "And that's why the room is locked."

"What do you mean?" I chased after him.

"People want to know more about what she's painted, but she doesn't have the answers," Finn said. "Or they want her to paint a particular spot in the future, and she can't. She has no control over what she sees."

"What's the point of it, then?" I asked. I quickened my pace to keep up with him, staring at his profile while he continued to stare straight ahead.

"She thinks it's a punishment."

"For what?"

"Everybody has something to be punished for." He shook his head vaguely.

"So . . . she has no idea what will happen to me? Or how to prevent it?"

"No."

"That's horrible," I said, more to myself than him. "That's even worse than not knowing anything."

"Precisely." Finn looked at me and slowed down, then stopped completely.

"Will I be able to do that? Have precognitive painting?" I asked.

"Maybe, maybe not." His eyes searched mine, in that soft way they did sometimes, and if I hadn't been worrying about my impending doom, I would've felt my stomach flutter.

"Do you know what my abilities will be?"

"No. Only time will tell for sure." He looked away, staring off at nothing. "Based on your parentage, they'll be very strong."

"When will I know for sure?"

"Later. After your training starts, and maybe when you get a bit older." Finn smiled thinly at me. "You have much to look forward to."

"Like what?"

"Like everything." He smiled more genuinely, and turned to walk away again. "Come on. I want to show you something."

ELEVEN

secret garden

Finn led me through the house and down a hall I didn't know existed. We went out the side door and stepped onto a narrow gravel trail lined with tall hedges. It curved around the house, leading us down the bluffs before it opened into a beautiful garden. The house and balcony hung over part of it, leaving half of it in shadows, but the rest was bathed in the warm bright glow of the sun.

Brick walls covered in thick flowered vines kept the garden blocked off from the rest of the world. Apple, pear, and plum trees blossomed all over the garden, making it more of an orchard than a garden. Flowers of pink and purple and blue sprang out in small beds, and mossy greens like creeping Charlie grew in patches along the ground.

It was on a hillside, so the whole thing tilted down. As we walked down the trail, I slipped a bit, and Finn took my hand to steady me. My skin flushed warmly, but the second I caught my balance, he let go of my hand. Still, I refused to let it dampen my mood.

"How is this possible?" I asked as butterflies and birds flitted about the trees. "None of these things are in season. They shouldn't be flowering."

"They always flower, even in winter," Finn said, as if that made more sense.

"How?" I repeated.

"Magic." He smiled and walked ahead.

I looked up at the house towering above us. From where I stood, I couldn't see any of the windows. The garden had been built in the perfect spot so it wasn't visible from the house, leaving it hidden among the trees. It was a secret garden.

Finn was ahead of me, and I hurried to catch up to him. The sound of the wind in the trees and the river flowing echoed through the bluffs, but over that I heard laughter. I walked around a hedge and saw a pond that inexplicably included a small waterfall.

I found the source of the laughter on two curved stone benches poised around it.

Rhys lay on his back on one bench, laughing and looking up at the sky, and Finn stood next to him, admiring the sparkling pond. A girl looking a little bit older than me sat on the other bench, a Mountain Dew bottle in her hand. Her hair was shiny red, her eyes sparkled green, and she had a nervous smile. When she saw me, she stood up and paled a little.

"You got here just in time, Wendy." Rhys smirked, sitting

up. "We were having a show. Rhiannon was just about to burp the alphabet!"

"Oh, my gosh, Rhys, I was not!" the girl protested, her cheeks flushing with embarrassment. "I just drank the Mountain Dew too fast and I said excuse me!" Rhys laughed again, and she looked apologetically at me. "I'm sorry. Rhys can be such an idiot sometimes. I wanted to make a better first impression than this."

"You're doing okay so far." I wasn't used to the idea of anybody trying to impress me . . . ever, and I couldn't imagine that this girl would have to try too hard. She already had a certain likable quality to her.

"Anyway, Wendy, this is Rhiannon, the girl next door." Rhys gestured from one to the other of us. "Rhiannon, this is Wendy, future ruler of everything around you."

"Hi, nice to meet you." She set down her pop and came over to me so she could shake my hand. "I've heard so much about you."

"Oh, yeah? Like what?" I asked.

Rhiannon floundered helplessly for a minute, looking to Rhys for help, but he just laughed.

"It's okay. I was just kidding," I told her.

"Oh. Sorry." She flashed an embarrassed smile.

"Why don't you come have a seat, Rhiannon, and relax for a bit?" Rhys patted the seat next to him, trying to ease her discomfort. She felt awkward because of me, and I still couldn't wrap my head around the concept.

"Is this new?" Finn asked Rhys and pointed to the pond.

"Uh, yeah." Rhys nodded. "I think Elora had it put in while you were gone. She's getting everything all fancied up, 'cause of everything that's coming."

"Mmm," Finn said noncommittally.

I went over to inspect the pond and waterfall myself. The waterfall should've drained the pond, since the pond had no other water flowing into it. I admired the way it sparkled brightly under the sun, and thought it shouldn't even be possible. But then again, none of this should be possible.

Rhys continued to tease Rhiannon about everything, and she kept blushing and making apologies for him. Their relationship resembled a normal healthy sibling relationship, and I had to push the thought away before I had a chance to think of Matt.

I sat down on the bench across from them, and Finn took a seat next to me. Rhys tended to dominate the conversation, with Rhiannon interjecting when he said things that were categorically untrue or apologizing when she thought he was being rude. He never was, though. He was funny and lively and kept things from ever feeling awkward.

Occasionally Finn would look over at me and make quiet comments when Rhys and Rhiannon were otherwise engaged in some kind of debate. Every time he did, I felt his knee brush against mine.

At first I assumed it was a simple accident because of our close proximity, but he had actually tilted himself toward me, leaning in closer. It was a subtle move, one that Rhys and Rhiannon probably wouldn't catch, but I definitely had.

"You are such a pest!" Rhiannon grumbled playfully after Rhys had flicked an unwanted flower at her. She twirled it in her hands, admiring the beauty of it. "You know you're not even supposed to pick these flowers. Elora will kill you if she finds out."

"So what do you think?" Finn asked me, his voice low. I leaned toward him so I could hear him better, and his dark eyes met mine.

"It's really lovely." I smiled, gesturing to the garden around us, but I couldn't look away from him.

"I wanted to show you that it's not all cold and intimidating," Finn explained. "I wanted you to see something warm and beautiful." A small smile played on his lips. "Although, when you're not around, it's not quite as nice here."

"You think so?" I asked, trying to make my voice sound sexier somehow, but I completely failed. Finn smiled wider, and my heart nearly hammered out of my chest.

"Sorry for interrupting your playtime," Elora spoke from behind us. Her voice wasn't that loud, but somehow it seemed to echo through everything.

Rhys and Rhiannon immediately stopped their fighting, both of them sitting up rigidly and staring down at the pond. Finn moved away from me, at the same time turning around to face Elora, making it look like that had been his intention. The way she looked at me made me feel guilty, even though I was pretty sure I hadn't done anything wrong.

"You weren't interrupting anything," Finn assured her, but I sensed nervousness below his calm words. "Were you planning to join us?"

"No, that'll be quite all right." Elora surveyed the garden with distaste. "I needed to speak with you."

"Would you like us to be excused?" Rhys offered, and Rhiannon promptly stood up.

"That won't be necessary." Elora held up her hand, and Rhiannon blushed as she sat back down. "We will be having guests for dinner." Her eyes went back to Rhys and Rhiannon, and Rhiannon seemed to cower under Elora's gaze. "I trust that you two will find a way to make yourselves useful."

"When they come over here, I'll go over to Rhiannon's," Rhys suggested cheerily. Elora nodded at him, indicating that his response was sufficient.

"As for you, you will be joining us." Elora smiled at me, but couldn't mask the unease behind it. "The guests are very good friends of our family, and I expect you to make a good impression on them." She gave Finn that intense look, staring at him so long I felt uncomfortable, and he nodded in understanding. "Finn will be in charge of preparing you for the dinner."

I nodded, figuring that I had better say something. "Okay."

"That is all. Carry on." Elora turned and walked away, her skirt flowing behind her, but nobody said anything until she was long gone.

Finn sighed, and Rhiannon practically shivered with relief. She was clearly even more terrified of the Queen than I was, and I wondered what Elora had done to make the girl so afraid. Only Rhys seemed to shake it off as soon as she had left.

"I don't know how you can stand that creepy mind-speak

thing she does with you, Finn." Rhys shook his head. "I would freak out if she was in my head."

"Why? There's nothing in your head for her to get into." Finn stood up, and Rhiannon giggled nervously.

"What did she say to you, anyway?" Rhys pressed, looking up at him.

Finn dusted off his pants, ridding them of dirt and leaves from the bench, but he didn't respond.

"Finn? What'd she say?"

"It's nothing to concern yourself with," Finn admonished him quietly, then turned to me. "Are you ready?"

"For what?"

"We have a lot to go over." He glanced warily at the house, then back at me. "Come on. We better get started."

As we walked back to the house, I realized that whenever Elora left, I was able to breathe again. Whenever she was present, it was as if she took all the oxygen from the room. Breathing deeply, I ran my hand up and down my arm to stifle the chill that ran over me.

"Are you holding up all right?" Finn asked, noticing my unease.

"Yeah, I'm great." I tucked some of my curls behind my ears. "So . . . what's going on with you and Elora?"

"What do you mean?" Finn looked at me from the corner of his eye.

"I don't know." I shrugged, thinking of what Rhys had said after she'd left. "It just seems like she looks at you intently a lot, and like you understand exactly what she means." As soon as it came out of my mouth, it dawned on me. "That's one of her abilities, isn't it? Talking inside your head? Kind of like what I can do, but less manipulative. 'Cause she's just telling you what to do."

"Not even telling me what to do. She's just talking," Finn corrected me.

"Why doesn't she talk to me like that?" I asked.

"She wasn't sure if you'd be receptive. If you're not accustomed to it, hearing another person's voice in your head can be unsettling. And she didn't really need to."

"But she needed to with you?" I slowed down, and he matched my pace. "She was talking to you privately about me, wasn't she?"

Finn paused, and I could see that he was considering lying to me. "Some of it, yes," he admitted.

"Can she read minds?" I felt slightly horrified at the thought.

"No. Very few can." When he looked over at me, he smiled crookedly. "Your secrets are safe, Wendy."

We went into the dining room, and Finn set about preparing me for dinner. As it turned out, I wasn't completely socially stunted and had a basic understanding of manners. Most of what Finn said amounted to commonsense things, like always say please and thank you, but he also encouraged me to keep my mouth shut whenever possible.

I think his task had been less about preparing me for the dinner and more about keeping me in line. The secret things

Elora had been telling him had just been a warning to babysit me—or else.

Dinner was at eight, and the company was arriving at seven. About an hour or so before that, Rhys popped in to wish me good luck and let me know he was heading over to Rhiannon's, in case anybody cared. Shortly after I got out of the shower, Finn came in, looking even sharper than usual.

He was clean-shaven for the first time since he'd stopped going to school, and he wore black slacks and a black button-down shirt with a narrow white tie. It should've been too much with all that black, but he managed to pull it off, all the while looking incredibly sexy.

I had on only my bathrobe, and I wondered why nobody here thought it was inappropriate for boys to barge in when I wasn't dressed. At least I was doing something semi-sexy: sitting on the edge of my bed putting lotion on my legs. I did it every time I showered, but since Finn was in the room, I tried to play it off as being sensual when it really wasn't.

Not that Finn even noticed. He knocked once, opened my bedroom door, and only gave me a fleeting glance as he headed straight to my closet. After a little while, I sighed in frustration and hurriedly rubbed the rest of the lotion in while Finn continued to rummage through my clothes.

"I don't think I have anything in your size," I said and leaned farther back on my bed, trying to see what he was doing in there.

"Funny," he muttered absently.

"What are you doing in there?" I asked, watching him, but he didn't even look at me.

"You are a Princess, and you need to dress like one." He went through my dresses and pulled out a long white sleeveless gown. It was gorgeous and much too fancy for me. When he came out of the closet, he handed it to me. "I think this might work. Try it on."

"Isn't everything in my closet suitable?" I tossed the dress on the bed next to me and turned to look at him.

"Yes, but different things are better for different occasions." He came over to the bed to smooth out the dress, making sure it didn't have any wrinkles or creases. "This is a very important dinner, Wendy."

"Why? What makes this one so important?"

"The Stroms are very good friends of your mother's and the Kroners are very important people. They affect the future." Finn finished smoothing the dress and turned to me. "Why don't you continue getting ready?"

"How do they affect the future? What does that mean?" I pressed.

"That's a conversation for another day." Finn nodded toward the bathroom. "You need to hurry if you're going to be ready in time for dinner."

"Fine." I sighed, getting up off the bed.

"Wear your hair down," Finn commanded. My hair was wet, so it was behaving now, but I knew that as soon as it dried, it would turn into a wild thicket of curls.

"I can't. My hair is impossible."

"We all have difficult hair. Even Elora and I. It's the curse of being Trylle," Finn said. "It's something you must learn to manage."

"Your hair is nothing like mine," I said dourly. His hair was short and obviously had some product in it, but it looked smooth, straight, and obedient.

"It most certainly is," Finn replied.

I meant to prove him wrong, so impulsively I reached out and touched his hair, running my fingers through the hair at his temple. Other than being stiff with product, it felt like my hair.

It wasn't until I had done it that I realized there was something inherently intimate about running my fingers through another person's hair. I had been looking at his hair, but then I met his dark eyes and realized exactly how close I was to him.

Since I was short, I was standing on my tiptoes, leaning up to him as if I were about to kiss him. Somewhere in the back of my mind I thought that would be a very good course of action right about now.

"Satisfied?" Finn asked. I retracted my hand and took a step back. "There should be hair products in your bathroom. Experiment."

I nodded my compliance, still too flustered to speak. Finn was unnaturally calm, and at times like that, I really hated how aloof he could be. I barely even remembered to breathe until I was in my bathroom.

Being that near to him made me forget everything but his dark eyes, the heat from his skin, his wonderful scent, the feel of his hair beneath my fingers, the smooth curve of his lips . . .

I shook my head, clearing it of any thoughts of him. That had to be the end of that.

I had a dinner tonight to worry about, and somehow I had to do something with my hair. I tried to remember what Maggie had used in my hair before I went to the dance, but that felt like a lifetime ago.

Thankfully, my hair magically decided to behave itself tonight, making the whole process go easier. Finn seemed to think my hair looked better down, so I left the length of it hanging in the back and pulled the sides back with clips. To top off the ensemble, I got a diamond necklace from my jewelry box.

The dress turned out to be trickier than my hair. It had one of those stupid zippers that refused to move higher than my lower back, and no matter how I contorted myself, I couldn't win. After struggling with it so long my fingers hurt, I had to get help.

Tentatively, I pushed open the bathroom door. Finn had been looking out the window at the sun setting over the bluffs. When he turned, his eyes rested on me for a full minute before he finally spoke.

"You look like a Princess," he said with a crooked smile.

"I need help with the zipper," I said meekly, gesturing to the open slit down my back.

He walked over, and it was almost a relief to have my back to him. The way he looked at me made my stomach swirl with nervous butterflies. One of his hands pressed warmly on my bare shoulder to steady the fabric as he zipped me up, and I shivered involuntarily.

When he had finished, I went over to the mirror to investigate for myself. Even I had to admit that I looked lovely. With the white dress and the diamond necklace, I almost looked too lavish. Maybe it was too much for just a dinner.

"I look like I'm getting married," I commented and glanced back at Finn. "Do you think I should change?"

"No, it's perfect." He looked pensively at me, and if I didn't know better, I'd say he looked almost sad. The doorbell chimed loudly, and Finn nodded. "The guests have arrived. We should greet them."

TWELVE

introductions

We walked down the hall together, but at the top of the stairs, Finn deliberately fell a few steps behind me. Elora and three people I guessed were the Kroners were standing in the alcove as I descended the stairs, and they all turned to look up at me. It was the first grand entrance I had ever made in my life, and there was something wonderful about it.

The Kroners consisted of a stunningly beautiful woman in a floor-length dark green dress, an attractive man in a dark suit, and an attractive boy about my age. Even Elora looked more extravagant than usual. Her dress had more detailing and her jewelry was more pronounced.

I could feel them appraising me as I walked toward them, so I was careful to keep my steps as smooth and elegant as possible.

"This is my daughter, the Princess." Elora smiled in a way

that almost looked loving and held her hand out to me. "Princess, these are the Kroners. Aurora, Noah, and Tove."

I smiled politely and did a small curtsy. Immediately after, I realized that they were probably the ones who should be curtsying to me, but they all continued to smile pleasantly at me.

"It's such a pleasure to meet you." Aurora's words had a syrupy tone that made me wonder whether or not I should trust her. A few dark curls fell artfully from her elegant updo, and her chestnut eyes were large and stunning.

Her husband, Noah, gave me a small bow, as did her son, Tove. Both Noah and Aurora looked appropriately respectful, while Tove looked vaguely bored. His mossy green eyes met mine very briefly, then darted away, as if eye contact made him uncomfortable.

Elora ushered us into the sitting parlor to talk until supper. The conversation was overly polite and banal, but I suspected there were undercurrents that I didn't fully understand. Elora and Aurora did most of the talking, with Noah adding very little. Tove said nothing at all, preferring to look anywhere but directly at anyone.

Finn was more in the background, speaking only when spoken to. He was poised and polite, but from the disdainful way Aurora looked at him, I gathered she didn't approve of his presence.

The Stroms were fashionably late, as Finn had predicted they would be. He'd briefed me extensively on both them and the Kroners earlier in the day, but he was much more familiar with the Stroms and talked of them in much more affectionate tones.

Finn had been a tracker for Willa, so he knew her and her father, Garrett, quite well. Garrett's wife (Willa's mother) had died some years earlier. Finn claimed that Garrett was easygoing, but that Willa was a tad high-strung. She was twenty-one, and prior to living in Förening, she'd been privileged to the point of excess.

When the doorbell rang, interrupting the irritatingly dull conversation between Aurora and my mother, Finn immediately excused himself to answer the door and returned with Garrett and Willa in tow.

Garrett was a rather handsome man in his mid-forties. His hair was dark and disheveled, making me feel better about my own imperfect hair. When he shook my hand with a warm smile, he immediately put me at ease.

Willa, on the other hand, had that snobby look as if she were simultaneously bored and pissed off. She was a waif of a girl with light brown waves that fell neatly down her back, and she wore an anklet covered in diamonds. When she shook my hand, I could tell that her smile was at least sincere, making me hate her a little less.

Now that they had arrived, we adjourned to the dining room for supper. Willa attempted to engage Tove in conversation as we walked into the other room, but he remained completely silent.

Finn pulled my chair out for me before I sat down, and I enjoyed it since I couldn't remember a single time that anyone had ever done that for me. He waited until everyone was sitting before taking a seat himself, and this deference would be the standard for the evening.

As long as at least one person was standing, so would Finn. He was always the first to his feet, and even though the chef and a butler were on staff tonight, Finn would offer to get anyone anything they needed.

The dinner dragged on much more slowly than I had imagined it could. Since I wore white, I barely ate out of fear of spilling anything on my dress. I had never felt so judged in my entire life. I could feel Aurora and Elora waiting for me to screw up so they could pounce, but I wasn't sure how either of them would benefit from my failure.

I could tell that on several occasions Garrett tried to lighten the mood, but his attempts were rebuffed by Aurora and Elora, who dominated the conversation. The rest of us rarely spoke.

Tove stirred his soup a lot, and I became mildly hypnotized by that. He'd let go of his spoon, but it kept swirling around the bowl, stirring the soup without any hand to guide it. I must have started to gape because I felt Finn gently kick me under the table, and I quickly dropped my eyes back to my own food.

"It is so nice to have you here," Garrett told me at one point, changing the entire topic of conversation. "How do you like the palace so far?"

"Oh, it is not a *palace*, Garrett," said Elora with a laugh. It wasn't a real laugh, though. It was the kind of laugh rich people use whenever they talk about new money people. Aurora tittered right along with it, and that quieted Elora down somehow.

"You're right. It's better than a palace," Garrett said, and Elora smiled demurely.

"I like it. It's very nice." I knew I was making bland conversation, but I was afraid to elaborate more.

"Are you adjusting here all right?" Garrett asked.

"Yes, I think so," I said. "I haven't been here that long, though."

"It does take time." Garrett looked at Willa with affectionate concern. His easy smile returned quickly and he nodded at Finn. "But you've got Finn there to help you. He's an expert at helping the changelings acclimate."

"I'm not an expert at anything," Finn said quietly. "I just do my job the best I can."

"Have you had a designer come over to make the dress yet?" Aurora asked Elora, taking a polite sip of wine. It had been a minute since she'd last spoken, so it was time for her to assert herself once more in the conversation. "That dress the Princess has on is very lovely, but I can't imagine that it was made specifically for her."

"No, it was not." Elora gave her a plastic smile and cast a very small but very distinct glare at my dress. Until just that second it had felt like the most beautiful thing I had ever worn. "The tailor is set to come over early next week."

"That is cutting it a bit short for next Saturday, isn't it?" Aurora questioned, and I could see Elora bristling just below the surface of her perfect smile. "That's just over a week away."

"Not at all," Elora said in an overly soothing tone, almost as if she were talking to a small child or a Pomeranian. "I am using Frederique Von Ellsin, the same one who designed Willa's gown. He works very quickly, and his gowns are always impeccable."

"My gown was divine," Willa interjected.

"Ah, yes." Aurora allowed herself to look impressed. "We have him on reserve for when our daughter comes home next spring. He's much harder to get then, since that is the busy season for when the children return."

There was something vaguely condescending in her voice, as if we had done something tacky by having me arrive here when I did. Elora kept on smiling, despite what I now realized was a steady stream of polite barbs from Aurora.

"That is one major benefit of having the Princess come home in the fall," Aurora continued, her words only getting more patronizing as she spoke. "Everything will be so much easier to book. When Tove came home last season, it was so difficult to get everything just right. I suppose you'll have everything you want on hand. That should make for a stunning ball."

Several things were setting off alarms in my head. First, they were talking about both me and Tove as if we weren't even there, although he didn't seem to notice or care about anything going on around him.

Second, they were talking about something going on next Saturday that I apparently needed a specially designed dress for, and yet nobody had bothered to mention it to me. Then again, this shouldn't surprise me. Nobody told me anything.

"I haven't had the luxury of making plans a year in advance the way most people do, since the Princess came home most unexpectedly." Elora's sweet smile dripped with venom, and Aurora smiled back at her as if she didn't notice.

"I can certainly lend you a hand. I just did Tove's, and as I said, I'm already preparing for our daughter's," Aurora offered.

"That would be delightful." Elora took a long drink of her wine.

Dinner continued that way, Elora and Aurora's conversation barely masking how much they detested each other. Noah didn't say much, but at least he managed not to look awkward or bored.

Willa and I ended up watching Tove quite a bit, but for entirely different reasons. She stared at him with unabashed lust, although I couldn't figure out what he'd done to deserve that, other than being attractive. I kept watching because I was certain he was moving things without touching them.

The Kroners didn't linger after dinner, but the Stroms did. I assumed that was because Elora actually liked Garrett and Willa.

Elora, Finn, and I walked the Kroners out, with Finn coming along only to open the doors for them. When saying their good-byes, Aurora and Noah bowed before us, making me feel quite ridiculous. There was absolutely no reason why anyone should bow to me.

To my astonishment, Tove gently took my hand in his, kissing it softly when he bowed. When he straightened up, his eyes met mine, and very seriously he said, "I look forward to seeing you again, Princess."

"And I, you." I was so pleased that I had said something

that sounded completely perfect for the moment. And then I smiled much too wide, I'm sure.

Once they departed into the night, oxygen seemed to return to the house, and Elora let out an irritated sigh. Finn rested his forehead against the door for a moment before turning back around to face us. I felt much better knowing that everyone else had found the evening exhausting too.

"Oh, that woman." Elora rubbed her temples and shook her head, then pointed at me. "*You.* You do not bow to anyone, ever. Especially not that woman. I know you thrilled her endlessly, and she's going to be telling everyone about the little dim-witted Princess who didn't know enough not to bow before a Marksinna." I looked at the floor, feeling any sense of pride vanish. "You don't even bow before me, is that clear?"

"Yes," I said.

"You are the Princess. *Nobody* is higher than you. Have you got that?" Elora snapped, and I nodded. "Then you need to start acting like it. You need to command the room! They came here to see you, to gauge your power, and you need to show them. They need to have confidence that you will be able to lead them all when I am gone."

I kept my eyes locked on the floor, even though I knew that probably offended her, but I was afraid I would cry if I looked at her yelling at me.

"You sit there like some beautiful, useless jewel, and that's exactly what she wants." She sighed disgustedly again. "Oh, and the way you gaped at that boy—"

At that, she abruptly stopped. She shook her head, as if too weary to continue, then turned and walked back to the sitting parlor. I swallowed back my feelings, and Finn gently touched my arm, smiling at me.

"You did just fine," he assured me quietly. "She's upset with Aurora Kroner, not you."

"It sure sounded like she was upset with me," I muttered under my breath.

"Don't let her get to you." He squeezed my arm, sending warming tingles through me, and I couldn't help but return his smile. "Come on. We need to get back to the guests."

In the sitting parlor, Garrett and Willa waited for us, the entire atmosphere far more relaxed than it had been at dinner. Finn even loosened his tie. Her outburst seemed to have calmed Elora completely, and she lounged on the chair next to Garrett. He seemed to capture a disproportionate amount of her attention, but I didn't mind.

Soon a whole other side of Finn emerged. He sat next to me, his leg crossed over his knee, making charming small talk with the group. He was still gracious and respectful, but he chatted easily. I bit my tongue, afraid to say the wrong thing, happy to let Finn entertain Garrett and Willa. Even Elora looked pleased.

Garrett and Elora started talking politics, and Finn became more engaged in the conversation. Apparently, Elora had to appoint a new Chancellor in six months. I didn't even know what that was, and I thought asking would only make me look foolish.

As the night progressed, Elora had to excuse herself because of a migraine. Garrett and Finn offered their sympathy, but neither of them seemed particularly surprised or concerned. When they continued with the whole Chancellor business again, it became clear that Willa had grown bored. She said she needed fresh air and invited me to join her.

We went down a long hall to a small alcove with nearly invisible glass doors. They led out to the balcony that ran from one end of the house to the other, lined with a thick black railing that reached up to my chest.

I froze, remembering the painting I had seen in Elora's locked room. It was this marble balcony I had been lying on, my hand outstretched at nothing, my face contorted in horror. I looked down at my dress, but it didn't feel right. This one was lovely, but the dress in the picture had shimmered. Broken glass had littered the ground also, and I didn't see any.

"Are you coming?" Willa glanced back at me.

"Uh, yeah." I nodded and, taking a deep breath, I followed her out.

Willa went over to the farthest corner and leaned on the railing. Out here, the view was even more intimidating. The balcony hung over a hundred-foot drop. Below us the tops of maples, oaks, and evergreens stretched out as far as the eye could see. The secret garden remained hidden from sight.

Farther down the bluff I could see the tops of houses, and way down at the bottom the turbulent river ran past us. Just then a breeze blew across the balcony, sending a cold chill down my bare arms, and Willa sighed.

"Oh, knock it off!" Willa grumbled, and at first I thought she was talking to me.

I was about to ask what she meant when she lifted her hand and waved her fingers lightly in the air. Almost instantly her hair, which had been blowing back in the breeze, settled on her shoulders. The wind had died away.

"Did you do that?" I asked, trying not to sound as awed as I felt.

"Yeah. That's the only thing I can do. Lame, isn't it?" Willa wrinkled her nose.

"No, actually, I think it's pretty cool," I admitted.

She controlled the wind! Wind was an unstoppable force, and she just wiggled her fingers, and magically it stopped.

"I kept hoping I'd get a *real* ability someday, but my mother only had command over the clouds, so at least I did better than that." Willa shrugged. "You'll see when your abilities start coming in. Everybody hopes for telekinesis or at least some persuasion, but most of us are stuck with basic use of the elements, if we're lucky. The abilities aren't what they used to be, I guess."

"Before you came here, did you know you were something?" I asked, looking over my shoulder at her. She had her back against the railing, and she leaned over it, letting her hair hang down over the edge.

"Oh, yeah. I always knew I was better than everyone else." Her eyes fluttered shut and she waved her fingers again, stirring up a light breeze to flow through her hair. "What about you?"

"Um . . . kind of." Different, yes. Better, not at all.

"You're younger than most of us, though," Willa commented. "You're still in school, aren't you?"

"I was." Nobody had made any mention of school since I got here, and I had no idea what their intentions were for the remainder of my education.

"School sucks anyway." Willa stood up straight and looked at me solemnly. "So why did they get you early, anyway? Is it because of the Vittra?"

"What do you mean?" I asked nervously.

I knew what she meant, but I wanted to see if she'd tell me. Nobody seemed that keen on talking about the Vittra, and Finn hadn't even mentioned their attack since I'd come here. Inside the compound I assumed I was safe, but I didn't know if they still wanted me.

"I've heard stories that the Vittra have been prowling around lately, trying to catch Trylle changelings," Willa said casually. "I figured you'd be a top priority 'cause you're the Princess, and that's kind of a big deal here."

She looked thoughtfully at her bare toes and mused, "I wonder if I'd be a top priority. My dad's not a King or anything like that, but we are kind of royalty. What's lower than a Queen in the human world? Is that a Duchess or something?"

"I don't know." I shrugged. I knew nothing of monarchy and titles, which was ironic, considering that I was now integral to a monarchy.

"Yeah, I think I'm like that." Willa narrowed her eyes in concentration. "My official title is Marksinna, and that's like a Duchess. My dad is a Markis, which is just a male Marksinna.

We're not the only ones, though. There are maybe six or seven other families in Förening alone with the same title. The Kroners were next in line for the crown if you didn't come back. They're real powerful, and that Tove is a catch."

While he was attractive, nothing had impressed me about Tove other than his telekinesis. Still, it felt weird knowing that they were vying for my spot, and we had just eaten dinner with them.

"I don't have to worry that much about it, though." Willa yawned loudly. "Sorry. Boredom makes me sleepy. Maybe we should go inside."

It was getting cold, so I was happy to oblige. As soon as we went back in, Willa lay on the couch and all but fell asleep, so Garrett excused himself shortly after. He went to say goodbye to Elora, and then helped Willa out to the car.

The butler was cleaning everything up, so Finn suggested that we head up to our respective rooms. The night had been surprisingly tiring, so I was eager to comply.

"What's going on?" I asked after the Stroms left. It was the first chance I'd had all evening to really talk to him. "What is this ball or party or whatever that's happening next Saturday?"

"It's the Trylle equivalent of a debutante ball, except that boys go through it too," Finn explained as we climbed the stairs.

Dully, I remembered how grand I had felt coming down the stairs a few hours earlier. For the first time I had felt almost like a Princess, and now I felt like a child playing dress-up.

Aurora had seen through my fancy trappings (which she didn't even find all that fancy) and realized that I wasn't special.

"I don't even know what a debutante ball is." I sighed. I knew nothing of high society.

"It's a coming-out party, your presentation to the world," Finn elaborated. "Changelings aren't raised here. The community doesn't know them. So when they come back, they're given a small amount of time to acclimate, and then they're introduced to society. Every changeling has one, but most are very small. Since you are the Princess, you will have guests from all over the Trylle community. It is quite an ordeal."

I groaned. "I'm not ready for that at all."

"You will be," Finn assured me.

We walked in silence the rest of the way to my bedroom as I fretted and worried about the upcoming party. It hadn't been that long ago that I had gone to my very first dance, and now I was expected to be the center of a formal ball.

I could never pull that off. Tonight had only been a semi-formal dinner, and I hadn't even performed well at that.

"I trust you'll sleep well this evening," Finn said as I opened the bedroom door.

"You need to come in with me," I reminded him, then pointed to my dress. "I can't unzip this thing on my own."

"Of course."

Finn followed me into the darkened room and flipped on the lights. The glass wall worked as a mirror thanks to the black night. In the reflection, I still thought I looked nice, and then I realized that was probably because I had other people picking out my clothes. My judgment was too flawed. I turned away from the glass and waited for Finn to unzip me.

"I really botched things tonight, didn't I?" I asked sadly.

"No, of course not."

Finn's hand pressed warm on my back, and I felt the dress loosen as he pulled the zipper down. I wrapped my arms around myself to keep it up, then turned to look at him. Some part of me was distinctly aware that we were only a few inches apart, my dress was barely on, and his dark eyes were fixed on me.

"You did exactly what I told you," Finn said. "If anyone ruined things, it was me. But the night wasn't ruined. Elora is just sensitive about the Kroners."

"Why? Why does she let them get to her so much? She's the Queen."

"Monarchs have been overthrown before," Finn answered calmly. "If you seem unfit for the position, the next in line can contest it and petition to take the title."

All the color drained from my face. There was suddenly way too much pressure on me to perform. I felt sick, and I swallowed hard. The ball had scared me enough before I knew that, if I failed, my mother could be overthrown.

"Don't worry. You'll be fine." His expression saddened again, and he added quietly, "Elora has a plan to appease them."

"What is it?" I asked.

Instead of answering, his eyes got far away and his expression blanked. His brow furrowed, and then he nodded.

"I am sorry," Finn said. "You're going to have to excuse me. Elora requires assistance in her room."

"Elora called you to her room?" I stumbled over the question, unable to hide my shock.

Somehow it seemed vaguely inappropriate that Finn would be making a late-night visit to her room. Maybe it was because she had just asked him inside his head, and I couldn't get a read on the exact nature of their relationship.

The fact that I was feeling jealous of my own mother was more than a little creepy, and that added a nauseous feeling on top of everything else.

"Yes. Her migraine is quite severe." Finn took a step away from me.

"All right, well, have fun with that," I muttered.

The door closed softly behind him, and I went into the bathroom to take off my jewelry and change into baggy pajamas. Sleep was difficult for me that night. I was too anxious about all the things I was expected to accomplish.

I knew nothing about this world or these people, and yet I was supposed to rule over them someday. That wouldn't have been so bad, except that I was supposed to master everything in less than a week so they would believe that I could rule.

If I didn't, everything my mother had worked so hard for would be taken away. Even though I wasn't that fond of Elora, I was even less fond of Aurora, and I didn't like the idea of ruining my family's entire legacy.

THIRTEEN

being trylle

Lazy Sundays happened even in Förening, thankfully. I woke up late and was happy to learn the chef was still on hand to make breakfast. I saw Finn briefly, passing him in the hall, but it was no more than a nod hello.

I flopped back onto my bed, thinking I would spend the day bored out of my mind. Then Rhys knocked on my door, interrupting my plans for moping, and invited me over to his room to watch movies with him and Rhiannon.

His room was a masculine version of mine, which made sense since he had decorated my room. A huge overstuffed couch sat in front of his TV, the one big difference between our rooms. We ended up watching *The Lord of the Rings* trilogy because Rhys insisted it was much funnier once I'd spent time with actual trolls.

Rhys sat between us on the couch. When the first movie started, he was directly in the middle, but somewhere around three or four hours into the marathon I noticed he'd moved closer to me, not that I minded.

He talked and joked a lot with Rhiannon, and they had a way of making me feel comfortable. After spending the weekend failing to be the perfect little princess Elora wanted me to be, it felt good to just relax and laugh.

Rhiannon left right after the third movie started, saying she had to get up early in the morning. Even after she'd gone, Rhys didn't move away from me. He sat so close to me on the couch that his leg pressed against mine.

I thought about moving away, but I didn't really have any reason to. The movie was fun, he was foxy, and I enjoyed being with him. It wasn't too long before his arm "casually" went around my shoulders, and I almost laughed.

He didn't make my heart race, not the way Finn did, but his arm felt nice. Rhys made me feel normal in a way that I never had before, and I couldn't help but like him for it. Eventually I leaned in to him and rested my head on his shoulder.

What I didn't realize was that watching all three extended-edition versions of *Lord of the Rings* in one sitting ends up being over eleven hours of movie viewing. At one in the afternoon on a boring Sunday, that sounded genius. But by the time midnight rolled around, it became a war on sleep, and I eventually lost.

In the morning, while I slept soundly on the couch in Rhys's room, I had no idea that a commotion was going on in the house. I would've been happy to sleep through it too, but Finn threw open the door in a panic, jolting me awake.

"Oh, my gosh!" I shouted, jumping up off the couch. Finn had scared the hell out of me, and my heart pounded in my chest. "What's going on? Is everything okay?"

Instead of answering, Finn just stood there glaring at me. Behind me, Rhys was waking up much more slowly. Apparently, Finn hadn't terrified him the way he had me.

I glanced back at Rhys, who was dressed in a T-shirt and sweats that somehow managed to look good on him, and it dawned on me how this must have looked to Finn when he first burst in.

I still wore my lazy-day comfy clothes, but Rhys and I had been curled up together. And even if Finn hadn't noticed that detail, there was no denying that I'd spent the night in here. My mind scrambled to think of an excuse, but at that moment even the innocent truth escaped me.

"She's in here!" Finn called out flatly.

Rhys groaned, so I knew things weren't good. He looked completely alert now, and he stood sheepishly next to me. I wanted to ask what was going on and why Finn looked so pissed off, but Elora didn't give me a chance.

She appeared in the doorway, her emerald robe flaring out behind her in a dramatic billow, and her hair hung down her back in a thick braid. She stood behind Finn, but she somehow managed to eclipse everything else.

Several times before I had thought she looked unhappy, but that was nothing compared to the severe expression she had on now. She scowled so deep it looked painful, and her eyes were filled with fury.

"What do you think you're doing?" Elora's voice echoed painfully inside my head, and she had added some of her psychic voice to make it more intense.

"Sorry," I said. "We were just watching movies and fell asleep."

"It was my fault," Rhys added. "I put the—"

"I don't care what you were doing! Do you have any idea how inappropriate this behavior is?" Her eyes narrowed on Rhys, and he shrank back even more. "Rhys, you know this was completely unacceptable." She rubbed her temples as if this were giving her another headache, and Finn looked at her with concern. "I don't even want to deal with you. Get ready for school, and stay out of my sight!"

"Yes, ma'am." Rhys nodded. "Sorry."

"As for you—" Elora pointed a finger at me but couldn't find the words to finish. She just looked so disappointed and disgusted with me. "I don't care how you were raised before you came here. You still know what kind of behavior is ladylike and what isn't."

"I wasn't—" I began, but she held up her hand to silence me.

"But to be honest, Finn, you disappoint me the most." She had stopped yelling, and when she looked at Finn, she just sounded tired. He lowered his eyes in shame, and she shook her head. "I can't believe you allowed this to happen. You know you need to keep your eyes on her at all times."

"I know. I won't let it happen again." Finn bowed apologetically to her.

"You most certainly won't. Now fix this mess by educating

her in the ways of the Trylle. In the meantime, I do not want to see any of you for the rest of the day." She held her hands up, like she was done with the lot of us, and then shook her head and left the room.

"I am so sorry," Rhys apologized emphatically. His cheeks were red with shame, and somehow that only made him cuter.

Not that I was really paying attention to how he looked just then. My stomach was twisted in knots, and I was thankful that I hadn't started to cry. I didn't even fully understand what I'd done. I knew sleeping in a boy's room wasn't ideal, but they were acting like it was a capital offense.

"You need to get ready for school," Finn snapped, glaring at Rhys. Then he pointed to the hall and turned to me. "You. Out. *Now.*"

I gave him a wide berth on my way out the door. Normally I loved being close to him, but not today. My heart pounded erratically, but not for any pleasurable reason. Finn tried to keep his face expressionless, but tension and anger radiated from his body. I slunk across the hall to my room, and Finn barked something at Rhys about behaving himself.

"Where are you going?" Finn demanded when I opened my bedroom door. He had just emerged from Rhys's room and slammed the door behind him, making me jump.

"To my room?" I pointed at my room and looked confused.

"No. You need to come to my room with me," Finn said.

"What? Why?" I asked.

A very small part of me felt excited about the prospect of going to his room with him. That sounded like the start of a fantasy I might have. But the way he was looking at me now, I was afraid he might kill me once we were in private.

"I need to get ready for the day, and I can't very well let you out of my sight." He wore pajama pants and a T-shirt, and his dark hair wasn't as sleek as it normally was.

I nodded and hurried after him. He walked fast and pissed off, and I fell about a step or two behind.

"I really am sorry, you know," I said. "I didn't mean to fall asleep there. We were just watching movies, and it got late. If I had known it would be like this, I would've made sure I was in my room."

"You should've known, Wendy!" Finn exclaimed, exasperated. "You should know that your actions have consequences and the things you do matter!"

"I am sorry!" I repeated. "Yesterday was so boring and I just wanted to do *something*."

Finn whirled on me suddenly, startling me so I took a step backward. My back hit the wall, but he stepped closer to me. He rested an arm against the wall on the side of me, his face only a few inches from mine. His dark eyes were blazing, but somehow his voice remained calm and even.

"You know how it looks when a girl spends the night alone with a boy. I know you understand that. But it is *so* much worse when a *Princess* spends the night alone with a *mänsklig*. It could put everything in jeopardy."

"I-I don't know what that means," I fumbled. "None of you will tell me."

Finn continued to glare at me for another painful minute,

then sighed and took a step back. As he stood there, rubbing his eyes, I swallowed back tears and caught my breath.

When he looked back at me, his eyes had softened a bit, but he didn't say anything. He just walked to his room and, uncertainly, I followed him.

His room was smaller than mine, but a much more comfortable size. Even though the blinds were shut, I could tell one of his walls was made entirely of glass. Dark blankets covered his bed, and books overflowed from several bookshelves. In one corner he had a small desk with a laptop on it.

Like me, he had an adjoining bathroom. When he went in it, he left the door open, and I heard the sound of him brushing his teeth. Tentatively, I sat on the edge of his bed and looked around.

"You must stay here a lot," I commented. I knew that he stayed here on and off, but to have a room full of stuff implied a more permanent living situation.

"I live here when I'm not tracking," Finn said.

"My mother is quite fond of you," I said dimly.

"Not right now she's not." Finn turned off the water and came out, leaning on the doorframe to his bathroom. Sighing, he lowered his eyes. "I'm sorry for yelling at you."

"It's okay." I shrugged. I still didn't understand why he'd been *that* mad, but he had a point. I was a Princess now, and I had to start behaving like one.

"No, you didn't deserve it." He scratched his temple and shook his head. "My anger was misdirected. When you weren't in your room this morning, I panicked. With everything going on with the Vittra . . ." He shook his head again.

"What's going on with the Vittra?" I asked, my heart speeding up.

"It's nothing to concern yourself with," Finn said. "My point is that my emotions were high when I couldn't find you, and I snapped at you. I apologize."

"No, it's my fault. You guys were right," I said. Finn just stood there looking away from me, and then I realized something. "How did you even know I wasn't in my room?"

"I checked on you." Finn gave me a look like I was an idiot. "I check on you every morning."

"You check on me when I'm sleeping?" I gaped at him. "Every morning?"

He nodded.

"I didn't know that."

"Why would you know that? You're sleeping," Finn pointed out.

"Well . . . it just feels weird." I shook my head. Matt and Maggie used to check on me, but it felt strange knowing that Finn would come in and watch me sleep, even if it was only for a second.

"I have to make sure you're safe and sound. It's part of my job."

"You sound like a broken record sometimes," I muttered wearily. "You're always just doing your job."

"What else do you want me to say?" Finn countered, looking at me evenly.

I just shook my head and looked away. My pants suddenly became very fascinating, and I picked lint off them. Finn kept looking at me, and I expected him to finish getting ready. When he didn't, I decided that I had to fill the silence.

"What is a mänsklig?" I looked at Finn again, and he exhaled.

"The literal translation for mänsklig is 'human.' " He tilted his head, resting it against the doorframe, and watched me. "Rhys is human."

I shook my head. "I don't understand. Why is he around?"

"Because of you," Finn said, and that only confused me more. "You're a changeling, Wendy. You were switched at birth. Meaning that when you took the place of another baby, that baby had to go somewhere else."

"You mean . . ." I trailed off, but it was incredibly obvious once Finn said it. "Rhys is Michael!"

Suddenly my crush on him felt very weird. He wasn't my blood brother, but he was my brother's brother, even though Matt wasn't really my brother either. It still felt . . . not right, somehow.

And really, I should've noticed sooner. I couldn't believe I didn't. Rhys and Matt looked so much alike—their sandy hair, blue eyes, even the way their faces were shaped. But Matt's worry had hardened him, while Rhys was quick to smile and laugh.

Maybe that's why I hadn't noticed it. The complete contrast between their personalities had thrown me off.

"Michael?" Finn looked perplexed.

"Yeah, that's what my mother—Kim, my fake mom—named him. She knew she had a son, and that's Rhys." My mind swirled. "But how . . . how did they do it? How did they switch us?"

"It's relatively simple," Finn explained, almost tiredly. "After Rhys was born, Elora induced labor with you, and using persuasion on the family and hospital staff, she switched you out for him."

"It can't be that simple. The persuasion didn't really work on Kim," I pointed out.

"We normally do same-sex exchanges, a girl for a girl, a boy for a boy, but Elora had her mind set on the Everlys. It doesn't work as well when you do a boy-to-girl switch like that. Mothers are more likely to pick up on something being wrong, as was the case with your host mother."

"Wait, wait!" I held up my hands and looked at him. "She knew it was more dangerous, that Kim would be more likely to snap? But she did it anyway?"

"Elora believed that the Everlys would be the best for you," Finn maintained. "And she wasn't completely wrong. Even you freely admit that the aunt and the brother were good to you."

I had always kind of hated Kim. I thought she had been terrible and cruel like so many of my classmates, but she had known that I wasn't her child. Kim had actually been an insanely good mother. She had remembered her son, even when she shouldn't have been able to, and she refused to give up on him. The whole thing was tragic, when I thought about it.

"So that's why they don't want me with the mänsklig? 'Cause he's like a stepbrother?" I wrinkled my nose at the thought.

"He's not your brother," Finn emphasized. "Trylle and mänsklig have absolutely no relation. The problem is that they're human."

"Are we, like . . . physically incompatible?" I asked carefully.

"No. Many Trylle have left the compound to live with humans and have normal offspring," Finn said. "That's part of the reason our populations are going down."

"What happens to Rhys now that I'm back?" I asked, ignoring the clinical way Finn addressed everything. He was nothing if not professional.

"Nothing. He can live here for as long as he wants. Leave if he decides to. Whatever he chooses." Finn shrugged. "Mänsklig aren't treated badly here. For example, Rhiannon is Willa's mänsklig."

"That makes sense." I nodded. Rhiannon seemed so skittish and nervous, but also rather normal, unlike everyone else. "So . . . what do they do with mänsklig?"

"They aren't exactly raised as real children, but they are given everything to keep them happy and content," Finn said. "We have schools set up for the mänsklig, and while they aren't as nice the schools you've gone to, the mänks do get an education. They even have a small trust fund set up for them. When they're eighteen, they're free to do as they please."

"But they're not equals," I realized. Elora tended to talk down to everyone, but she was worse with Rhys and Rhiannon. I couldn't imagine that Willa was much nicer either.

"This is a monarchy. There are no equals." For an instant Finn looked almost sad, then he walked over and sat on the bed next to me. "As your tracker, I am expected to educate you, and as Elora pointed out, I should've started sooner. You need to understand the distinct hierarchy here.

"There is royalty, of which you are at the top." Finn gestured to me. "After Elora, of course. Below you there are the Markis and Marksinna, but they can become Kings and Queens through marriage. Then there are your average Trylle, the common folk, if you will. Below that there are trackers. And at the very bottom, there are mänsklig."

"What? Why are trackers so low?"

"We are Trylle, but we only track. My parents were trackers, and their parents before them, and so on," Finn explained. "We have no changeling population. Ever. That means that we have no income. We bring nothing into the community. We provide a service for other Trylle, and in return we are provided with a home and food."

"You're like an indentured servant?" I gasped.

"Not exactly." Finn tried to smile, but it looked forced. "Until we retire from tracking, we don't need to do anything else. Many trackers, such as myself, will work as a guard for some of the families in town. All of the service jobs, like the nannies, the teachers, the chefs, the maids, are almost entirely retired trackers, and they make an hourly wage. Some are also mänsklig, but they stick around less and less."

"That's why you always bow to Elora," I said thoughtfully.

"She is the Queen, Wendy. Everyone bows to her," Finn corrected me. "Except for you and Rhys. He's rather impossible, and host parents don't usually force their mänks to bow to them."

"It's nice to know that being the Princess has some perks, like not bowing," I said, smirking.

"Elora may seem cold and aloof, but she is a very powerful woman." Finn looked at me solemnly. "*You* will be a very powerful woman. You will be given every opportunity the world has to offer you. I know you can't see it now, but you will have a very charmed life."

"You're right. I can't see it," I admitted. "It probably didn't help that I just got in trouble this morning, and I don't feel very powerful."

"You're still very young," Finn said with a trace of a smile.

"I guess." I remembered how angry he had been earlier and I turned to him. "I didn't do anything with Rhys. You know that, right? Nothing happened."

Finn stared thoughtfully at the floor. I studied him, trying to catch a glimpse of something, but his face was a mask. Eventually he nodded. "Yes. I know that."

"You didn't this morning, though, did you?" I asked.

This time Finn chose not to answer. He stood up and said

he needed to shower. He gathered his clothes and went into the bathroom.

I thought this might be a good time to explore his room, but I suddenly felt very tired. He'd woken me early, and this whole morning had been incredibly draining. Lying back down, I rolled over and curled up in his blankets. They were soft and smelled like him, and I easily fell asleep.

FOURTEEN

kingdom

Other than the garden out back, I'd seen little of the palace grounds. After breakfast, Finn took me outside to show me around. The sky was overcast and gloomy, and he stared up at it with a skeptical eye.

"Is it going to rain?" I asked.

"You never can tell around here." He sounded annoyed, then shook his head and walked on, apparently deciding to risk it.

We'd gone out the front door of the mansion this time, stepping out on the cobblestone driveway. Trees overshadowed the palace, arching high into the sky. Immediately at the edge of the driveway, lush ferns and plants filled in the gaps between the pines and maples.

Finn walked into the trees, pushing the plants aside gently to make a pathway. He'd insisted I wear shoes today, and as I followed behind him, I understood why. A rough trail had been made, but it was overgrown with moss, and twigs and stones littered the ground.

"Where are we going?" I asked, as the path climbed upward.

"I'm showing you Förening."

"Haven't I already seen Förening?" I stopped and looked around. Through the trees I couldn't see much of anything, but I suspected it all looked about the same.

"You've barely seen anything yet." Finn glanced back at me, smiling. "Come on, Wendy."

Without waiting for my answer, he climbed on. The trail already had a steep incline, and it looked slick with mud and moss. Finn maneuvered it easily, grabbing on to the occasional branch or protruding root.

My climb wasn't anywhere near as graceful. I slipped and stumbled the whole way up, scraping my palms and knees on several sharp rocks. Finn didn't slow and rarely glanced back. He had more faith in my abilities than I did, but I suppose that was nothing new.

If I hadn't been so busy mastering a slippery slope, I might've enjoyed the time. The air smelled green and wet from all the pine and leaves. The river below seemed to echo through everything, reminding me of the time I put a conch shell to my ear. Over it, I heard birds chirping, singing a fevered song.

Finn waited for me next to a giant boulder, and when I reached him, he made no comment about my slow pace. I didn't have a chance to catch my breath before he grabbed a small handhold in the boulder and started pulling himself up.

"I'm pretty sure I can't climb up that," I said, eyeing the slick surface of the rock.

"I'll help you." He had his feet in a crevice, and he reached back, holding his hand out to me.

Logically speaking, if I grabbed on to him, my body weight would pull him back off the boulder. But he didn't doubt his ability to pull us both up, so neither did I. Finn had this way of making me believe anything, and it scared me sometimes.

I took his hand, barely getting a chance to enjoy how strong and warm it felt before he started pulling me up. I squealed, which only made him laugh. He directed me to a crevice, and I found myself hanging on to the boulder for dear life.

Finn climbed up, always keeping one hand out for me to grab if I slipped, but I did most of the actual climbing myself. I was surprised when my fingers didn't give and my feet didn't slide. When I pulled myself up to the top of the boulder, I couldn't help but feel a bit of pride.

Standing up on the massive rock, wiping mud off my knees, I started to make some comment about my amazing agility, but then I caught sight of the view. The top of the boulder had to be the highest point atop the bluffs. From here I could see everything, and somehow it was even more amazing than the view from the palace.

Chimneys stood out like dots among the trees, and I could see the plumes of smoke blowing away in the wind. Roads curved and wound through the town, and a few people walked along them. Elora's palace was masked with vines and trees, but it still looked startlingly large hanging on the edge of its bluff.

The wind whipping through my hair made the whole thing exhilarating. Almost like I was flying, even though I was just standing there.

"This is Förening." Finn gestured to the hidden houses peeking out among the green foliage.

"It is breathtaking," I admitted. "I'm totally in awe."

"It's all yours." His dark eyes met mine, emphasizing the solemnity of his words. Then he looked away, scanning the trees. "This is your kingdom."

"Yeah, but . . . it's not actually mine."

"Actually, it kind of is." He offered me a small smile.

I looked back down. In terms of kingdoms, I knew this one was relatively small. It wasn't as if I'd inherited the Roman Empire or anything, but it still felt strange to me that I might possess any kind of kingdom.

"What's the point?" I asked softly. When Finn didn't answer, I thought my words might have been carried away by the wind, so I asked louder. "Why do I get this? What am I to do with it?"

"Rule over it." Finn had been standing behind me, but he stepped closer, moving next to me. "Make the decisions. Keep the peace. Declare the wars."

"Declare the wars?" I looked at him sharply. "That's really something we do?"

He shrugged.

"I don't understand," I said.

"Most things will already be decided when you take the throne," Finn said, staring down at the houses instead of me.

"The order is already in place. You just have to uphold it, enforce it. Mostly, you live in the palace, attend parties, trivial governmental meetings, and occasionally decide on something substantial."

"Like what?" I asked, not liking the hard tone his voice had taken on.

"Banishments, for one." He looked thoughtful. "Your mother once banished a Marksinna. It hadn't been done in years, but she's entrusted with making the decisions that best protect our people and our way of life."

"Why did she banish her?" I asked.

"She corrupted a bloodline." He didn't say anything for a minute, and I looked at him questioningly. "She had a child with a human."

I wanted to ask him more about that but I felt a drop of rain splash on my forehead. I looked up to the sky to be certain I'd felt rain, and the clouds seemed to rip open, pouring water down before I had a chance to shield myself.

"Come on!" Finn grabbed my hand, pulling me.

We slid down the side of the rock, my back scraping against the rough surface of it, and fell heavily into a thicket of ferns. Rain had already soaked through my clothes, chilling my skin. Still holding my hand, Finn led me to shelter underneath a giant pine tree.

"That came on really suddenly," I said, peering out from under the branches. We weren't completely dry under the tree, but only a few fat drops of rain made their way through.

"The weather is so temperamental here. The locals blame

it on the river, but the Trylle have more to do with it," Finn explained.

I thought back to Willa, and her complaint that she could only control the wind, and her mother, the clouds. The garden behind the palace bloomed year-round thanks to Trylle abilities, so it wouldn't be hard to fathom that they could make it rain too.

The birds had fallen silent, and over the sound of the rainfall I couldn't hear the river. The air smelled thick with pine, and even in the middle of the rainstorm I felt oddly at peace. We stood there watching the rain in companionable silence for a while longer, but soon the growing chill began to affect me, and my teeth started to chatter.

"You're cold."

I shook my head. "I'm fine."

Without further prompting, Finn put his arm around me, pulling me closer to him. The abruptness of it made me forget to breathe, and even though he felt no warmer than I did, the strength of his arm wrapped around me sent warmth spreading through me.

"I suppose I'm not much help," he said, his voice low and deep.

"I've stopped shivering," I pointed out quietly.

"We should get back inside, so you can change into dry clothes." He breathed deeply, looking at me a moment longer.

Just as abruptly as he had grabbed me, he pulled away and started heading back down the bluff. The rain came down fast and cold, and without him to warm me, I had no urge to stay in it longer than I had to. I went down after him, half running half sliding to the bottom.

We ran inside the front doors, skidding on the marble floors, and water dripped off us into rapidly growing puddles. I only had a second to catch myself when I realized we weren't alone in the entryway.

Elora walked toward us, carrying herself with her usual regality. Her gown swam around her, making her appear to float as she moved. With her was an obese balding man, his jowls jiggling as he walked.

"How good of you to arrive now, as I'm showing the Chancellor out," Elora said icily, glaring at both Finn and me. I wasn't sure which of us she was more angry with.

"Your Majesty, I can stay and talk," the Chancellor said, looking up at her with small, fevered eyes. He wore a white suit that I couldn't imagine looking good on anyone, but it made him look like a giant, sweaty snowball.

"Chancellor, I'm sorry we missed your visit," Finn said, doing his best to compose himself. Even dripping wet, he looked collected and eager to please. I, on the other hand, hugged my arms around myself and tried not to shiver.

"No, you've given me much to consider, and I don't want to waste your time further." Elora smiled thinly at the Chancellor, and her eyes burned with contempt.

"You will take it under advisement, then?" He looked up at her hopefully and stopped walking. She'd been trying to usher him to the door, and her smile grew strained when he stopped.

"Yes, of course." Elora sounded too sweet, and I assumed she was lying. "I take all of your concerns very seriously."

"My sources are very good," the Chancellor went on. Elora had gotten him walking again, urging him closer to the door. "I have spies all over, even in the Vittra camps. That is how I got my position."

"Yes, I remember your platform." Elora appeared to suppress an eye roll, but his chest puffed up as if she'd complimented him.

"If they say there's a plot, then there's a plot," the Chancellor said with conviction. Next to me I saw Finn tense up, narrowing his eyes at the Chancellor.

"Yes, I'm sure there is." Elora nodded to Finn, who held the door open for the Chancellor. "I'd love to talk with you more, but you must hurry if you want to beat the worst of this storm. I don't want you to get stranded."

"Oh, yes, quite right." The Chancellor looked at the sheets of rain coming down, and his face paled slightly. He turned back toward Elora. Bowing, he took her hand and kissed it once. "My Queen. I'm at your service, always."

She smiled tightly at him while Finn wished him a safe journey. The Chancellor barely even glanced in my direction before diving out into the rain. Finn shut the door behind him, and Elora let out a sigh of relief.

"What were you doing?" Elora looked at me with disdain, but before I could answer, she waved me off. "I don't care. You're just lucky the Chancellor didn't realize you were the Princess."

I glanced down at my dirty, soaking-wet clothes, knowing I looked nothing like royalty. Somehow Finn still looked high-class, and I had no idea how he managed that.

"What was the nature of the Chancellor's visit?" Finn asked.

"Oh, you know the Chancellor." Elora rolled her eyes and started walking away. "He always has some conspiracy theory brewing. I should really change the laws so I have total say about who is appointed the Chancellor, instead of letting the Trylle vote. The people always fall for idiots like him."

"He mentioned something about a Vittra plot," Finn pressed. He followed her, staying a few steps behind, and I trailed in their wake.

"I'm sure it's nothing. We haven't had Vittra come into Förening in years," Elora said with an eerie confidence.

"Yes, but with the Princess—" Finn began, but she held up her hand, silencing him. She turned to him, and by the look on her face I knew she was speaking in his mind. After a minute he took a deep breath and spoke. "All I am proposing is that we take extra precautions, have extra guards on duty."

"That's why you're around, Finn." She smiled at him, something that almost looked genuine, but with a weird malicious edge to it. "It's not just for your pretty face."

"Your Majesty, you put too much faith in me."

"Now that I can believe." Elora sighed and started walking away. "Go change out of those clothes. You're dripping all over everything."

Finn watched her retreating figure for a minute, and I

waited next to him until I was certain she was out of earshot. Although, if I thought about it, I wasn't sure that Elora was ever out of earshot.

"What was that about?" I whispered.

"Nothing." Finn shook his head. He glanced over at me, almost as if he'd forgotten I was there. "You need to change before you get sick."

"That wasn't nothing. Is there going to be an attack?" I demanded, but Finn only turned and started walking toward the stairs. "What is it with you people? You're always walking away from questions!"

"You're soaking wet, Wendy," Finn said matter-of-factly, and I jogged to catch up to him, knowing he wouldn't wait for me. "And you heard everything I heard. You know what I know."

"That's not true! I know she did that creepy mind-speak with you."

"Yes, but she only told me to keep quiet." He climbed the stairs without looking back at me. "You'll be safe. You're the Princess, the most important asset this kingdom has right now, and Elora won't risk you. She just hates the Chancellor."

"Are you sure I'm safe?" I asked, and I couldn't help but think of that painting in Elora's hidden room. The one that showed me terrified and reaching for nothing.

"I would never do anything to put you at risk," Finn assured me when we reached the top of the stairs. He gestured down the hall to my room. "We still have much to go over. It'd be best if you forgot about this and changed into something warmer."

FIFTEEN

education

After I had changed, Finn directed me to a sitting room on the second floor, down the hall from my room. The vaulted ceiling had a mural, all clouds and unicorns and angels. Despite that, the furniture looked modern and normal, unlike the expensive antiques that filled most of the house.

Finn explained that this had once been Rhys's playroom. When he'd outgrown it, they had turned it into a room for him, but he rarely used it.

Lying on my back on the couch, I stared up at the ceiling. Finn sat in an overstuffed chair across from me with a book splayed open on his lap. Stacks of texts sat on the floor next to him, and he tried to give me a crash course on Trylle history.

Unfortunately, despite the fact that we were some type of mythical creatures, Trylle history wasn't any more exciting than human history had been.

"What are the roles of the Markis and Marksinna?" Finn quizzed me.

"I don't know. Nothing," I replied glibly.

"Wendy, you need to learn this." Finn sighed. "There will be conversations at the ball, and you need to appear knowledgeable. You can't just sit back without saying anything anymore."

"I'm a Princess. I should be able to do whatever I want," I grumbled. My legs were draped over the arm of the couch, and I swung my feet back and forth.

"What are the roles of the Markis and Marksinna?" Finn repeated.

"In other provinces, where the King and Queen don't live, the Markis and Marksinna are the leaders. They're like governors or something." I shrugged. "In times when the King or Queen can't fulfill their duties, a Markis can step up and take their place. In places like Förening, their title is mostly just a way of saying that they're better than everyone else, but they don't really have any power."

"That is true, but you can't say that last part," Finn said, then flipped a page in the book. "What is the role of the Chancellor?"

"The Chancellor is an elected official, much like the prime minister in England," I answered tiredly. "The monarchy has the final word and wields the most power, but the Chancellor serves as their adviser and helps give the Trylle commoners a voice in the way the government is run.

"But I don't get it," I said, looking at him. "We live in

America, and this isn't a separate country. Don't we have to follow their laws?"

"Theoretically, yes, and for the most part Trylle laws coincide with American laws, except that we have more of them. However, we live in separate pockets unto ourselves. Using our resources—namely, cash and persuasion—we can get government officials to look the other way, and we conduct our business in private."

"Hmm." I twirled a lock of hair on my finger and thought over what he was saying. "Do you know everything about Trylle society? When you were talking with Garrett and Elora, it was like there was nothing you didn't know."

I'm sure he would've easily won the Kroners over if he had tried. Instead he had assumed it was his role to hide in the background when they were around, so he'd kept his mouth shut. But everything about him was more refined than me. Cool, collected, intelligent, charming, and handsome, he seemed much more like a leader than I did.

"A foolish man thinks he knows everything. A wise man knows he doesn't," Finn replied absently, still looking down at the book.

"That's such a fortune-cookie answer," I said with a laugh, and even he smirked at me. "But seriously, Finn. This doesn't make any sense. You should be a ruler, not me. I don't know anything, but you're all set to go."

"I'll never be a ruler." Finn shook his head. "And you are right for the job. You just haven't had the training that I've had."

"That's stupid," I grumbled. "It should be based on your abilities, not lineage."

"It *is* based on abilities," Finn insisted. "They just happen to come with lineage."

"What are you talking about?" I asked, and he shut the book on his lap.

"Your persuasion? That comes from your mother," Finn elaborated. "The Markis and Marksinna are what they are because of the abilities they have, and they are passed down through their children. Regular Trylle have some abilities, but they've faded with time. Your mother is one of the most powerful Queens we've had in a very long time, and the hope is that you will continue the tradition of power."

"But I can barely do anything!" I sat up. "I have mild persuasion, and you said it wouldn't even work on you!"

"Not yet, no, but it will," Finn corrected me. "Once you start your training, it will make more sense to you."

"Training? What training?"

"After the ball this weekend. Then you will begin working on your abilities," Finn said. "Right now your only priority is preparing for the ball. So . . ." He flipped open the book again, but I wasn't ready to go back to studying.

"But *you* have abilities," I countered. "And Elora prefers you to me. I'm sure she'd like it better if you were Prince." I realized sadly that that was true, and I lay back down on the couch.

"I'm sure that isn't true."

"It is too," I said. "What is the deal with you and Elora?

She definitely likes you better than me, and she seems to confide in you."

"Elora doesn't really confide in anyone." Finn fell silent for a moment, and then exhaled. "If I explain this to you, do you promise to get back to studying?"

"Yes!" I answered immediately and looked over at him.

"What I say to you cannot leave this room. Do you understand?" Finn asked gravely, and I nodded, gulping, afraid of what he was going to tell me.

I had been growing more and more preoccupied with Finn and Elora's relationship. She was an attractive older woman, and he was definitely a foxy guy, and I could see her digging her cougar claws into him. That was what I was afraid of, anyway.

"About sixteen years ago, after your father was gone, *my* father came under the employ of your mother. He had retired from tracking, and Elora hired him to guard her and the estate." His eyes darkened and his lips tightened, and my heart raced.

"Elora was in love with my father. No one knew, except for my mother, who is still married to him. Eventually, my mother convinced him to leave. However, Elora remained quite fond of my father and, in turn, rather fond of me." He sighed and continued casually, as if he were talking about the weather. "She has personally requested my services over the years, and because she pays well, I have accepted."

I stared at him, feeling nauseous and nervous. Since his father became involved with my mother after I was born, I could safely assume that we weren't siblings, so at least that was something.

Everything else made it feel rather disturbing, and I wondered if Finn secretly hated me. He had to hate Elora, and he must only be here because of how much she paid him. Then I wondered if he was some kind of glorified gigolo, and I had to fight to keep from vomiting.

"I am not sleeping with her, and she has never made any advances of the sort," Finn clarified, looking at me evenly. "She is fond of me because of her feelings for my father. I don't blame her for what happened between them. It was a long time ago, and my father was the one who had a family to think of, not her."

"Huh." I looked up at the ceiling because it was easier than looking at him.

"I have distressed you. I'm sorry," Finn apologized sincerely. "This is why I was hesitant to say anything to you."

"No, no, I'm fine. Let's just go on," I insisted unconvincingly. "I have a lot to go over and all that."

Finn remained silent for a minute, letting me absorb what he had just told me, but I tried to push it from my mind as quickly as possible. Thinking about it made me feel dirty, and I already had too much on my mind.

Eventually Finn continued on with the texts, and I tried harder to pay attention. If I was thinking about what exactly a Queen's job entailed, I wasn't thinking about my mother crushing on his father.

Frederique Von Ellsin, the dress designer, came over the next day. He was excited and flamboyant, and I couldn't tell for sure whether or not he was Trylle. I wore only a slip as he took my measurements and sketched like mad in a notepad. Finally, he declared that he had the perfect gown in mind, and he dashed out of my room to get working on it.

All day long there was an irritating succession of people. They were all staff of some kind, like caterers and party planners, so most of them ignored me. They just trailed after Elora as she rattled off an inconceivable amount of information about what she expected them to do, and they all scurried to write it down or punch it into their BlackBerrys.

Meanwhile, I had the pleasure of camping out in my sweats all day. Whenever Elora saw me, she glared at my apparel with disgust, but she was always too busy making demands on somebody else to complain about me.

Everything that I managed to overhear only made my coming-out festivities sound even more terrifying. The most horrific thing I heard as she zipped by: "We'll need seating for at least five hundred." Five hundred people were going to be at a party where I would be the center of attention? Splendid.

The only upside of the day was that I got to spend the entire thing with Finn. But that became less enjoyable because Finn refused to talk about anything that wasn't related to my performance at the party.

We spent two hours going over the names and pictures of the more prominent guests. Two whole hours spent poring over a yearbook-type thing trying to memorize the faces, names, and notable facts of about a hundred people.

Then there was the hour and a half spent at the dinner table. Apparently I did not know how to eat properly. There were certain ways to hold the fork, tilt the bowl, lift the glass, and even place the napkin. Up until that time I had never mastered any of those skills, and from what I gathered about the way Finn regarded me, I still hadn't.

Eventually I gave up. Pushing my plate back, I laid my head down and pressed my cheek against the cold wood of the table.

"Oh, my God, has he killed you?" Willa asked, sounding appalled.

I lifted my head to see her standing at the end of the dining room table, hands on her fashionable hips. She wore too much jewelry, her necklaces and bracelets overly adorned and jangly, but perhaps that was part of being a troll. They all seemed to have a fondness for trinkets, something I had somehow missed, other than my obsession with my thumb ring.

"He bored me to death too." Willa smiled at me, and I couldn't believe I felt relieved to see her. No way would she try to drill me about the names of the past three hundred monarchs.

"And yet you look as alive as ever," Finn said dryly, leaning back in his chair. "Perhaps I didn't try hard enough with you."

"Is that some kind of burn, *stork*?" Willa pulled back her lip in some kind of snide grimace, but she didn't completely pull it off.

"If you're feeling a burn, I suggest you look to your former sexual partners." Finn gave her a small smile, and I gaped at him. I'd never heard him speak like that to anyone before.

"Funny." Willa tried to keep a straight face, but I got the impression she was amused. "Anyway, I'm here to rescue the Princess."

"Really?" I asked a little too brightly. "Rescue me how?"

"Fun stuff." She shrugged in a cute way, and I looked to Finn to see if I could leave.

"Go." He waved vaguely at me. "You've worked hard and you need a break."

I didn't think I'd ever be happy to get away from Finn, but I nearly scampered after Willa. She looped her arm through mine, leading me away from the dining room and toward my room. I instantly felt bad about leaving Finn, but I couldn't take another lecture on silverware.

Willa chatted with me the whole way to my room in one endless stream of commentary about how dreadful her first few weeks were. She'd been certain that Finn would stab her with a fork before they even made it through the dining service, or vice versa.

"This is the worst part," she said solemnly as we walked into my bedroom. "The whole boot camp before the ball." She wrinkled her nose. "It's *horrid.*"

"Yeah, I'm not enjoying it," I admitted tiredly.

"But I made it through, so you'll definitely make it through." She walked into my bathroom, and when I didn't follow, she looked back at me. "Are you coming?"

"To the bathroom with you?"

"To practice hairstyles." She gave me a *duh* look, and reluctantly I walked in after her. Out of the frying pan and into the fire.

"Hairstyles?" I asked as Willa ushered me over to the stool in front of the vanity.

"Yeah, for the ball." She sifted through the hair products on the counter and stopped, meeting my eyes in the mirror. "Unless your mother is going to help you with it."

"Not that I know of." I shook my head.

"She's definitely not the nurturing type," Willa agreed, somewhat sadly. Picking a bottle of something and a brush, she turned to me. "Do you want your hair up or down?"

"I don't know." I thought back to when I'd first met Willa, and Finn had told me to wear it down. "Down. I guess."

"Good choice." She smiled and pulled out my hair tie, painfully taking my hair down. "So, did Frederique come today?"

"Uh, yeah, a few hours ago," I said between gritted teeth as she raked a comb through my hair.

"Excellent," Willa said. "When you have your fitting, you should take a picture and send it to me. I'd love to see what it looks like."

"Yeah, sure thing."

"I know how ridiculous and confusing everything is at first." Willa teased and primped my hair, all the while chatting happily. "And Finn knows pretty much everything, but he can be a little . . . cold, at times. And I'm sure the Queen isn't much better."

"Not really," I admitted. But cold wouldn't be how I described Finn. Sometimes he was standoffish, but other times, when he looked at me just so, he was anything but cold.

"I'm just letting you know that I wanna help you." She stopped pulling at my hair long enough to meet my eyes in the mirror again. "And not like that backstabbing bitch Aurora

Kroner, or because my father told me to, although he did. Or even like Finn because it's his job. I just know what it's like to be you. And if I can help, I want to."

She gave me a crooked smile, and the sincerity in it startled me. Underneath her vapid pretense, she was actually a kind person. So few people here seemed to genuinely care about anyone else, and it was nice to have finally found one.

Immediately after that moment, Willa launched into a lengthy monologue about gowns. She could describe every gown she'd seen since coming to Förening three years ago, and she only liked one or two of them.

So my training with Willa didn't turn out to be that much more interesting than that with Finn. She had a lot more gossip, about who dated whom and who was engaged and all that. But since I didn't know who any of the people were, it wasn't that interesting.

Willa was thus far single, and it didn't sit well with her. She kept saying that her father needed to arrange something, and mentioned a few guys she'd had her eye on who'd slipped by. She spoke very fondly of Tove Kroner. Although she did point out that by missing out on him, she'd also miss out on a monster of a mother-in-law.

Still, by the end of the day I had a hairstyle picked out, a makeup "plan" in order, and I felt like I knew a little bit more about Trylle royalty. She made it all sound a lot like high school, which would've been comforting, except I hadn't done that well at high school.

SIXTEEN

further instruction

They had taken an interest in me, and I knew I should feel flattered, but I wished they'd just left me alone. Elora and Aurora Kroner stood on the opposite side of the table. A seating chart stretched across the giant oak surface, and they both leaned over it, staring with intense scrutiny.

I had a feeling Elora had just dragged me with her because misery loves company. As for Aurora, I didn't really get why she was interested in me. The best I could figure was that she hoped to understand me in order to bring about my demise. The too-big way she smiled at me kept making me want to cringe.

Finn had snuck into my room early in the morning, and my initial excitement faded when I saw how frantically he picked out my clothes. He instructed me to get ready with lightning speed and to be on my best behavior all day. I hated the way he treated me like I was five and it was my first day of kindergarten.

But sitting there, watching them analyze every minute detail of a flippin' seating chart, I really felt like a five-year-old. One who had gotten in trouble and had to sit in a very agonizing time-out. I tried to look studious and interested in all of this, but I didn't know any of these people.

We were in the War Room in the south wing where walls were plastered with maps. Red and green patches speckled all of them, indicating other tribes of trolls. I'd been trying to study them while Elora and Aurora talked, but Elora kept snapping my attention back every time it wandered.

"If we put the Chancellor here, then Markis Tormann will have to move from this table entirely." Aurora tapped the paper.

"I don't see another way around it." Elora smiled as sweetly as she could manage, and Aurora matched it perfectly.

"He's traveling a great distance to be here for this." Aurora batted her eyes at Elora.

"He'll still be near enough where he can hear the christening," Elora said and turned her attention to me. "Are you ready for the christening ceremony?"

"Um, yeah," I said. Finn had mentioned it to me, but I hadn't been paying that much attention. I couldn't say that to Elora, though, so I just smiled and tried to look confident.

"A Princess doesn't say 'um.'" Elora narrowed her eyes at me, and Aurora did a poor job of trying to mask a snicker.

I sighed. "Sorry."

Elora looked like she wanted to chastise me further, but Aurora watched us both like a hawk. Elora pursed her lips, biting her tongue so she wouldn't show any sign of weakness.

I didn't understand what Aurora was doing here or what Elora had to fear from her. She was the Queen, and as far as I could tell, Aurora's only ability seemed to be making backhanded compliments and veiled threats.

The Marksinna looked radiant, wearing a long burgundy gown that made me feel incredibly underdressed in a simple skirt. Aurora's beauty nearly overshadowed Elora's, and that was really saying something, but I don't think that kind of thing mattered to Elora.

"Perhaps you should continue your training elsewhere," Elora suggested, glaring at me.

"Yes. Excellent idea." I jumped to my feet so quickly I almost knocked the chair over behind me. Aurora's amused expression changed to downright disgust, and Elora rolled her eyes. "Sorry. I'm very excited about all of this."

"Contain yourself, Princess."

Using restraint, I left the room as calmly as I could. I wanted to rush out, feeling much like a kid on the last day of school. I wasn't sure that I knew my way back, and I had no idea where Finn was, but as soon as I thought it was safe, I picked up my pace, nearly jogging away.

I'd made it a little ways down the hall, past several closed doors, when somebody stopped me.

"Princess!" a voice called from one of the few open doors.

I stopped, tentatively peering inside the room. It appeared to be more of a den, with a lush red rug in the center surrounded by leather chairs. One wall was made of glass, but the shades had been pulled shut over most of it, leaving the room in shadows.

A heavy mahogany bar sat in the corner, and a man leaned in front of it, holding a glass in his hand. I squinted, trying to get a better look at him. His hair looked disheveled, and he was dressed nice but casual.

"Don't you recognize me, Princess?" He had a smile in his voice, so I thought he might be teasing.

"It's just hard to see," I said, stepping into the room.

"Garrett Strom. Willa's father," he told me, and I could see his grin widening.

"Oh, right. It's good to see you." I smiled back, feeling more at ease. I'd only met him at dinner the other night, but I liked him. "Can I help you with something?"

"Nope. I'm just waiting for your mother, but I'm assuming it'll be a long day, so I got a jump start." Garrett motioned to the drink in his hand.

"Nice."

"Do you want something to drink?" Garrett offered. "I'm sure you need one, with Elora putting you through your paces."

I chewed my lip, thinking. I'd never drank before, other than a glass of wine with dinner, but after the last few days I definitely could use something to take the edge off. However, Elora would kill me if she found out, and Finn would be more than disappointed in me.

"No, I'm good." I shook my head. "Thanks, though."

"Don't thank me. It's your liquor," he pointed out. "You do look worn out. Why don't you take a load off?"

"All right." I shrugged and sat down in one of the chairs. The leather may have looked distressed, but the chair had the hard buoyancy of being brand-new. I moved around, trying to get comfortable, before eventually giving up.

"What is she having you do?" Garrett asked, sitting down across from me.

"I don't know. She's making a seating chart." I leaned my head against the back of the chair. "I don't even know why she wanted me there, except to point out what I was doing wrong."

"She just wants you to feel included in all of this," Garrett said between sips of his drink.

"Well, I'd rather not be included," I muttered. "Between her and Aurora giving me icy glares and judging everything I say and do, I'm perfectly happy to be left out."

"Don't let her get to you," Garrett advised.

"Which one?"

"Both," he said with a laugh.

"Sorry. I don't mean to dump on you."

"Don't be sorry." He shook his head. "I know how hard this can be, and I'm sure Elora isn't making it any easier on you."

"She expects me to know everything and be perfect already, and I haven't been here that long."

"You're strong-willed. You get that from her, you know." Garrett smiled. "And as strange as it sounds, everything she's doing—it's to protect you."

It was the first time anyone had drawn any kind of comparison between Elora and me, and it warmed me in a weird way. I realized that he was one of very few people I'd met who called her "Elora" instead of "Queen," and I wondered exactly how well he knew her.

"Thanks," I said, unsure what else to say.

"I heard Willa visited you last night." His eyes settled on me. My vision had adjusted to the darkness of the room, and I could see the softness in his gaze.

"Yeah, she did. She's been very helpful."

"Good. I'm glad to hear it." Garrett looked relieved at that, and I wondered what he'd been expecting me to say. "I know she can be a little"—he wagged his head, searching for the right word—"*Willa* at times, but she means well."

"Yeah, Finn filled me in."

"I've been working on her to lighten up on the mänks. But it's a work in progress."

"Why is she so hard on Rhiannon?" I hadn't seen Willa talk to her much, but what little she said had been filled with jabs and snide remarks, even worse than Aurora's.

"Rhiannon got to live with me nineteen years before Willa did," Garrett explained. "Willa's always been secretly afraid that I preferred Rhiannon over her, but the fact is, while I love Rhiannon, I only have one daughter."

I had never thought about him loving Rhiannon, or anyone loving the mänsklig left behind. I looked in the direction of the War Room, as if I could see Elora through the wall. I couldn't imagine her loving anyone.

But the only babies among the Trylle elite were mänsklig, and at some point parental instincts had to take over. Certainly not with everyone, but it made sense that some, like Garrett, would feel as if the child they raised was their own.

"Do you think Elora loves Rhys?" I asked.

"I think Elora is an incredibly hard woman to get close to," Garrett allowed carefully, then he smiled at me. "I know she loves you, though."

"Yeah, I can tell," I said dryly, unwilling to even consider what he'd said, let alone believe it. I'd been burned by enough crazy moms already.

"She speaks very fondly of you. When you're not around, of course." He gave a small chuckle. Something about the way he said that, I felt a sense of intimacy in it.

An image flashed before me. Elora sitting at her vanity, wearing a robe, and putting on jewelry. Garrett was behind her, still lying in her bed with the sheets covering him. She made some offhand comment about me being prettier than she expected, and before he could agree, she told him he needed to hurry and get dressed.

I shook my head, clearing it of the thought.

"Are you dating Elora?" I asked directly, even though I already knew the answer.

"I definitely wouldn't call it dating," he scoffed and took a long drink. "Let me put it this way: I'm about as close to her as anyone can get. Well, at least anyone can get *now*."

"'Now'?" I furrowed my brow. "What do you mean by that?"

"Elora wasn't always the cool, collected Queen you know

and fear." There was a bitter edge to his words, and I wondered how long he'd been seeing her. Had it been while she was married to my father? Or when she was in love with Finn's father?

"What made her change?" I asked.

"The same thing that makes everyone change: experience." He turned his glass in his hands, admiring what little liquor he had left.

"What happened to my father?"

"You're really digging deep, aren't you?" Garrett cocked an eyebrow at me. "I do not have enough alcohol for this conversation." He knocked back the rest in one swallow.

"Why? What happened?" I pressed, leaning forward in my chair.

"It was a very long time ago." He took a deep breath, still looking down. "And Elora was devastated."

"She really loved him, then?" I still found it weird to think that she'd ever loved anyone. She didn't seem capable of any emotion deeper than anger.

"I honestly don't know. I didn't know her that well back then." Garrett abruptly got up from his chair and walked over to the bar. "My wife was still alive, and we only had a casual acquaintance with the Queen." He poured himself another drink, keeping his back to me. "If you want to know more about all of this, you'll have to talk to Elora."

"She won't tell me anything." I sighed and leaned back in the chair.

"Some things are better forgotten," Garrett mused. He

took a long drink, still keeping his back to me, and I realized belatedly that I'd upset him.

"Sorry." I stood up. I didn't know how to correct the situation, so I thought leaving might be the best way to fix it.

He shook his head. "No need to be sorry."

"I should get back, anyway." I edged toward the door. "Finn is probably looking for me by now."

Garrett nodded. "Probably." I'd almost made it out the door when he stopped me. "Princess?" He turned his head to the side, so shadows darkened his profile. "Elora's hard on you because she's afraid to care about you. But she'll fight to the death for you."

"Thanks," I mumbled.

The light in the hallway felt too bright after the dimness of the den. I didn't know what I'd said that had upset Garrett so much. Maybe bringing up memories of his dead wife. Or maybe reminding him that while Elora couldn't openly care for him now, she had cared once, for another man.

I tried to push away the confusion Garrett had made me feel. I wasn't sure if I could trust the things he'd said about Elora. I didn't think he was a liar, but he'd wanted to make me feel better. Convincing me that I had a mother who actually loved me probably would help, but I had long since stopped holding out for that dream.

I found Finn in the front hall, directing several of Elora's aides with the planning for the ball. He had his back to me, so he didn't notice me right away. I stood there for a moment, just watching him direct and take control. He knew exactly what do with everything, and I couldn't help but admire him for it.

"Princess." Finn caught sight of me when he glanced over his shoulder, then he turned fully to me with a smile. An aide asked him something, and he gestured vaguely to the dining hall before walking over to me. "How did this morning go?"

I shrugged. "It could've been worse."

"That doesn't sound promising." He raised an eyebrow. "But I suppose you've earned a bit of a reprieve."

"A reprieve?" It was my turn to look skeptical.

"Yeah, I thought we'd do something fun for a while." Finn smiled.

"Fun?" I remembered yesterday, how he'd tried to convince me his mind-numbing training had been fun. "Do you mean fun fun? Or do you mean looking at pictures for two hours fun? Or Using a Fork 101 fun?"

"Something that at least resembles actual fun," Finn answered. "Come on."

SEVENTEEN

jealousy

As Finn led me down a hall to the south wing, I realized that I'd never seen any of this before. When Garrett had teased Elora about this being a palace, he wasn't kidding. There were so many places I had yet to see. It was astounding.

Finn gestured to a few rooms, pointing out the library, meeting halls where business was conducted, the opulent dining hall where we would hold the dinner on Saturday, and then, finally, the ballroom.

Pushing open the doors, which seemed to be two stories high, Finn led me into the grandest room I had ever seen. Massive and exquisite, the ceiling seemed to stretch on forever, thanks in part to the fact that the entire thing was skylight. Gold beams ran across it, holding up glittering diamond chandeliers. The floors were marble, the walls were off-white with gold detailing, and it looked every bit the ballroom from a Disney fairy tale.

The decorators had started bringing things in, and stacked chairs and tables now leaned against one of the walls. Tablecloths, candlesticks, and all sorts of decorations were piled around them. The only other thing in the room was a white grand piano sitting in the opposite corner. Otherwise the room was empty except for Finn and me.

I hated how taken I was with the splendor. I hated even more that the room was so magnificent and I looked like I did. My hair was in a messy bun, and my skirt felt far too plain. Finn wasn't exactly dressed to the nines either, but his standard button-down shirt and dark wash jeans looked much more fitting.

"So what's the fun part?" I asked, and my voice echoed off the walls.

"Dancing." Finn's lip twitched with a smile, and I groaned. "I've danced with you before, and I know that it needs some improvement."

"The slow circles don't cut it?" I grimaced.

"Unfortunately, no. A proper waltz should be enough, though. If you can master that, you'll be set for the ball on Saturday."

"Oh, no." My stomach dropped as I realized something. "I'm going to have to dance with these people, aren't I? Like strangers and old men and weird handsy boys?" Finn laughed at that, but I wanted to curl up in a ball and die.

"I could lie to you, but to be honest, those are probably the only people who will ask you to dance," Finn admitted with a wry smirk.

"You're enjoying this more than I've ever seen you enjoy anything," I said, and that only deepened his smile. "Well, I'm glad you find this funny. Me being felt up by complete strangers and tripping all over them. What a great time."

"It won't be so bad." He motioned for me to come over. "If you learn the basic steps, at least you won't be tripping over them."

I sighed loudly and walked over to him. Most of my trepidation about dancing with strangers melted away the instant Finn took my hand in his. It suddenly occurred to me that before I had to dance with them, I got to dance with *him*.

After a few directions from him and a rough start by me, we were dancing. His arm was around me, strong and reassuring. He instructed me to keep my eyes locked on his so I wouldn't get in the habit of watching my feet while I danced, but I wouldn't have looked anywhere else anyway. His dark eyes always mesmerized me.

We were supposed to keep a certain distance between our bodies, but I found it impossible. His body nearly pressed against mine, and I delighted in the sensation. I was certain we weren't going as fast as we should, but I didn't care. This moment with him seemed entirely too perfect to be real.

"Right, okay." Finn suddenly stopped and took a step away from me. Disappointed, I let my hands fall to the side. "You've got that down pretty well, but there's going to be music. So you should see how you do with that."

"Okay?" I said unsurely.

"Why don't I play the piano, and you count out the steps

yourself?" Finn had already started backing away to the piano, and I wondered what I had done wrong that made him stop so suddenly. "That might be a better way for you to learn."

"Um, okay." I shrugged uncertainly. "I thought I was doing fine before."

"We weren't going fast enough. The music will help you keep time."

I frowned at him, wishing he would just come back and dance with me. I remembered how he once told me I was a terrible dance partner, and wondered if maybe that was the problem.

He sat down at the piano and started playing a beautiful, elaborate waltz. Of course he could play. He could do anything. I just stood there staring at him, until he directed me to start dancing.

I whirled around on the dance floor, but it definitely wasn't as fun as it had been with him. In fact, it wasn't really that fun at all. It might have been if I weren't trying to figure out what I did wrong that always made Finn back away from me.

It was hard to concentrate on that, though, when Finn kept barking out corrections at me. Funny, he hadn't noticed any of my mistakes when we had been dancing together.

"Nope, that's it," I panted after what felt like an eternity.

My feet and legs were getting sore, and a sheen of sweat covered my body. I had had my fill of dancing for the day. I sat down heavily on the floor, then leaned back, sprawling out on the cool marble.

"Wendy, it hasn't even been that long," Finn insisted.

"Don't care. I'm out!" I breathed deeply and wiped the sweat from my forehead.

"Haven't you ever worked at anything?" Finn complained. He got up from the piano bench and walked over to me so he could lecture me up close. "This is important."

"I'm aware. You tell me every second of every day."

"I do not." Finn crossed his arms and looked down at me.

"This is the hardest I've ever worked at anything," I said, staring back up at him. "Everything else I've quit before this, or I never even tried. So don't tell me I'm not putting effort into this."

"You've never tried harder than this? At anything?" Finn asked incredulously, and I shook my head. "That brother you had never made you do anything?"

"Not really," I admitted thoughtfully. "He made me go to school, I guess. But that's about it." Matt and Maggie encouraged me to do many things, but there was very little they actually made me do.

"They spoiled you more than I thought." Finn looked surprised at that.

"They didn't spoil me." I sighed, then quickly amended, "They didn't spoil me rotten. Not the way Willa was spoiled, and I'm sure a lot of the other changelings were. They just wanted me to be happy."

"Happiness is something you work for," Finn pointed out.

"Oh, stop with that fortune-cookie crap," I scoffed. "We worked for it just like anybody else. They were just really careful with me, probably because my mom tried to kill me. It set them up to treat me more gently than they would've otherwise."

"How did your mother try to kill you?" Finn asked, startling me. I hadn't told him much about it, but he rarely wanted to talk about my past.

"It was my birthday, and I was being my usual bratty self. I was angry because she'd gotten me a chocolate cake, and I hated it," I said. "We were in the kitchen, and she snapped. She started chasing after me with this giant knife. She called me a monster, and then she tried to stab me but she just managed to cut my stomach pretty badly. Then my brother Matt rushed in and tackled her, saving my life."

"She cut open your stomach?" Finn furrowed his brow with concern.

"Yeah." I pulled up my shirt, revealing the scar that stretched across it.

Immediately after I'd done that, I regretted it. Lying on the floor and flashing Finn the fattest part of my body did not seem like a good idea.

Finn crouched on the floor next to me, and tentatively his fingertips traced along the mark etched on my belly. My skin quivered underneath his touch, and nervous warmth spread through me. He continued to stare intently at the scar, then he laid his hand flat on my belly, covering it. His skin felt hot and smooth, and inside, my stomach trembled with butterflies.

He blinked and, seeming to realize what he was doing, he pulled his hand back and got to his feet. Quickly I pulled my shirt back down. I didn't even feel that comfortable lying down anymore, so I sat up and fixed my bun.

"Matt saved your life?" Finn asked, filling that semi-awkward silence that had shrouded us. He still had a contemplative look on his face, and I wished I knew what he was thinking.

"Yeah." I got to my feet. "Matt always protected me, ever since I could remember."

"Hmm." Finn looked thoughtfully at me. "You bonded so much more with your host family than the changelings normally do."

" 'Host family'?" I grimaced. "You make me sound like a parasite."

Then I realized that I probably was. They had dropped me off with the Everlys so I would use their resources, their money, their opportunities, and bring them back here. That's exactly what a parasite did.

"You're not a parasite," Finn said. "They loved you, and you genuinely loved them in return. It is unusual, but that's not a bad thing. In fact, it's a very good thing. Maybe it's given you a compassion that Trylle leaders have been lacking for a very long time."

"I don't think I'm very compassionate." I shook my head.

"I see how it bothers you the way Elora talks to people. Elora thinks the only way to command respect is to command fear, but I have a feeling that you will have an entirely different way of ruling."

"And how will I rule?" I arched my eyebrow at him.

"That is for you to decide," Finn said simply.

He ended our lesson after that, saying I needed to rest up for tomorrow. The day had exhausted me, and I was eager to curl up in my blankets and sleep until Sunday, straight through the ball and all the angst that accompanied it.

Sleep didn't come easy, though. I found myself tossing and turning, thinking about the way it felt dancing with Finn, and his hand resting warmly on my stomach.

But I would always end up thinking of Matt and how much I still missed him. I had expected that to lessen the longer I was here, but it only seemed to get worse. After all this, I really needed to know that someone had my back and cared about me unconditionally.

I woke up early the next morning. Actually, I'd been waking up all night long, and at six I finally just gave up. I got up with the intention of sneaking downstairs to grab a bite to eat, but when I hit the top of the stairs, Rhys came barreling up them to meet me, chomping on a bagel.

"Hey, what are you doing up?" He grinned, swallowing down his bite.

"Couldn't sleep." I shrugged. "You?"

"Same. I have to get ready for school soon anyway." He pushed his hair out of his eyes and leaned back against the stair railing. "Are you worrying about this Saturday?"

"Kind of," I admitted.

"It is pretty intense," Rhys said, his eyes wide. I nodded

noncommittally. "Is something else bothering you? You look pretty . . . upset, I guess."

"No." I shook my head and sighed, then sat down on the top step. I didn't feel much like standing anymore, and I wanted to cry. "I was just thinking about my brother."

"Your brother?" Something flashed across Rhys's face, and slowly he sat down next to me. He seemed almost breathless. At first I didn't understand, but then it dawned on me.

This must be so weird for Rhys. His whole life he had known that this wasn't his real family, and it wasn't even the same as being adopted. His family hadn't wanted to give him up. He had been stolen, and not even by a family that had wanted him. They had just wanted me to have his life.

"Yeah. I mean . . . *your* brother, actually," I corrected myself, and it felt painful saying that. Matt would always be my brother, no matter what our genetics were.

"What's his name?" Rhys asked quietly.

"Matt. He's pretty much the nicest guy in the whole world."

"Matt?" Rhys repeated in an awed tone.

"Yeah." I nodded. "He's the bravest guy ever. He would do anything to protect the people he cares about, and he's completely selfless. He always puts everybody else first. And he's really, really strong. He's . . ." I swallowed and decided that I couldn't talk about him anymore. I shook my head and looked away.

"What about my mom and dad?" Rhys pressed, and I didn't know how to answer that.

"Dad died when I was five," I said carefully. "My mother took it pretty hard, and, um . . . she's been in the hospital ever since. For psychiatric problems. Matt and my dad's sister, Maggie, they raised me."

"Oh." His face contorted with concern.

I suddenly hated Kim even more. I knew that she had done everything because she loved Rhys, but that didn't make her actions any less inexcusable. I didn't have it in me to tell him what she'd done or that she'd never be able to have a life with him because she'd always be locked up.

"I'm sorry." I placed my hand gently on his, to comfort him. "It's hard to explain how I know it, but your mom really loved you. She really wanted you. And I think she always hated me because she knew I wasn't you."

"Really?" There was something hopeful and sad in his eyes when he looked at me.

"Yeah. It kind of sucked for me, actually." I smiled wanly at him, and he laughed.

"Sorry about that." Rhys smiled back at me. "I guess I'm too hard to forget."

"Yeah, I guess you are," I agreed. Rhys moved his hand so it was actually holding mine.

"So what about this Maggie? What's she like?" Rhys asked.

"She's pretty cool. A little overly attentive sometimes, but cool," I said. "She put up with a lot of crap from me. They both did, really." I thought about how strange this all was, that they weren't my family anymore. "This is so weird. They're your brother and your aunt."

"No, I understand. They're your family too," Rhys said. "They loved you and raised you. That's what family is, right?"

I had needed someone to say that to me for so long, and I squeezed his hand gratefully. I still loved them and always would, and I just needed that to be okay.

"Wendy!" Finn came down the hall, still dressed in his pajamas. Instinctively I pulled my hand back, and Rhys stood up. "What are you doing?"

"I just woke up. We were just talking." I looked up at Rhys, who nodded in agreement.

Finn glared at us both, and I felt like we'd just been caught robbing a bank.

"I suggest you get ready for school," he said icily.

"Yeah, that's what I was doing anyway," Rhys said, then smiled down at me. "I'll see you later, Wendy."

"Yeah, okay." I smiled back at him.

"What are you doing?" Finn hissed, glowering down at me.

"I already told you," I insisted and stood up. "We were just talking."

"About what?" Finn asked.

"My family." I shrugged. "What does it matter?"

"You cannot talk to him about your host family," Finn said. "Mänsklig cannot know where they come from. If they did, they would be tempted to track down their families, and that would completely ruin our entire society. Do you understand that?"

"I didn't really tell him anything!" I said, but I felt stupid that that hadn't occurred to me. "I missed Matt, and I just said stuff about how neat he was. I didn't tell Rhys where he lived or anything like that."

"You have to be more careful, Wendy."

"Sorry. I didn't know." I didn't like the way he was glaring at me, so I turned and started walking down the hall toward my room.

"Wait." Finn grabbed my arm gently so I would stop and look at him.

He took a step closer to me so he was right in front of me, but I was trying to be mad at him, so I refused to look at him. I could still feel his eyes on me and the heat from his body, and it did little to help me maintain my anger.

"What?" I asked.

Finn lowered his voice. "I saw you holding his hand."

"So?" I said. "Is that a crime?"

"No, but . . . you *can't* do that. You cannot get involved with a mänsklig."

"Whatever." I pulled my arm from his grip, irritated that the only thing he ever thought about was his job. "You're just jealous."

"I am not jealous." Finn took a step back from me. "I am watching out for your well-being. You don't understand how dangerous it would be to get involved with him."

"Yeah, yeah," I muttered and started walking back to my room. "I don't understand anything."

"That's not what I said." Finn followed me.

"But it's true, isn't it?" I countered. "I don't know anything."

"Wendy!" Finn snapped, and grudgingly, I turned back to

look at him. "If you don't understand things, it's because I didn't explain them well enough."

He swallowed hard and looked down at the floor, his dark eyelashes falling on his cheeks. There was something more that he wanted to say to me, so I crossed my arms, waiting.

"But you were right." He was clearly struggling with the words, and I watched him carefully. "I was jealous."

"What?" My jaw fell open, and my eyes widened with surprise.

"That does not affect the job I have to do, nor does it change the fact that you absolutely cannot become involved with a mänsklig," Finn said firmly, still looking at the floor instead of at me. "Now go get ready. We have another long day ahead of us." He turned around and started to walk away.

"Wait, Finn!" I called after him, and he paused, half looking back at me.

"The matter is not open for discussion," he replied coolly. "I promised I would never lie to you, so I didn't."

I stood in front of my bedroom door, reeling from his confession. For the first time, he had actually admitted that at least some of his feelings for me had nothing to do with the job at hand. Yet somehow I was supposed to forget all that and go about as if everything were normal.

EIGHTEEN

intimidation

I spent a long time getting ready, still making sense of what Finn had told me. It thrilled me that he cared enough to feel jealous, but I also realized how pointless it was. He'd never do anything that conflicted with his sense of honor and duty.

Even with me taking so much time, Finn never came to get me. Eventually, I perched at the top of the spiral staircase to wait for him. I thought about going down to his room, but I didn't really feel comfortable with that. Besides, he'd probably send me away.

From the top of the stairs, I watched in surprise as Tove Kroner pushed open the front door. He hadn't knocked or anything, and he raked a hand through his messy hair, looking around.

"Can I help you?" I called down. As Princess, I felt like I ought to be hospitable, even if I felt flustered and confused as hell.

"Uh, yeah. I'm looking for you." He shoved his hands in his pockets and walked to the bottom of the steps, but didn't go any farther.

"What for?" I wrinkled my nose, then, realizing I'd sounded rude, shook my head. "I mean, I beg your pardon?"

"Just to help." Tove shrugged.

I walked slowly down the stairs, watching his eyes search the room. He never did seem comfortable looking at me.

As I approached him, I took in the soft natural highlights coursing through his dark hair. It was long and unruly, hitting just above his shoulders.

His tanned skin had a subtle mossy undertone, the green complexion that Finn had told me about. Nobody else had skin like that, except maybe his mother, but hers was fainter than Tove's.

"Help me with what?" I asked.

"What?" He'd taken to chewing on his thumbnail. He glanced up at me, still biting it.

"What are you here to help me with?" I spoke slowly and carefully, my tone bordering on condescending, but I don't think he noticed.

"Oh." He dropped his hand and stared off, as if he'd forgotten why he'd come. "I'm psychic."

"What? You can read minds?" I tensed up, trying to block him from reading any of my thoughts.

"No, no, of course not." He brushed me off and walked away, admiring the chandelier hanging from the ceiling. "I can sense things. And I can move things with my mind. But I can't read your thoughts. I can see auras, though. Yours is a bit brown today."

"What does that mean?" I crossed my arms over my chest, as if I could hide my aura that way. I didn't even really know what an aura was.

"You're unhappy." Tove sounded distracted, and he glanced back at me. "Normally it's orange."

"I don't know what that means either." I shook my head. "I don't know how any of this is supposed to help me."

"It's not really." He stopped moving and looked up at me. "Has Finn talked to you about training?"

"You mean the Princess training I'm doing now?"

"No." He shook his head, chewing the inside of his cheek. "For your abilities. It won't start until after the christening. They think if you had any handle on them *before* you were indoctrinated, you'd run wild." He sighed. "They want you calm and docile."

"This is you calm?" I raised a skeptical eyebrow.

"No." Tove stared off at nothing again, then turned back to me, his green eyes meeting mine. "You intimidate me."

"*I* intimidate you?" I laughed, unable to stop myself, but he wasn't offended. "I'm the least intimidating person ever."

"Mmm." His face hardened in concentration. "Maybe to some people. But they don't see what I see or know what I know."

"What do you know?" I asked gently, startled by his confession.

"Have they told you?" Tove eyed me again.

"Told me what?"

"Well, if they haven't told you, I'm certainly not going to." He scratched at his arm and turned his back to me, walking away and looking around the room again.

"Whatever it is you're doing, it's not helping," I said, growing frazzled. "You're only confusing me more."

"My apologies, Princess." Tove stopped moving and bowed at me. "Finn wanted me to talk to you about your abilities. He knows you can't start your real training until after the ball, but he wants you to be prepared."

"Finn asked you to come over?" My heart thumped in my chest.

"Yes." His brow creased with confusion. "Does this upset you?"

"No, not at all," I lied. Finn had probably asked Tove over so he wouldn't have to deal with me. He was avoiding me.

"Do you have questions?" Tove stepped closer, and I was once again struck by the subtle green tinge to his skin. On a less attractive guy it might've been creepy. But on him it managed to look strangely exotic.

"Tons," I said with a sigh. He cocked his head at me. "You'll have to be more specific."

"You have nothing to be afraid of, you know." Tove watched me closely, and I think I might've preferred it when he was scared to look at me.

"I'm not afraid." It took effort not to squirm under his gaze.

"I can tell when you lie," he said, still watching me. "Not because I'm psychic, but because you're so obvious about it. You should probably work on that. Elora is very good at lying."

"I'll practice," I muttered.

"That's probably for the best." Tove spoke with an intense sincerity that I found disarming. His disjointed insanity even had its own charm. He looked down at the floor, his expression turning sad. "I rather like you this way. Honest and flustered. But it'd never work for a Queen."

"No, I don't suppose it would," I agreed, feeling a bit melancholy myself.

"I'm a bit scattered too, if you hadn't noticed." He gave me a small, crooked smile, but his green eyes stayed sad. With that, he crouched down, picking up a small oval stone off the floor. He flipped it around in his hand, staring down. "I find it hard to stay focused, but I'm working on it."

"So . . . not to sound mean or anything, but why did Finn want *you* to help?" I rubbed my arms, hoping I didn't upset him by asking.

"Because I'm strong." Tove tossed the stone aside, apparently tiring of it. "And he trusts me." He looked back at me. "So let's see what you can do."

"With what?" I asked, confused by the abrupt change of subject.

"Anything." He spread his arms wide. "Can you move stuff?"

"With my hands, yeah."

"Obviously." He rolled his eyes. "You're not a paraplegic, so I assumed you were physically capable."

"I can't do much. Just persuasion, and I haven't used it since I've been here."

"Try." Tove pointed to the chandelier dangling above us. "Move that."

"I don't want to move that," I said, alarmed.

An image flashed in my mind. The painting I had seen in Elora's room, all dark smoke and red fires around broken chandeliers. Except the image in my mind seemed much more vivid, as if I could smell the smoke and see the fire raging, casting new shadows in the painting. The sound of glass shattering echoed in my ear.

I swallowed hard and shook my head, taking several steps back from the chandelier. I hadn't been underneath it exactly, but I wanted to get farther away.

"What was that?" Tove asked, cocking his head at me.

"What?"

"Something happened." He studied me, trying to decipher my reaction, but I just shook my head. It felt like too much to explain, and I wasn't sure that I hadn't imagined it. "Interesting."

"Thanks," I mumbled.

"I hate to do this, since you look so frightened, but I need to get you out of my head." He looked up at the chandelier, and my eyes followed his.

My heart raced in my chest, and my throat felt dry. The crystal shards twinkled and chimed and started to shimmer. I took several steps back, wanting to yell at him to stop, but I didn't even know if he'd listen. Then the whole chandelier started to sway, and I couldn't hold back.

"Stop!" I shouted, my voice echoing through the front hall. "Why are you doing that?"

"I am sorry." He exhaled deeply, and looked back down at me. I kept my eyes locked on the chandelier until I was certain it'd stopped moving. "I had to do something, and there was nothing else in the room I could move, except for you yourself, and I didn't think you'd like that either."

"Why did you have to move anything?" I snapped. My panic had started to fade, replaced by a pulsating anger, and I clenched my fists at my sides.

"When you get frightened like that, you project it so intensely." He held up his hands, pushing them out to demonstrate. "Most people can't hear it or feel it anymore, but I'm particularly sensitive to emotion. And when I move things, it helps focus me. It kinda shuts off the noise for a while. You were too strong. I had to silence it." He shrugged. "I'm sorry."

"You didn't need to freak me out like that." I calmed a bit, but my words still came out hard. "Just don't do that again, please."

"It's such a shame." Tove watched me, looking both bemused and rueful. "They won't even be able to see what you really are. They've all gotten so weak that they won't be able to tell how powerful you are."

"What are you talking about?" I momentarily forgot my anger.

"Your mother is so powerful." Tove sounded almost awed

by it. "Probably not as much as you, and maybe not as much as me, but it's in her blood, crackling like electricity. I feel her walking through a room, and she's almost magnetized. But the rest of them . . ." He shook his head.

"You mean the other Trylle?" I clarified, since Tove insisted on being so cryptic.

"We used to move the earth." He sounded wistful, and his whole demeanor had changed. He was no longer pacing or looking around, and I realized that moving the chandelier really had done something to him.

"Are you speaking literally or metaphorically?" I asked.

"Literally. We could make mountains, stop rivers." He moved his arms dramatically, as if he could do those things now. "We created everything around us! We were magic!"

"Aren't we still magic?" I asked, surprised by the passion in his voice.

"Not the way we were before. Once the humans created their own magic with technology, the dependence switched. They had all the power and the money, and we started to depend on them to raise our children," he scoffed. "Changelings stopped coming back, when they realized we didn't have that much to offer them anymore."

"We came back," I pointed out emptily.

"Your gardener, who makes the flowers bloom, she's a Marksinna!" Tove pointed to the back of the house where the garden lay. "A *gardener*! I'm not one for class, but when one of the most powerful members of your population is the gardener, you know it's a problem."

"Well . . . why is she a gardener, then?" I asked.

"Because. Nobody else can do it." He looked at me, his green eyes burning with something. "Nobody can do anything anymore."

"You can. I can," I said, hoping to alleviate whatever distressed him.

"I know." He sighed and lowered his eyes. "Everyone's just gotten too fixated on the human system of monarchy. With designer dresses and expensive jewels." His lip curled with disgust. "Our obsession with riches has always been our downfall."

"Yeah." I nodded. "But your mother seems to be the worst with it."

"I know." Tove raised his eyebrows with weary acceptance. Something softened, and he looked almost apologetically at me. "I'm not against humans. It sounds like I am, doesn't it?"

"I don't know. It sounds like you're passionate," I said.

When I'd first met him, I'd mistaken his inattention as boredom and arrogance. But I was starting to think his abilities had something to do with it, giving him a kind of power-related ADD. Behind that, he had a fearless honesty that few Trylle seemed to possess.

"Maybe." He smiled and lowered his eyes, looking slightly embarrassed.

"How old are you?" I asked.

"Nineteen. Why?"

"How do you know so much about the past? You talked about the way things were like you were there, like you saw it happen. Or like you're a major history buff or something."

"My mother is keen on me studying, in case I ever get a chance for the throne," Tove said, but the idea seemed to tire him. I doubted he was any more excited about the prospect of ruling than I was. Aurora's scheming for the crown must be entirely her idea.

"What'd you see when you looked at the chandelier?" Tove asked, bringing me back to his reason for being here.

"I don't know." I shook my head. I wanted to answer honestly, but I didn't know how to. "I saw . . . a painting."

"Some people see the future." He stared up at the chandelier, the light twinkling above us. "And some people see the past." He paused, thinking. "In the end, they're not all that different. You can't prevent either of them."

"How profound," I said, and he laughed.

"I haven't helped you at all, have I?"

"I don't know," I admitted.

"You're too much for one afternoon, I'm afraid," Tove said.

"How do you mean?" I asked, but he just shook his head.

"I know you have a lot to go over, and you don't need me wasting your time. I don't know that I can help you much right now." He walked toward the door.

"Hey, wait," I said, and he stopped. "You said that normally they don't want us tapping into our abilities until after the christening. But Finn wanted you to help prepare me now. What for? Is something going on?"

"Finn's a protector. It's his job to worry," Tove explained, and my heart twisted. I hated it when people pointed out that

I was just part of Finn's job. "He needs to know that in any event, you'll be taken care of. Whether he's there or not."

"Why wouldn't he be there?" I asked, feeling fear ripple through me.

"I don't know." Tove shrugged. "But when something really matters to you, you make sure it's safe."

With that, Tove turned and walked out of the house. I was grateful for his help, though I wasn't even sure what he'd done. Other than confuse me more. And now I felt a new sense of dread settling over me.

I had no idea what was going on with Finn, and my thoughts insisted on going back to the painting I'd seen in Elora's secret room. I had been reaching off the balcony, looking horrified. Tove's words echoed through my mind, sending a chill down my spine.

You can't prevent the future.

I looked up at the chandelier. I'd been too terrified to even try to move it, thinking it would collapse and I'd bring Elora's painting into life. But I hadn't, and nothing terrible had come to pass.

Had I changed the future? Or was the worst still to come?

NINETEEN

christening

On Friday, with the party only twenty-four hours away, Elora felt the need to check on my progress, not that I blamed her. Her plan was a dress rehearsal for dinner, testing my ability to converse and eat, apparently.

She didn't want a massive audience to witness my possible failure, so she just invited Garrett, Willa, and Rhiannon over to join her, Finn, Rhys, and me. It was the biggest group she could assemble without risk of embarrassment. Since I had already met these people, I didn't feel all that nervous, even though Elora informed me beforehand that I needed to act the same way I would tomorrow night.

Everyone had been instructed similarly, and they all appeared far more regal than normal. Even Rhys had dressed in a blazer, and he looked rather handsome. As usual, Finn was unnecessarily attractive.

Thanks to Finn's random confession of jealousy, I wasn't

entirely sure how to act around him. He had come into my room before dinner to make sure that I was getting ready, and I couldn't help but feel that he was purposely avoiding looking at me.

When I reached the dining hall, Elora instructed us where to sit, with her at one end of the table and me at the other. Rhys and Finn flanked me, and Rhiannon, Garrett, and Willa, took their places in between.

"Who will I be sitting by tomorrow?" I asked between careful sips of wine.

"Between Tove Kroner and I." Elora narrowed her eyes at the drink in my hand. "Hold the glass by the stem."

"Sorry." I thought I had been, but I moved my fingers, hoping I was holding it more correctly now.

"A Princess never apologizes," Elora corrected me.

"Sorry," I mumbled, then realized what I had just done and shook my head. "That was an accident. It won't happen again."

"Don't shake your head; it's not ladylike," Elora chastised me. "A Princess doesn't make promises either. She might not be able to keep them, and she doesn't want them held against her."

"I wasn't really making a promise," I pointed out, and Elora narrowed her eyes more severely.

"A Princess is never contrary," she said coolly.

"I've only been a Princess for like a week. Can't you give me a little break?" I asked as kindly as I could.

I'd grown frustrated by all the Princess talk. Nearly every

sentence she'd said to me in the past two days had started with "A Princess" and was followed by things that a Princess never or always did.

"You've been a Princess your entire life. It's in your blood." Elora sat up even straighter in her chair, as if she were trying to loom over me. "You should know how to behave."

"I am working on it," I grumbled.

"Speak up. Use a clear strong voice no matter what it is you're saying," Elora snapped. "And you don't have time to work on it. Your party is tomorrow. You must be ready *now.*"

I wanted to snap back at her, but both Rhys and Finn were giving me warning stares to keep my mouth shut. Rhiannon stared nervously at her plate, and Garrett just went about munching his food politely.

"I understand." I exhaled deeply and took another drink of my wine. I'm not sure if I held the glass right this time, but Elora didn't say anything.

"So, I got your picture of the dress." Willa smiled at me. "It was really stunning. I'm a little jealous, actually. You only get to be the belle of the ball once, and you definitely will be tomorrow. You're going to look amazing."

She was coming to my aid, changing the subject from things I was doing wrong to something I was doing right. Even if she was a bitch to Finn and Rhiannon, I just couldn't bring myself to hate her.

"Thank you." I smiled back at her gratefully.

My final fitting had been earlier in the day, and since

Willa had asked me to the other night, I sent her a picture. Finn took it on his camera phone.

I felt very awkward posing for the photo, and it didn't help that he never reassured me that I looked good in the dress. It felt like too much for me to pull off, and I would've liked a little boost just then. But Finn had simply snapped the picture, and that had been the end of that.

"Have you seen the dress?" Willa turned to Elora, who nibbled primly at a piece of broccoli.

"No. I trust Frederique's designs, and Finn has final approval," she answered absently.

"I'm going to insist on being involved in the process when my daughter gets her gown," Willa offered thoughtfully. Elora bristled almost imperceptibly at that, but Willa didn't notice. "But I've always loved dresses and fashion. I could spend my whole life at a ball." She looked wistful for a moment, then smiled at me again. "That's why it's so great that you're here. You're going to have such a monumental ball."

"Thank you," I repeated, unsure how else to respond.

"You had a lovely party yourself," Garrett interjected, slightly defensive about the party he had thrown for his daughter. "Your gown was fantastic."

"I know." Willa beamed immodestly. "It was pretty great." Finn made a noise in his throat, and both Elora and Willa glared at him, but neither of them said anything.

"My apologies. Something caught in my throat," Finn explained, taking a sip of his wine.

"Hmm," Elora murmured disapprovingly, then cast a look

back at me. "Oh, that reminds me. I have been too busy this week to ask you. What were your plans for your name?"

"My name?" I asked, tilting my head to the side.

"Yes. At the christening ceremony." She looked at me for a moment, then turned sternly to Finn. "I thought Finn told you about it."

"Yes, but isn't that name already decided?" I was definitely confused. "I mean, Dahl is the family name, isn't it?"

"Not the surname." Elora rubbed her temples, clearly annoyed. "I meant your first name."

"I don't understand. Why wouldn't my name be Wendy Dahl?"

"That isn't a proper name for a Princess," Elora scoffed. "Everyone changes their names. Willa used to be called something different. What was it, dear?"

"Nikki," Willa said. "I took the name Willa, after my mother."

Garrett smiled at that, and Elora tensed up slightly, then turned her focus back to me.

"So what is it? What name would you like?" Elora pressed, possibly using me to deflect the tension.

"I . . . I don't know."

Irrationally, my heart had started pounding in my chest. I didn't want to change my name, not at all. When Finn had told me that about the christening ceremony, I had assumed it would only be my last name. While I wasn't thrilled about that, I didn't care much. Eventually I would probably get married and change my name anyway.

But Wendy, that was *my* name. I turned to Finn for help, but Elora noticed and snapped my attention back to her.

"If you need ideas, I have some." Elora spoke in a clipped tone, and she was cutting her food with irritated fervor. "Ella, after my mother. I had a sister, Sybilla. Those names are both lovely. One of our longest-running Queens was Lovisa, and I've always thought highly of that name."

"It's not that I don't like any of those," I explained carefully. Although, really, I thought Sybilla was quite terrible. "I like my name. I don't know why I have to change it."

Elora waved off the idea. "Wendy is a ridiculous name. It's entirely improper for a Princess."

"Why?" I persisted, and Elora glared at me.

I flat-out refused to change my name, no matter what Elora said. It's not that I thought Wendy was a particularly fabulous name, but Matt had given it to me. He was one of the only people who had ever wanted me, and I wasn't going to get rid of the one thing that I had left of him.

"It is the name of a mänsklig," Elora said through gritted teeth. "And I have had enough of this. You will find a name to suit a Princess, or I will choose one for you. Is that clear?"

"If I am a Princess, then why can't I decide what is proper?" I forced my voice to stay even and clear, trying not to let it shake with anger and frustration. "Isn't that part of the glory of being a Princess, of ruling a kingdom? Having some say in the rules? And if I want my name to be Wendy, why is that so wrong?"

"No Princess has ever kept her human name, and none

ever will." Her dark eyes glared severely at me, but I met them firmly. "My daughter, the Princess, will not carry the name of a *mänks*."

There was a bitter edge dripping from the word "mänks," and I saw Rhys's jaw tense. I knew what it was like to grow up with a mother who hated me, but I had never been required to sit quietly while she openly made derogatory remarks about me. My heart went out to him, and I had to struggle even harder to keep from shouting at Elora.

"I will not change my name," I insisted. Everyone had taken to looking down at their plates while Elora and I stared each other down. This dinner had to be considered an epic failure.

"This is not the proper place to have this discussion," Elora said icily. She rubbed her temple, then sighed. "It's no matter. There isn't a discussion to be had. Your name will be changed, and clearly I will be picking it for you."

"That's not fair!" Tears welled up in my eyes. "I've done everything you've asked of me. I should at least be able to keep my own name."

"That's not the way things are done," Elora replied. "You will do as I say."

"With all due respect," Finn interrupted, startling everyone. "If it is as the Princess wishes, then perhaps it's as it should be. Her wishes are going to be the highest order of the land, and this is such a simple one that I can't imagine anyone would find offense with it."

"Perhaps." Elora forced a thin smile at him, giving him a hard look, but he stared back at her, his eyes meeting hers unabashedly. "But right now my wishes are still the highest order, and until that has changed, my word will remain final."

Her smile deepened, growing even more menacing as she continued. "With all due respect, *tracker*, perhaps you care too much for her wishes and too little for her duties." His expression faltered momentarily, but he quickly met her eyes again. "Was it not your duty to inform her of the specifics of the christening and have her completely ready for tomorrow?"

"It was," Finn replied without any trace of shame.

"It seems you have failed," Elora surmised. "I'm beginning to question how exactly you've been filling your time with the Princess. Has any of it been spent on training?"

Suddenly Rhys knocked over a glass of wine. The glass shattered and liquid splattered everywhere. Everyone had been too busy staring at Elora and Finn to notice, but out of the corner of my eye I saw him do it on purpose.

Rhys started apologizing and rushing about to clean it up, but Elora had stopped glaring at Finn, and he no longer had to defend himself. Rhys had come to his rescue, and I couldn't be more relieved.

After the mess was cleaned up, Willa, who had never seemed that fond of Rhys, suddenly began chatting incessantly with him, and he eagerly reciprocated. They talked just so that Elora and Finn couldn't.

Elora still managed to squeeze in a few biting comments toward me, such as, "Really, Princess, you must know how to use a fork." But as soon as she finished her sentence, Willa would pipe up with a funny story about this girl she knew or this movie she saw or this place where she went. It was endless, and in general we were all grateful.

When dinner was over, Elora claimed she had a migraine brewing and a million things to do for tomorrow. She apologized that dessert would not be served tonight, but she didn't leave her seat at the head of the table. Unsure of what else to do, everybody started to excuse themselves. Garrett suggested that they should be heading out, and she nodded noncommittally.

"I will see you tomorrow evening," Elora replied hollowly. She stared into space instead of looking at him, and he tried not to look troubled by this.

"Take care of yourself," Garrett said, touching her shoulder gently.

Finn, Rhys, and I rose to see Garrett, Willa, and Rhiannon to the door, but Elora's voice stopped me cold. I think it stopped everyone else too, but they did a better job of playing it off.

"Finn?" Elora said flatly, still staring off at nothing. "Would you escort me to my drawing room? I'd like to have a word with you."

"Yes, of course," Finn replied, giving her a small bow.

I froze and looked to him, but he refused to look at me. He just stood stoically, hands behind his back, and waited for Elora to ask for further assistance.

I might've stood there until Elora dismissed me, but Willa looped her arm through mine and started to drag me away.

Rhys and Rhiannon were just ahead of us, whispering

quietly to each other. Garrett stole one last glance at Elora and walked on to the front door.

"So, I'll come over about ten tomorrow morning," Willa said, purposely keeping her tone light and cheery.

"What for?" I asked, feeling somewhat dazed.

"To help you get ready. There is *so* much to do!" Willa said and then shot a look in the direction of the dining room. "And your mother doesn't seem to be the helpful type."

"Willa, don't talk bad about the Queen," Garrett said without conviction.

"Well, anyway, I'll be over to help you with everything. You'll be fabulous." She gave me a reassuring smile and squeezed my arm right before she left with her father.

Soon Rhys and I were alone, standing in the entryway.

"You okay?" he asked.

"Yeah, I'm fine," I lied.

I felt oddly shaky and ill, and I was pretty sure that I didn't want to be a Princess anymore, if I ever did. There weren't many more dinners like this I could handle. I took a step away, preparing to tell Elora just that, but I felt Rhys's hand warm on my arm, stopping me.

"If you go in there, you'll just make it worse," Rhys insisted gently. "Come on."

He put his hand on the small of my back and ushered me over to the stairs. When we reached them, I expected him to try to push me up the stairs to my room, but he didn't. He knew that I had to wait for Finn to find out what had happened.

I peered in the direction of the dining room, hoping to catch a glimpse of something. I wasn't sure what that would help, but I thought if I could just *see* what was happening, I could somehow make it okay.

"That was a rough dinner," Rhys said with a joyless laugh and sat down on the stairs. I couldn't see anything, so I gave up. Pulling my skirt underneath me, I sat next to him.

"I'm sorry," I said.

"Don't be sorry. It wasn't your fault," Rhys assured me with his lopsided grin. "You just made this house a whole lot more interesting."

Elora had purposely pulled Finn aside to make a public spectacle. Otherwise, she would've lectured him privately, inside his head. For some reason, she had wanted me to witness that. I didn't understand what exactly he had done wrong, except disagree with her. But he had been respectful and hadn't said anything that wasn't true.

"What do you think she's saying?" I asked.

"I don't know," Rhys said. "She's never really yelled at me."

"You've got to be kidding." I stared at him skeptically. Rhys was always flouting the rules, and Elora was about as strict as they came.

"No, seriously." Rhys laughed at my shock. "She's snapped at me to knock stuff off when she's around me, but do you know how often she's even around? I was raised by nannies. Elora made it perfectly clear from day one that she wasn't my mother and she never wanted to be."

"Did she ever want to be a mother at all?" From what little

I knew of her, she seemed to be lacking even the slightest bit of maternal instinct.

"Honestly?" Rhys debated whether or not to tell me, before sadly replying, "No. I don't think she did. But she had a lineage to carry on. A duty."

"I'm just part of her job," I muttered bitterly. "For once, I just wish that somebody actually wanted me around."

"Oh, come on, Wendy," Rhys admonished me softly and leaned in closer. "Lots of people want you around. You can't take it personally that Elora's a bitch."

"It's a little hard not to." I fidgeted with my dress. "She's my mother."

"Elora is a strong, complicated woman that you and I can't even begin to understand," Rhys explained tiredly. "She is a Queen above all else, and that makes her cold and distant and cruel."

"What was it like growing up with that?" I glanced over at him, suddenly feeling guilty for moping about my life when he'd had it even harder. At least I had Matt and Maggie.

"I don't know." He shrugged. "Probably like growing up in a boarding school with a strict headmistress. She was always lurking in the background, and I knew that she had the final say on everything. But her interaction with me was at an absolute minimum." He looked at me again, this time uncertainly.

"What?"

"She's not quite as secretive as she thinks, though. This is a big house, but I was a sneaky little kid." He bit his lip and fiddled with a button on his blazer. "You know she used to sleep with Finn's dad?"

"I do," I said quietly.

"I thought he would tell you." Rhys fell silent for a minute, chewing his lip. "Elora was in love with him. She's strange when she's in love. Her face is different, softer and more radiant." Rhys shook his head, lost in a memory. "It was almost worse seeing her like that, knowing that she's capable of kindness and generosity. It made me feel gypped that all I ever got were icy glares from across the room."

"I'm sorry." I put my hand gently on his arm. "I wish I could say something to make you feel better. But to be honest, I can't imagine how horrible it must have been to grow up like that."

He forced a smile, then shrugged, pushing away the memory.

"Anyway. Finn's father left Elora, for his wife, which was just as well." Rhys looked thoughtful for a moment. "Although I bet she would've thrown it all away to be with him, if he had really loved her. But that's not the point."

"What is the point?" I asked shakily.

"Rumor has it she keeps Finn around because she still loves his old man, even though he never loved her. Nothing's ever happened between Finn and Elora, I'm sure." Rhys let out a heavy sigh. "But . . ."

"But what?"

"Finn's dad never looked at her the way Finn looks at you." He let it hang in the air for a second as I tried to figure out what he meant. "So you've got that strike against you too. She never wanted to be a mother, and you're getting the one thing she never had."

"What are you talking about? I haven't gotten anything she never had, and I definitely don't have Finn. I . . . we never . . . it's just official business."

"Wendy." Rhys looked at me with a sad smile. "I know that I wear my heart on my sleeve, but you're just as bad."

"I-I don't know what you're talking about," I stuttered and looked away from him.

"All right." Rhys laughed. "Whatever you say."

To lighten the moment, Rhys made some joke that I didn't really catch. My mind raced and my heart pounded. Rhys must be imagining things. And even if he wasn't, surely Elora wouldn't punish Finn for that. Would she?

TWENTY

resignation

Finn reached the stairs, and I scrambled to my feet. He had probably only been with Elora for fifteen minutes, but in my mind it seemed like forever. Rhys had been sitting next to me, but he got up much slower than I had. Finn looked over us with disdain, then turned and started walking up the stairs without a word.

"Finn!" I jogged after him, but Rhys rather smartly made his escape to the kitchen. "Wait! Finn! What happened?"

"A conversation," Finn replied glibly. I scurried to keep up with him, but he made no effort to slow down, so I grabbed his arm, stopping him halfway up the stairs. He glanced back over his shoulder as if looking for Rhys, clearly avoiding my gaze. "I thought I told you to stay away from the mänsklig."

"Rhys was just sitting with me while I waited for you," I said. "Get over it."

"It's very dangerous for you to be around him." Finn faced

the top of the stairs but looked at me from the corner of his eye. "It's dangerous for you to be around me." I didn't appreciate the way he wouldn't look at me directly. I missed his dark eyes.

"What's that supposed to mean?" I demanded.

"Let go of my arm," Finn said.

"Just tell me what's going on, and I'll leave you alone," I said, tightening my grip.

"I have been relieved of my duties," Finn answered carefully. "Elora no longer perceives a threat, and I have been insubordinate. I am to pack my things and leave the premises as soon as possible."

The air completely went out of my lungs. It was my worst fear. Finn was going to leave, and it was my fault. He had been defending me when I should've been defending myself. Or I should've just kept my mouth shut.

"What?" I gaped at him. "That's not right. You can't . . . You've been here for so long, and Elora trusts you. She can't . . . It's my fault! I'm the one who refused to listen!"

"No, it's not your fault," Finn insisted firmly. "You didn't do anything wrong."

"Well, you can't just leave! I have the ball tomorrow, and I don't know anything!" I continued desperately. "I'm not a Princess at all, Finn. You have so much left to help me with."

"I wouldn't be helping you after the ball anyway." Finn shook his head. "A tutor will be coming in to help you learn everything you need to know from here on out. You're ready for the ball, no matter what Elora says. You'll do wonderfully tomorrow."

"But you won't be here?"

He turned away from me and quietly said, "You don't need me."

"This is my fault! I'm gonna talk to Elora. You can't leave. She has to see that."

"Wendy, no, you can't—" Finn said, but I had already started back down the stairs.

There was an unbearable panic settling over me. Finn had forced me to leave the only people who had ever made me feel loved, and I had done it because I trusted him. Now he was going to leave me alone with Elora and a monarchy I wanted no part of.

Rhys would still be here, but I knew that it was only a matter of time before she sent him away as well. I was going to be more alone and isolated than I had ever been before, and I couldn't handle it.

Even as I was running down to Elora's drawing room, I knew it was more than that. I couldn't stand to lose Finn, and it didn't matter how Elora or anyone else treated me. A life without him just didn't seem possible anymore. I hadn't even realized how important he had become to me until Elora threatened to take him away.

"Elora!" I threw open the drawing room door without knocking. I knew it would piss her off, but I didn't care. Maybe, if I was insubordinate enough, she would send me away too.

Elora stood in front of the windows staring out at the black night, and she wasn't startled at all by the door slamming open. Without turning to look at me, she calmly said, "That's completely unnecessary, and it goes without saying that that is not at all how a Princess behaves."

"You're always going on about how a Princess should behave, but what about how a Queen should act?" I countered icily. "Are you such an insecure ruler that you can't handle the slightest bit of dissension? If we don't bow instantly to your opinion, you ship us off?"

Elora sighed. "I assume this is about Finn."

"You had no right to fire him! He did nothing wrong!"

"It doesn't matter if he did anything wrong, I can 'fire' anyone for any reason. I am the Queen." Slowly she turned to me, her face stunningly emotionless. "It is not the act of disagreeing that I had a problem with; it was why."

"This is about my stupid name?" I spouted incredulously.

"There is much you still have to learn. Please, sit." Elora gestured to one of the couches, and she lay back on the chaise lounge. "There's no need to get huffy with me, Princess. We need to talk."

"I don't want to change my name," I said as I sat down on the couch across from her. "I don't know why it's such a big deal to you. Names can't be that important."

"It's not about the name." Elora waved it off. Her hair flowed out like silk around her, and she played with it absently. "I know that you think I'm cruel and heartless, but I'm not. I care very deeply for Finn, more than a Queen should care for a servant, and I am sorry that I have been so negligent in the examples that I have set for you. It pains me to see Finn go, but I can assure you that I did it for you."

"You did not!" I yelled. "You did it because you were jealous!"

"My emotions played no part in this decision. Not even the way I feel about you factored into this." Her lips tightened, and she stared emptily at me. "I did what I had to do because it was best for the kingdom."

"How is getting rid of him best for anybody?"

"You refuse to understand that you are a Princess!" Elora paused and took a deep, fortifying breath. "It doesn't matter whether or not you understand the gravity of the situation. Everyone else does, including Finn, which is why he is leaving. He knows this is best for you too."

"I don't understand. How can his leaving possibly help me? I count on him for everything, and you do too. And now you're telling me you let him go, just like that?"

"I know you think this is all about money, but it's about something more powerful than that. Our bloodline is rich with tremendous abilities, far exceeding the general Trylle population." Elora leaned in closer to me as she spoke. "Unfortunately, Trylle have become less interested in our way of life, and the abilities have begun to weaken. It is essential to our people that the bloodline is kept pure, that the abilities are allowed to flourish.

"The titles and positions seem arbitrary," Elora continued. "But we are in power because we have the most power. For centuries, our abilities outshone every other family's, but the Kroners are rapidly overtaking us. You are the last chance for hanging on to the throne and retaining power for our family."

"What does this have to do with Finn?" I demanded, growing tired of political talk.

"Everything," Elora answered with a thin smile. "In order to keep the bloodlines as pure and powerful as possible, certain rules were put into effect. Not just for royalty, but for everyone. It's not merely as a repercussion for behaving outside of societal norms, but also so half-breed spawn won't weaken our bloodlines." Something about the way she said "spawn" sent a chill down my spine.

"Consequences vary in severity," Elora continued. "When a Trylle becomes involved with a mänsklig, they are asked to leave the community."

"There's nothing going on between Rhys and me," I interjected, and Elora nodded skeptically.

"While trackers are Trylle, they don't possess abilities in the conventional sense," Elora went on, and I began to realize what she was getting at. "Trackers are meant to be with trackers. If Trylle are involved with them, they are looked down upon, but it is allowed.

"Unless you are royalty." She looked severely at me. "A tracker can never have the crown. Any Marksinna or Princess caught with a tracker is immediately stripped of her title. If the offense is bad enough, such as a Princess destroying an essential bloodline, then they would both be banished."

I swallowed hard. If anything happened between Finn and me, I wouldn't be able to be a Princess, and I wouldn't even be able to live in Förening anymore. That was shocking at first, until I reflected that I didn't even want to be a Princess or live here. What did I care?

"So?" I said, and Elora looked momentarily surprised.

"I know that right now all of this means nothing to you." Elora gestured widely to the room around us. "I know you hate this, and I understand. But this is your destiny, and even if you don't see it, Finn does. He knows how important you are, and he would never let you ruin your future. That is why he offered up his resignation."

"He *quit*? That's impossible. Finn would never quit." Not when he knew how much I needed him.

And he had to know. That's why he stood up for me with Elora. He knew that I would be lost without him, and he couldn't do that to me. It would go against everything he believed in.

"It's a shame," Elora continued as if my refusal to believe didn't merit a response. "I blame myself because the signs were so obvious. And I blame Finn because he knows better than to get involved, better than anyone. But I commend him for realizing what the right thing was for you. He is leaving to protect you."

"There's nothing I need protection from!" I got to my feet. "He has no reason to leave because nothing's going on. I'm not involved with anyone."

"I would find that much more believable if you hadn't raced down here with tears in your eyes to plead for his job," Elora replied coolly. "Or if he had promised me he could keep things purely business from here on, I would've kept him." She looked down at the chaise, pulling at a loose thread in the fabric. "But he couldn't even do that. He didn't even try to convince me."

I wanted to argue with her, but I began to realize exactly what she was saying. Finn cared about me, and he'd admitted it to Elora, knowing how she would react. He cared about me so much he had been unable to continue doing his job. He couldn't keep things separate anymore, and he was upstairs packing right now.

I would've liked to yell at Elora more, blame her for everything horrible in my life and tell her that I was giving up the crown, but I didn't have time to waste. I had to catch him before he left, because I had no idea where he would go.

By the time I made it to his room, my breath was ragged. My hands were trembling, and that familiar butterfly feeling Finn gave me had spread throughout my body. I was in love with him, and I wasn't going to give him up. Not for anything in this world or the next.

When I opened his bedroom door, he was standing over his bed, folding clothes and putting them in a suitcase. He looked back at me, surprised by my appearance, then the expression in his dark eyes changed to something unreadable.

Dark stubble covered his cheeks, and there was something so ruggedly handsome about him, he was almost unbearable to look at. The top few buttons of his dress shirt were undone, revealing a hint of chest that I found strangely provocative.

"Are you all right?" Finn stopped what he was doing and took a step toward me.

"Yeah." I nodded, swallowing hard. "I'm going with you."

"Wendy . . ." His expression softened, and he shook his head. "You can't go with me. You need to be here."

"No, I don't care about here!" I insisted. "I don't want to be a stupid Princess, and they don't need me. I'm terrible at everything. My leaving is the best thing for everyone."

"They do need you. You have no idea how badly they need you." Finn turned away from me. "Without you, it will completely fall apart."

"That doesn't make any sense! I'm just one stupid girl who can't even figure out which fork to eat with! I have no abilities. I'm awkward and silly and inappropriate, and that Kroner kid is *much* better suited for this. I don't need to be here, and I'm not going to stay if you're not here!"

"There is much you have yet to learn," Finn said tiredly, almost to himself. He had started folding his clothes again, so I walked over to him and grabbed his arm.

"I want to be with you, and . . . I think you want to be with me." I felt sick to my stomach saying it aloud. I expected him to laugh at me or tell me that I was insane, but instead, he slowly looked at me.

In a rare moment of vulnerability, his dark eyes betrayed everything they had been trying to hide from me: affection and warmth, and something even deeper than that. His arm felt strong under my hand, and my heart pounded in my chest. Gently he placed his hand on my cheek, letting his fingers press warmly on my skin, and I stared hopefully at him.

"I am not worth it, Wendy," Finn whispered hoarsely.

"You are going to be so much more than this, and I cannot hold you back. I refuse to."

"But Finn, I—" I wanted to tell him more, but he pulled away.

"You have to go." He turned his back to me completely, busying himself with packing so he wouldn't have to look at me.

"Why?" I demanded, tears stinging my eyes.

"Because." Finn picked up some of his books off a shelf, and I followed right behind him, unwilling to relent in my pursuit.

"That's not a reason!"

"I've already explained it to you."

"No, you haven't. You've just made vague comments about the future."

"I don't want you!" Finn snapped.

I felt like I had been slapped. For a moment I stood in stunned silence, just listening to the sound of my heartbeat echo in my ears.

"You're lying." A tear slipped down my cheek. "You promised you would never lie to me."

"Wendy, I need you to leave!" he growled.

He breathed heavily, with his back to me, but he had stopped moving around. He leaned against the bookshelf, his shoulders hunched forward.

This was my last chance to convince him, and I knew it. I touched his back, and he tried to pull away from me, but I wouldn't move my hand. He whirled on me, grabbing my wrist. He pushed me until my back was against the wall, pinning me there.

His body pressed tightly against mine, the strong contours of his body against the soft curves of mine, and I could feel his heart hammering against my chest. He still gripped my wrist, restraining one of my hands against the wall.

I wasn't sure what he intended to do, but he looked down at me, his dark eyes smoldering. Then suddenly I felt his lips press roughly against mine.

He kissed me desperately, like he couldn't breathe without me. His stubble scraped against my cheeks, my lips, my neck, everywhere he dared press his mouth against me. He let go of my wrist, allowing me to wrap my arms around him and pull him even closer.

Seconds ago I had been crying, and I could taste the salt from my tears on his lips. Tangling my fingers in his hair, I pulled his mouth more eagerly against mine. My heart beat so fast it hurt, and an intense heat spread through me.

Somehow he managed to pull his mouth from mine. His hands gripped my shoulders, holding me to the wall, and he took a step back. Breathing hard, he looked at the floor instead of at me.

"This is why I have to go, Wendy. I can't do this to you."

"To me? You're not doing anything to me." I tried to reach out for him, but he held me back. "Just let me go with you."

"Wendy . . ." He lifted his hand back to my cheek, using his thumb to brush away a fresh tear, and looked at me intently. "You trust me, don't you?"

I nodded hesitantly.

"Then you have to trust me on this. You *need* to stay here, and I need to go. Okay?"

"Finn!"

"I'm sorry." Finn let go of me and grabbed his half-packed suitcase off his bed. "I stayed too long." He started walking to the door, and I ran after him. "Wendy! Enough!"

"But you can't just leave . . ." I pleaded.

He hesitated at the doorway and shook his head. Then he opened the door and left.

I could've followed him, but I didn't have any more arguments. His kiss had left me feeling dazed and disarmed, and I wondered dimly if that had been his plan all along. He knew his kiss would leave me too weak to chase after him and too confused to argue with him.

After he had gone, I sat down on the bed, which still smelled like him, and started to sob.

TWENTY-ONE

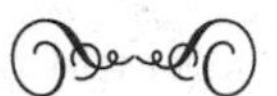

the ball

I'm not sure I had slept at all when Willa burst into my room the next day to wake me for the ball. My eyes were red and swollen, but she made very little comment about it. She just started in on getting me ready and talking excitedly about how much fun it was all going to be. I didn't believe her, but she didn't seem to notice.

Almost everything I did required verbal and physical prompts. She even had to remind me to rinse the shampoo from my hair, and I was just lucky that modesty had never been her strong suit.

It was impossible to combine fresh heartbreak with the fervor of a ball. Willa kept trying to get me excited or at least nervous about the whole thing, but her efforts were completely futile. The only way I managed to function was by being completely numb.

I couldn't understand how this had happened. When I

first met Finn, he had seemed creepy, and then he was just irritating. Repeatedly I had rejected him and told him that I didn't need him or want to be around him.

How had it turned into this? I had lived my whole stupid life without him, and now I could barely make it through an hour.

I sat on a stool, wrapped in my robe, while Willa did something to my hair. She had offered to style it in front of a mirror so I could see her progress, but I didn't care. Holding a bottle of spray in her hand, she stopped what she was doing and just looked at me.

"Wendy." Willa sighed. "I know Finn's gone, and you're obviously taking it pretty hard. But he's just a stork, and you are a *Princess*."

"You don't know what you're talking about," I mumbled.

I had considered defending him for a moment, but I was kind of pissed that he had left without me. There was no way that I could've left *him* after that kiss. As it was, it had been torture to stay behind. I just lowered my eyes and tried to close the subject.

"Fine." Willa rolled her eyes and went back to spraying my hair. "But you're still a Princess, and this is your night." I didn't say anything as she yanked and teased. "You're still young. You don't understand how many fish there really are in the sea, especially your sea. The most eligible, attractive men are gonna be all over you, and you're not even gonna remember that stupid stork who brought you here."

"I don't like fishing," I muttered dryly, but she ignored me.

"You know who *is* a catch? Tove Kroner." Willa made a pleased sound. "I wish my dad would set me up with him." She sighed wistfully and jerked on a lock of my hair.

"He's really foxy, really rich," Willa went on, as if I had asked her to tell me more. "He's like the highest Markis in the world, which is so weird. The Marksinna are usually the ones with all the abilities. Guys can do some things, but they pale in comparison to what women can do, yet Tove has more ability than anybody else. I wouldn't be surprised if he could read minds."

"I thought nobody could do that," I said, amazed that I was even following her. A few weeks ago, nothing she said would have made sense.

"No. Only very, very few can. So few it's almost the stuff of legends these days." She gently fluffed my hair. "But Tove is the stuff of legends, so that makes sense. And if you play your cards right, you'll be pretty damn legendary yourself." She whipped me around so I was facing her and smiled at her handiwork. "Now we just need to get you into your gown."

Somehow, while getting me ready, Willa had managed to ready herself. She had on a floor-length light blue gown that swept out at her hips, and she looked so beautiful, I had no hope of topping her.

After she had finally gotten me into my own dress, she forced me in front of the mirror, insisting that I looked too amazing to not see myself.

"Oh, wow." Saying that to my reflection felt egotistical, but

I couldn't help it. I had never looked better in my life, and I doubted that I would ever look this good again.

The gown was a shimmery silver and white that flowed around me. It was strapless in an elegant way, and the diamond necklace Willa had chosen set it off. My dark curls fell perfectly behind me, and subtle diamond clips sparkled in my hair.

"You're gonna rock it tonight, Princess," Willa promised with a sly smile.

That was the last calm moment of the night. As soon as we stepped out of my bedroom, we were swept off by aides and staff that I didn't even know Elora had. They gave me a rundown of the times when everything was set to happen and where I had to be and who I had to meet and what I had to do.

It was already more than I could comprehend, and at least momentarily I was spared the dull heartache I got from thinking of Finn. I looked helplessly at Willa, knowing that I would have to try to make this up to her later on. Without her, it would've been completely impossible for me to make it through.

First, there was some kind of meet-and-greet in the ballroom. Elora stood on one side of me, and thankfully, Willa stayed on my other side, taking on the role of some kind of assistant. The three of us stood at one end of the ballroom, flanked by security. A long line of people waited to meet me.

Willa filled in the names and titles as they approached. Most of them were famous in the Trylle world, but Elora explained that anybody could come meet me today, so the line was absolutely endless. My face hurt from smiling, and there were only so many different ways I could say, "Pleased to meet you" and "Thank you."

After that, we went to the dining hall for a more exclusive function. The table only seated a hundred (that's right—*only* a hundred), and with Willa sitting five places down from me, I felt lost.

Whenever I felt insecure, I instinctively searched for Finn, only to remember that he wasn't there. I tried to concentrate on eating my food properly, which wasn't that easy considering how nauseous I felt and how badly my jaw hurt from the forced smiles.

My mother sat to my right at the head of the table, and Tove Kroner sat next to me on my left. Throughout the dinner, he hardly said a thing, and Elora went about making polite conversation with the current Chancellor.

The Chancellor didn't seem to remember me from the other day when I'd come in drenched from the rain, and I was glad for it. The way he looked at me creeped me out, and I found it impossible to smile at him out of fear I might vomit.

"Drink more wine," Tove suggested quietly. Holding a wineglass in his hand, he leaned in a bit toward me to be heard over the din. His mossy eyes rested on mine briefly before he averted them, staring instead at an empty space across from us. "It relaxes the muscles."

"I beg your pardon?"

"From smiling." He gestured to his own mouth and forced a smile before quickly dropping it. "It's starting to hurt, right?"

"Yeah." I smiled lightly at him, feeling the soreness at the corners of my mouth.

"The wine helps. Trust me." Tove took a long drink from his wine, much longer than was polite, and I saw Elora eyeing him as she chatted with the Chancellor.

"Thanks." I took his suggestion, but I drank much more slowly than he did, afraid of inciting the wrath of Elora. I didn't think she'd do anything publicly, but I knew she wouldn't let me get away with anything either.

As the dinner wore on, Tove grew restless. He leaned back in his seat, laying his hand on the table. His wineglass would slowly slide over to his hand, then it would slowly slide away, without him ever touching it. I'd seen him perform a similar trick with his bowl of soup last week, yet I couldn't help but stare.

"You pretty on edge tonight?" Tove asked, glancing at me. I wasn't sure if he caught me watching his trick or not, but I looked down at my plate anyway.

I nodded. "Mmm, a little."

"Yeah, I can tell." He leaned forward, resting his elbows on the table, and I imagined Elora was livid.

"I'm trying to stay calm." I stabbed absently at some kind of vegetable I had no intention of eating. "I think I've been handling this very well, considering everything."

"No, you're acting fine. I can sense it." He tapped the side of his head. "I can't explain it, but . . . I know how tense you are." He chewed his lip. "You project your emotions so forcefully. Your persuasion is immensely powerful."

"Maybe," I allowed. His gaze was unnerving, and I didn't want to disagree with him.

"Here's a tip: use it tonight." Tove was barely audible over the chatter. "You're trying to please so many people and it's exhausting. You can't be everything to everyone, so I try not to be anything to anyone. My mother hates me for it, but . . ." He shrugged. "Just use it a little bit, and you'll charm everyone. Without really trying."

"It takes effort to use persuasion," I whispered. I could feel Elora listening to us, and I didn't think she'd approve of what we were saying. "It would be just as exhausting."

"Hmm," Tove mused, then leaned back in his seat.

"Tove, the Chancellor was just telling me that you had discussed working for him this spring," Elora interjected brightly. I barely glanced up at her, but in that second she managed to glower at me before returning to her overly cheery expression.

"My mother discussed it," Tove corrected her. "I've never said a word to the Chancellor, and I have no interest in the position."

I was increasingly becoming a fan of Tove, even if he weirded me out and I didn't understand what he meant most of the time. He just said whatever he wanted without fear of repercussion, and I admired it.

"I see." Elora raised an eyebrow, and the Chancellor started saying something about the wine they were drinking.

Tove managed to look bored and irritated the rest of the dinner, chewing his nails and looking at everything except me. There was something very strange and unstable about him. He belonged in this world even less than I did, but I imagined that there really wasn't any place that he'd fit in.

Soon we moved on to the ballroom for dancing. The ballroom looked positively magical when it was all done up, and I couldn't help but think of the brief dance I had shared with Finn a couple days before. That, of course, reminded me of the passionate kiss we had shared last night, making me feel weak and sick. I couldn't even force a smile when I thought of Finn.

Making matters worse, it soon became clear that dancing was by far the worst experience of the evening. The receiving line had been rough, but now I was being forced to make conversation with one weird man after another while they put their hands on me.

Garrett managed to steal a dance with me, and that was a relief. I had been dancing nonstop for an hour because everyone kept cutting in. He complimented me, but not in the creepy perv way everyone else seemed to be going for.

Every now and then I would catch Elora spinning around on the floor, or Willa would sneak me a smile as she twirled around with some foxy young guy. It was unfair that she got to pick who she danced with, but I was stuck with every stranger who asked.

"You're probably the most ravishing Princess we've ever had," the Chancellor told me after he cut in for a dance.

His pudgy cheeks were red from exertion, and I wanted to suggest that he sit down and take a break, but I thought Elora would disapprove. He held me much closer than was necessary, and his hand was like a massive ham on my back, pressing me to him. I couldn't pull away without making a scene, so I just tried to force a smile.

"I'm sure that's not true," I demurred. He sweated so badly, it had to be bleeding onto my dress. The beautiful silver and white fabric would be stained yellow after this.

"No, you really are." His eyes were wide with some kind of weird pleasure, and I wished someone would hurry up and cut in. We had just started dancing, but I couldn't take much more of this. "In fact, I've never seen anyone more ravishing than you."

"Now, that, I'm certain, cannot be true." I glanced around, hoping to spot Willa somewhere so I could try to pawn him off on her.

"I know that you'll be expected to start courting soon, and I'd just like you to know that I have a lot of things going for me," the Chancellor went on. "I'm very wealthy, very secure, and my bloodline is immaculate. Your mother would approve of this arrangement."

"I haven't made any arrangements yet . . ."

I craned my neck, knowing that if Elora saw me, she would accuse me of being rude. But I didn't know how else to react. This blubbery man had grabbed my ass during some kind of marriage proposal. I had to get out of there.

The Chancellor lowered his voice. "I've been told I'm an excellent lover, as well. I'm sure that you don't have any experience but I could definitely teach you."

His expression grew hungry, and his eyes had dropped

lower than my face. It was taking all my restraint not to push him off me, and in my head I screamed to get away from him.

"May I cut in?" Tove appeared at my side. The Chancellor looked disappointed at the sight of him, but before he could say anything, Tove had put his hand on the Chancellor's shoulder and taken my hand, pulling me away.

"Thank you," I breathed gratefully as we waltzed away from a very confused-looking Chancellor.

"I heard you calling for help." Tove smiled at me. "You seem to be using your persuasion more than you think." In my mind, I had been begging for a way out, but I hadn't uttered an actual word.

"You heard me?" I gasped, feeling pale. "How many other people heard me?"

"Probably just me. Don't worry. Hardly anybody can sense anything anymore," Tove said. "The Chancellor might've noticed if he hadn't been too busy staring at your chest, or if you were more skilled at it. You'll get the hang of it."

"I don't really care if I get the hang of it. I just wanted to get rid of him," I muttered. "I'm sorry if I'm wet. I'm probably covered in his sweat."

"No, you're fine," Tove assured me.

We danced the appropriate width apart, so he probably couldn't feel my dress to tell if it was soaked or not, but there was something relaxing about being with him. I didn't have to say anything or worry about being felt up or ogled. He barely looked at me and said nothing else at all, but the silence between us felt completely comfortable.

Elora finally interrupted the festivities. The christening ceremony would be happening in twenty minutes, and she noted that I needed a break from all the dancing. The dance floor emptied and everyone took seats at the tables edging the dance floor, or milled around the refreshments table.

I knew that I should sit down while I had the chance, but I was desperate to have a moment to breathe, so I went to a corner hidden behind extra chairs and leaned against the wall.

"Who are you hiding from?" Rhys teased, finding me in the corner. Dressed in a flashy tux, he looked dashing as he sauntered over to me, grinning.

"Everyone." I smiled at him. "You look really good."

"Funny, I was just gonna tell you the same thing." Rhys stood next me, putting his hands in his pockets and smiling even wider. "Although 'good' doesn't even begin to do you justice. You look . . . otherworldly. Like nothing else here can even compare to you."

"It's the dress." I looked down, hoping to keep my cheeks from blushing. "That Frederique is amazing."

"The dress is nice, but trust me, *you* make the dress."

Gently, he reached over and fixed a wayward curl that had fallen out of place. He let his hand linger there a minute, his eyes meeting mine, then dropped his hand.

"So, having fun yet?" Rhys asked.

"A blast." I smirked. "What about you?"

"I can't dance with the Princess, so I'm a little bitter," he said with a sad smile.

"Why can't you dance with me?" I would've loved to dance

with him. It would've been a blessed reprieve after everything I'd been through tonight.

"Mänks." He pointed his thumbs at himself. "I'm lucky I'm even allowed in."

"Oh." I looked down at the floor, thinking about what he'd just said. "Not to sound rude or anything, because I'm glad you're here, but . . . why are you here? Why aren't you banned or something equally ridiculous?"

"Didn't you know?" Rhys asked with a cocky grin. "I am the highest mänks in the land."

"And why is that?" I couldn't tell if he was teasing me or not, so I tilted my head, watching as his expression got more serious.

"Because I'm yours," he replied softly.

He was invited because he was my mänsklig, my opposite, but when he answered, that wasn't what he meant at all. Something in his eyes made me blush for real this time, and I smiled sadly at him.

One of Elora's aides burst into the corner, ruining what was left of the moment, and demanded that I take my seat at the head table with the Queen. The christening ceremony was about to start, and a knot formed in my stomach. I hadn't heard what my name was to be, and I was depressed about the idea of changing it.

"Duty calls." I smiled apologetically at Rhys and started to walk past him.

"Hey." Rhys grabbed my hand to stop me, and I turned to

look at him. "You're gonna be great. Everyone's raving about you."

"Thanks." I squeezed his hand gratefully.

A cracking echoed through the room, followed by a tinkling that I didn't understand. The sound was coming from everywhere, so it was hard to place right away. But then it looked like the ceiling was raining glitter, and the skylights crashed to the floor.

TWENTY-TWO

falling

Rhys realized what was happening before I did, and, still holding my hand, he yanked me behind him. We were in the corner, out of the way of most of the glass, but from the agonized screams, I gathered that everyone else wasn't so lucky.

Dark figures fell through the broken skylights, landing on the floor with surprising grace. Blood and broken glass layered the floor. Before I recognized them, I remembered the uniform. Matching long black trench coats, like a crime-fighting team.

The word seemed to swell through the room without anybody saying anything: *Vittra.*

Vittra had broken in, crashing through the ceiling, and Trylle guards circled them. In the very center I saw Jen, the tracker who had been so fond of hitting me, his eyes scanning the room.

"You are not invited. Please leave." Elora's voice boomed above everything else.

"You know what we want, and we're not leaving until we get it." Kyra stepped forward, Jen's accomplice from before. She walked on the glass with bare feet but didn't seem to notice. "She's got to be here. Where are you hiding her?"

Jen turned toward me, and his black eyes met mine over Rhys's shoulder. When he grinned wickedly, Rhys realized we were in trouble. He started to push me toward the door, but before we made it, Jen bolted toward us, and everyone burst into life. The Vittra scrambled, going after the guards and other Trylle.

Elora glared at Kyra, who collapsed on the ground, writhing in pain. Nobody had touched her, and based on the look in Elora's eyes, I figured that Kyra's agony had something to do with Elora's abilities.

I saw Tove bound over the table he was sitting at, using his powers to send Vittra flying without even touching them. People screamed, and I felt a strong wind blow through the room, surely Willa's attempt at helping.

Then Jen was in front of us, blocking out the chaos of the ballroom. Rhys stood his ground in front of me. He moved to defend me in some way, but Jen lunged forward and punched him, throwing him to the ground.

"Rhys!" I reached out for Rhys, but he didn't move. I wanted to make sure he wasn't dead, but Jen grabbed me around my waist, restraining me.

"That's what you have protecting you now?" Jen laughed. "Did we scare off Finn?"

"Let go of me!" I kicked at him and tried to pry his arm off me.

With his arm still gripping me, we both abruptly went flying backward, as if someone had pushed him. He slammed into the wall, and his arm loosened enough that I could scramble away from him on my hands and knees.

Dazed, I got to my feet and tried to figure out what had happened. Tove stood on the other side of a glass-strewn table, holding his hand palm-out at Jen.

I smiled appreciatively at him, but my smile disappeared as soon as I got a look at the room. The Vittra clearly had the upper hand. Even though the Trylle in the room outnumbered the Vittra attackers, most of them weren't fighting back. The trackers were throwing punches and pushing back against the Vittra, but most of the royalty appeared to do little more than cower in fear.

A visiting Trylle on the other side of the room had begun using fire, and I could feel Willa's wind whipping about. Garrett had no real powers of his own, but he was attempting hand-to-hand combat with the Vittra, even though they physically appeared to be much stronger.

Other than Tove, Willa, Elora and the Trylle using fire, none of the other Trylle really seemed to have abilities, or at least they weren't using them. The room was total pandemonium, and it was about to get worse. Even more Vittra streamed in through the ceiling.

"This is why you need to work on your persuasion." Tove looked at me evenly, and another Vittra charged at his back.

"Watch out!" I yelled.

Tove turned, throwing his hand back and tossing the Vittra across the room. I looked around to grab a weapon when I felt Jen's arms around my waist again. I yelled and fought as hard as I could, but his arms felt like granite around me.

Tove turned his attention back to me, but two other Vittra chased after him, so he only had a moment to send Jen flying back into the wall again. We hit even harder this time, and it jostled me painfully, but Jen let go.

My head throbbed from the impact, and I blinked to clear it. A hand took mine, helping me to my feet. I wasn't sure if I should accept it, but I did anyway.

"You've got to be more careful, Tove," he said.

"I was just trying to get her free!" Tove snapped, and another Vittra yelled as Tove sent him flying into a table across the room. "And I'm busy here!"

I turned back to see who had helped me, and all the air went out of my lungs. Wearing a black hoodie under a black jacket, Finn surveyed the mess around me. He stood right next to me, holding my hand, and I couldn't think or move.

"Finn!" I gasped, and he finally looked at me, his dark eyes a mixture of relief and panic.

"This is bedlam!" Tove growled.

A table had been flipped on its side, and it separated Tove from Finn and me. Using his abilities, Tove sent it sailing into a Vittra attacking the Chancellor, and then he rushed over to us. All the Vittra seemed to be busy, so he had a moment to catch his breath.

"It's worse than I thought." Finn pursed his lips.

"We've gotta protect the Princess," Tove said.

I squeezed Finn's hand and watched as Jen started to get up, only to be slammed back into the wall by Tove.

"I'll get her out of here," Finn said. "Can you handle it down here?"

"I don't have a choice." Tove barely had time to answer when Willa started screaming across the room. I couldn't see her, and that scared me even more.

"Willa!" I tried to run to see what was happening, but Finn wrapped his arms around me, pulling me back.

"Get her out of here!" Tove commanded as he took a step in the direction of Willa's screams.

Finn started dragging me out of the ballroom while I strained to see what was going on. Tove had disappeared, and I couldn't see Elora or Willa. As Finn pulled me, my feet hit Rhys's leg, and I remembered that he was lying unconscious, bleeding on the ground. I struggled against Finn's arms, trying to reach Rhys.

"He's fine! They won't touch him!" Finn tried to reassure me. He still had one arm around my waist, and he was much stronger than me. "You've got to get out of here!"

"But Rhys!" I pleaded.

"He'd want you to be safe!" Finn insisted and finally managed to get me to the ballroom doors.

I looked up from Rhys and was stunned to see the chaos of

the room. Then all the chandeliers suddenly crashed to the floor, and the only light came from the things that were in flames. People were screaming and yelling, and the sound was echoing off everything.

"The painting," I murmured, and my mind flashed on the picture I'd seen in Elora's drawing room. This was it. This was the exact scene.

And there was nothing I could have done to prevent it. I couldn't even understand it until it was too late.

"Wendy!" Finn shouted, trying to move me into action.

He let go of my waist and took my hand, yanking me out of the room. Using my free hand, I pulled up my dress to keep from tripping on it as we raced down the hallway. I could still hear the carnage from the ballroom, and I had no idea where we were running to.

I didn't have time to ask him where we were going or to feel thankful that I was with him again. My only consolation was that if I died tonight, I'd at least have spent the last few minutes of my life with Finn.

We rounded the corner toward the entryway, and Finn stopped sharply. Three Vittra were coming in the front doors of the palace, but they hadn't seen us yet. Finn changed direction, darting across the hall into one of the sitting rooms, pulling me with him.

He closed the door quietly behind us, leaving us in near darkness. Moonlight spilled in through the glass, and he ran to a corner between a bookcase and the wall. He pulled me tightly to him, shielding me with his body.

We could hear the Vittra outside. I held my breath, pressing my face into Finn's chest and praying they wouldn't come in the room.

When they finally ran past, Finn still didn't loosen his grip on me, but I could hear his heartbeat slow. Somewhere beneath all my panic and fear I became aware of the fact that Finn held me tightly in his arms. I looked up at him, barely able to make out his features in the light from the windows next to us.

"I saw that before," I whispered, looking up at him. "What happened in the ballroom. Elora painted it. She knew that was going to happen!"

"Shh," Finn said gently.

I lowered my voice. "But why didn't she stop it?"

"She didn't know when it would happen or how," Finn explained. "She just knew, and the only thing she could do to prevent it was to add more protection."

"So then why did you leave?" I asked softly.

"Wendy . . ." He pushed back stray curls from my face, and his hand lingered on my cheek as he looked down at me. "I never really left. I was just down the hill, and I never stopped tracking you. I knew what was happening as soon as you did, and I raced back here."

"Are we gonna be okay?" I asked

"I won't let anything happen to you. I promise."

I looked up at him, searching his eyes in the dim light, and I wanted nothing more than to stay in his arms forever.

The door creaked open, and Finn tensed instantly. He

pushed me back against the wall, wrapping his arms around me to hide me. I held my breath and tried to stop my heart from pounding. We heard nothing for a second, and then the light flicked on.

"Well, well, if the prodigal stork hasn't returned." Jen smirked.

"You won't get her," Finn said firmly.

He pulled away from me just enough so he could face Jen. I peered around him, watching Jen walk in a slow semicircle toward us. He walked in an oddly familiar way, like something I had seen on Animal Planet. And then I realized—Jen was stalking his prey.

"Maybe I won't," Jen allowed. "But getting you out of my way would probably make it easier, if not for me, then for somebody else. Because we won't stop coming for her."

"And we won't stop protecting her."

"You're willing to die to protect her?" Jen raised an eyebrow.

"You're willing to die to get her?" Finn challenged evenly.

In the ballroom, Tove had insisted they had to protect me, and I hadn't thought he even cared for me all that much. Was it just that I was the Princess? Had Elora endured similar attacks when she first came home?

I clenched the back of Finn's jacket and watched the two of them stare each other down. I didn't understand what was so damn important about me that so many Vittra were willing to kill, and, according to Finn, so many Trylle were willing to die.

"Neither one of you has to die," I said. I tried to slip around

Finn's arm, but he pushed me back. "I'll go, okay? I don't want anybody else to get hurt over this."

"Why don't you listen to the girl?" Jen suggested, wagging his eyebrows.

"Not this time."

"Suit yourself." Jen had apparently tired of talking and dove at Finn.

Finn was wrenched from my fingertips, and I screamed his name. They both went flying through the glass out onto the balcony, sending shards flying everywhere. I was barefoot, but I ran forward without regard.

Jen managed to land a few good blows, but Finn was much quicker and seemed to be stronger. When Finn hit him, Jen staggered back several feet.

"You've been working out." Jen wiped fresh blood from his chin.

"You could give up now, and I wouldn't think any less of you," Finn said.

"Nice try." Jen lunged forward, kicking Finn in the stomach, but Finn held his own.

I grabbed a giant shard of glass from off the balcony and moved around them, trying to find an opening to attack. I managed to slice open a finger, but I barely noticed. Jen knocked Finn to the balcony floor. He pounced on top of him and started hitting him in the face. Using all my might, I stabbed the glass into his back.

"Ow!" Jen shouted, but he sounded more irritated than wounded.

I stood behind him, panting. That was not the reaction I had expected and I didn't know what to do.

Jen whirled around, smacking me so hard across the face that I went flying to the edge of the balcony. I only had a moment to notice the dizzying drop below as my head hung over the edge, and then I was scrambling to my feet and gripping the railing.

Finn had already regained his feet and knocked Jen back down. Kicking him as hard as he could, Finn growled through gritted teeth, "Don't. Ever. Touch. Her. Again."

When Finn tried to kick him again, Jen grabbed his foot and yanked him back to the floor. I heard the sound of Finn's head cracking against the heavy concrete of the balcony. He withstood the blow, but it stunned him long enough for Jen to bend over and wrap his hands around Finn's throat. He lifted Finn off the floor by his neck.

I jumped on Jen's back, which wasn't as smart as I'd thought it would be, because Jen had the giant shard of glass sticking out of him. The glass cut through my dress and my side without actually impaling me. It was enough to make me bleed and hurt, but not enough to kill.

"Get off!" Jen growled, then jerked his arm back, elbowing me hard in the stomach and knocking me off him.

I landed on my feet but Jen already had Finn pressed back over the railing. The top half of Finn's body dangled over the edge, and if Jen let go, Finn would plummet to his death hundreds of feet below.

For a moment I couldn't breathe or move. All I could see

was the painting of me. The broken shards of glass glinting in the moonlight. My beautiful dress, which appeared stark white by the light of the moon, with the slit of blood in the side. The vast darkness that went on beyond the balcony, and the horrified look on my face as I reached for it.

"Stop!" I pleaded, tears streaming down my face. "I'll go with you! Please! Just let go of him! *Please!*"

Jen laughed. "I hate to break it to you, Princess, but you're going with me either way!"

"Not if I can help . . ." Finn barely managed to speak through Jen's hand clamped on his throat.

Finn kicked his leg up, planting it squarely between Jen's legs, and Jen groaned but didn't loosen his grip on Finn. Keeping his leg there, Finn started tilting backward. Jen realized what he was doing, but Finn had reached forward and grabbed Jen's jacket.

He had changed the weight ratio, and in a moment that felt oddly slow-motion, Finn went backward over the railing, pulling Jen with him.

"*No!*" I screamed and lunged toward them. I landed on my belly, sliding across the balcony with my hand outstretched, grabbing at empty air.

TWENTY-THREE

aftermath

As soon as I reached the railing, Finn floated up, coughing hoarsely. I gaped at him, too shocked to believe he was real. He drifted over the top of the railing, then dropped heavily onto the balcony.

Lying on his back, he coughed again, and I rushed to his side, kneeling next to him. I touched his face, checking to make sure he was real, and his skin felt soft and warm under my hands.

"That was quite the gamble," Tove remarked from behind me, and I turned to look at him.

Tove had lost his blazer, and his white shirt looked slightly burned and bloody. Other than that, he didn't look that bad as he took a step toward us.

"Nah, you always come through," Finn said. And I realized that when Finn had gone over the balcony, Tove had used his power to catch him and lift him back up, setting him down safely.

I went back to staring down at Finn, unable to believe that he was alive and here with me again. My hand was on his chest, above his heart, so I could feel it pounding. He placed his hand over mine, holding it gently, but he looked past me at Tove.

"What's going on in there?" Finn asked Tove and nodded to the house.

"They're retreating." Tove stood over us. "A lot of people were hurt, but Aurora is working on them. My father broke a few ribs, but he'll live. Unfortunately, that's more than I can say for some of the Trylle."

"Did we lose a lot of people?" Finn asked, his expression grim.

"I can't say yet for sure, but we lost a few." Tove grimaced. "But we could've avoided that completely if the Markis and Marksinna would learn to fight. They leave all of their protection in the hands of the trackers, but if the royalty would just get their hands dirty, they could've . . ." He shook his head. "Nobody needed to die today."

Finn pressed his lips together grimly, then looked at me. "What happened? Are you hurt?" His hand went to my side, where I bled all over my dress. I winced under his touch but shook my head.

"It's nothing. I'm fine."

"Have my mother look at it. She'll patch you both up," Tove said. When I gave him a confused look, he went on, "Aurora's a healer. She can touch you and fix you. That's her ability."

"Come on." Finn gave me a shaky smile and slowly sat up.

He tried to act like he was perfectly fine, but he had taken quite a beating and there was hesitation in his movements. Tove helped him to his feet, then took my hand and pulled me up.

I wrapped my arm around Finn's waist, and Finn put his arm around my shoulders, reluctantly putting some of his weight on me. We walked carefully through the broken glass back into the house, and Tove gave more details about the attack.

Other than the trackers who had been guarding, most of the Trylle had played defenseless, myself included. The Vittra might not have as many abilities, but they had mastered physical combat much better than the Trylle.

Thankfully, a few of the Trylle like Tove and Elora were strong enough and smart enough to fight back. What they lacked in physical prowess, they made up for in overwhelming abilities.

But Tove was quick to point out that if all the Trylle had stood up and used what abilities they had—no matter how weak—or simply fought back with their fists, the Vittra would have hardly stood a chance. We should've won this without any deaths and hardly any injuries.

The Trylle royals had grown too complacent, to the point where they believed that defending themselves was beneath them. They'd become too focused on social class to realize that they needed to handle some things themselves, instead of leaving the trackers and mänks to do all the dirty work.

The ballroom looked even worse than it had when we'd left it. Someone had lit lanterns around the edges of the room, so we could at least see better than before.

Willa ran over when she saw me and threw her arms around me. I hugged her back, feeling tremendous relief that she was alive. Despite a few scrapes and bruises, she looked okay.

She then launched into an excited tale about how she had blown a few Vittra out of the ceiling, and I told her I was proud. I wanted to listen to her talk, but the destruction was too overwhelming.

When Elora saw us, she pulled Aurora from where she was helping a bleeding man. I noted with dark satisfaction that the Chancellor had a nasty cut on his forehead, and I hoped that Aurora couldn't make time to fix him.

Elora didn't look any worse for the wear. If I hadn't known, I never would've thought she'd been here when the fight was going on. Aurora, on the other hand, though she still looked beautiful and regal, did show signs of the battle. Her dress was torn, her hair was a mess, and there was blood all over her hands and arms, though I doubted most of it was hers.

"Princess." Elora looked genuinely relieved when she walked over to us, delicately stepping over broken tables and a Vittra corpse. "I'm glad to see you're all right. I was very worried about you."

"Yeah, I'm fine."

She reached out and touched my cheek, but there was nothing affectionate about it. It was the way I would touch a strange animal that I'd been assured was safe though I didn't really believe it.

"I don't know what I would've done if something happened to you." She smiled wanly at me, then dropped her hand and looked at Finn. "I'm sure a thank-you is in order for saving my daughter."

"No need," Finn replied rather curtly, and Elora gazed at him intently for a moment, saying something in his mind. Then she turned and walked away, apparently to deal with something far more pressing than her daughter.

Aurora squeezed Tove's arms and looked at him warmly, making me feel a horrible pang at my own mother's reaction. Aurora had seemed like an ice queen too, but she could at least show signs of genuine happiness that her son hadn't died.

The moment passed quickly, and she moved on to me. She tore the hole in my dress wider so she could put her hand on my wound, and I gritted my teeth at the pain. Finn tightened his arm around my shoulders, a warm tingling sensation passed over my side, and moments later the pain stopped.

"Good as new." Aurora smiled tiredly at me.

She seemed to have aged since before she'd touched me, and I wondered how much all that healing took out of her. She started to step away, going back to help other people, and Finn leaned on me, clearly in pain.

"What about Finn?" I asked, and she looked back at me, startled. Apparently I had asked something wrong, and she didn't know how to react.

"No, no, I'm fine." Finn waved her off.

"Nonsense." Tove clapped him on the back and nodded at his mother. "Finn saved the day. He deserves a little help. Aurora, wanna take care of him?" She looked uncertainly at her son, then nodded and walked over to Finn.

"Of course," Aurora said.

She looked him over for wounds, trying to pinpoint what needed fixing. I glanced away from them, and I saw Rhys sitting on the edge of a table. He held a bloody cloth to his forehead and stared down at the floor.

"Rhys!" I shouted, and when he looked up and saw me, he smiled.

"Go see him," Finn suggested. Aurora poked at something painful in his side and he winced. "She's taking care of me."

"I got him." Tove took Finn's arm, so he would be leaning on Tove instead of me.

I looked back at Finn, but he nodded at me to go, clearly trying not to let on how much pain Aurora was causing him.

I really didn't want to leave Finn, but I felt like I should at least say hi to somebody who tried to save my life. Especially since Rhys had been the only person all night who had told me I looked beautiful without sounding really creepy about it.

"You're alive!" Rhys grinned. He tried to stand up, but I gestured for him to sit back down. "I wasn't sure what happened to you." He looked past me at Finn, and his expression faltered. "I didn't know Finn was back. If I had, I wouldn't have worried."

"*I* was worried about *you*." I reached out and carefully touched his forehead. "You took quite the punch there."

"Yeah, but I couldn't get one in," Rhys grumbled, looking down at the floor. "And I couldn't stop him from taking you."

"Yes, you did!" I insisted. "If you hadn't been there, they would've hauled me off before anybody had a chance to do anything about it. You kind of saved the day."

"Yeah?" His blue eyes were hopeful when he looked at me.

"Definitely." I smiled back at him.

"You know, back in the day, when a guy saved a Princess's life, she would reward him with a kiss," Rhys commented.

His smile was light, but his eyes were serious. If Finn hadn't been standing a few feet behind me, watching, I probably would've kissed him. But I didn't want to do anything to spoil having Finn back, so I just shook my head and smiled.

"Maybe when I slay the dragon. Then I'll get a kiss?"

"I promise," I agreed. "Would you settle for a hug?"

"A hug from you is never settling."

I leaned over and hugged him tightly. A woman sitting nearby looked aghast at the new Princess openly hugging a mänsklig. Things were really going to have to change when I was Queen.

After Aurora patched up Finn, she suggested we both get some rest. The room was still a disaster, but Tove insisted that he and his mother were taking care of everything. I wanted to protest and help more, but I was exhausted, so I didn't put up a fight.

Using his abilities during the fight had focused Tove. His entire personality shone through, and he took control of the situation with ease. I had a feeling that for the first time I was seeing the real Tove, and not the kid trapped behind the noise of his powers.

In a sense, we worked in opposite ways. I projected intensely, which was why my persuasion was strong, whereas Tove received everything. He could pick up on my emotions and thoughts whether he wanted to or not. But I imagined that he sensed other people too, and his mind had to be a fog of everyone's emotions.

Finn went with me to my room, just in case it wasn't completely safe. Before we even reached the stairs, Finn had taken my hand in his. Most of the way I was silent, but when we got close to my door I felt like I had to say something.

"So . . . are you and Tove like pals or something?" I was teasing, but I was curious. I had never really seen them even speak before, but there seemed to be a kind of familiarity between them.

"I'm a tracker," Finn answered. "I tracked Tove. He's a good kid." He looked over at me, smiling a little. "I told him to keep an eye on you."

"If you were so worried about me, why didn't you stay in the palace?" I asked more sharply than I meant to.

Finn shook his head. "Let's not talk about that now." We had stopped in front of my bedroom door, and there was a playful glimmer in his dark eyes.

"What should we talk about, then?" I looked up at him.

"How beautiful you look in that dress." Finn looked me over appreciatively, and he put his hands on my sides.

I laughed, and then he was pushing me against the door. His body was so tight against me I could barely breathe, and his mouth searched for mine. He kissed me in the same frantic way he had before, and I loved it.

I wrapped my arms around him and pushed myself against him eagerly. He reached around me, opening the door, and we tumbled into my room. He caught me before I actually fell, then lifted me easily into his arms and carried me.

Gently, he tossed me onto the bed, and then lowered himself on top of me. His stubble tickled my neck and shoulders as he covered me in kisses.

Sitting back, he peeled off his jacket and hoodie, and I expected him to take off his T-shirt, but he stopped, looking down at me. His black hair was slightly disheveled, but his expression was completely foreign to me. He just stared at me, making my skin redden with shame.

"What?"

"You're just so perfect," Finn said, but he sounded distressed about it.

"Oh, I am not." I blushed and laughed. "You know I'm not."

"You can't see what I see." He leaned over me again, his face right above mine but not kissing me. After a minute's hesitation, he kissed my forehead and my cheeks, and then, very tenderly, kissed my lips. "I just don't want to disturb you."

"How are you going to disturb me?"

"Mmm." A smile played on his lips and then he sat up, climbing off me. "You should go change into pajamas. That dress can't be comfortable."

"What do I need pajamas for?" I sat up. I tried to sound flirty, but I knew there was a panicked edge to my voice. As soon as we'd come in here, I thought things were going to go much further than pajamas would allow.

"I'll stay with you tonight," Finn tried to reassure me. "But nothing more can happen except for sleep."

"Why?"

"I'm here." Finn looked at me intently. "Isn't that enough?"

I nodded and carefully climbed off of the bed. I stood in front of him so he could unzip my dress, enjoying the way his hands lingered on my skin. I didn't understand what was going on, but I would be happy for anything I could have with him.

I went into the bathroom and changed into my pajamas, then came back and climbed into bed. He continued sitting on the edge for a minute, then, almost reluctantly, he came over to me. I curled up in his arms, burying my head in his chest, and he held me tightly to him.

Nothing had ever felt better than being with him like that, and I tried to stay awake so I could relish every minute, but eventually my body gave in and I passed out.

In the morning, I woke up to Elora coming in my room for the first time ever. She was wearing pants, something I had never seen her in. I was still curled up in Finn's arms, and she didn't seem surprised or offended by that.

"I trust you slept well." Elora looked around the room, but not in a nervous way. She had just never been here before. "And I trust that Finn was a gentleman."

"He always is." I yawned.

He had started pulling away from me and getting out of the bed. I furrowed my brow but didn't say anything. It wasn't that shocking that she'd be upset that we were together, so I didn't think much of it when Finn started to gather up his jacket and sweatshirt.

"Thank you for protecting my daughter," Elora said without looking at him.

Finn paused at the doorway to look back at me, his dark eyes conflicted. He nodded, then turned and walked out of my room, shutting the door behind him.

"Well, you took that much better than I thought you would," I admitted, sitting up.

"He's not coming back."

"What?" I stared at the door in dismay.

"He saved your life, so I gave him last night to say goodbye to you," Elora explained. "I will be transferring him out of here as soon as possible."

"You mean he knew?" I gaped at her.

"Yes. I made the agreement with him last night," Elora said. He had known and hadn't let me in on it, and hadn't tried to steal me away.

"But . . . he saved my life!" I insisted, feeling a terrifying pain growing in my chest. It screamed that I couldn't possibly survive without Finn. "He should be here to protect me!"

"He is emotionally compromised and unsuitable for the job," Elora explained flatly. "Not only that, if he stayed around, you would be banished from Förening. He doesn't want that, and neither do I." She sighed.

"I shouldn't have even given him last night, but . . . I don't want to know what you did with him. Don't tell me. Don't tell anyone. Is that clear?"

"Nothing happened." I shook my head. "But I want him back. He'll protect me better than anyone!"

"Let me put it to you this way: he will do anything to keep you alive, Princess." Elora looked at me evenly. "That means he would die to save you, without hesitation. Do you really want that? Do you really want him to die because of you?"

"No . . ." I trailed off, looking dazedly at my blankets. I knew she was right. Last night he had almost died to save me. If Tove hadn't come out onto the balcony, he would be dead.

"Very well. It's in his best interest that he's not around you either," Elora said. "Now you need to get up and get ready. We have much to go over."

TWENTY-FOUR

good-bye

The next few days were an endless stream of defense meetings. There had never been an attack on Förening this severe. The body count was well into the double digits, including several visiting higher royal Trylle. Any loss of powerful Trylle was devastating for the kingdom.

Elora and Aurora led all the meetings, while Tove and I sat quietly in the back. He was the most powerful and should've had more of a say, but he didn't seem that interested.

The twenty or so other people who always seemed to be in attendance offered advice that was completely pointless. Tove just said that our best defense was to get our abilities under control. Willa took this advice to heart and busied herself with self-defense classes and getting a better control of her wind ability. Elora barely spoke to me, and never uttered a kind word.

The one positive was that I'd been spared the christening ceremony, and Elora decided to allow me to keep my own name.

I wandered around in a fog. I didn't care whether I lived or died. If they attacked again, I would deal with whatever happened.

"You're gonna have to snap out of this one day," Rhys said.

I lay in my bed, staring at the ceiling, while he leaned against the doorway. He still had a nasty cut above his eyebrow, since Aurora wouldn't resort to healing a mänks. The wound was slowly getting better, but it pained me to see it. It was just a reminder that he had gotten hurt for me.

"Maybe." I didn't feel like I ever would, and I hoped I wouldn't.

"Oh, come on." Rhys sighed and came over to sit on the bed next to me. "I know that everything that's happened has really taken its toll on you, but it's not the end of the world."

"I never said it was," I muttered. "I just hate this house. I hate my mother. I hate being a Princess. I hate everything about being here!"

"Even me?" Rhys asked.

"No, of course not you." I shook my head. "You're about the only thing I like anymore."

"I feel privileged." He smiled at me, but when I didn't smile back, his quickly faded. "Look, I hate it here too. It's a hard place to live in, especially this house, with Elora. But . . . what else are we gonna do? Where else can we go?"

That's when it occurred to me. I absolutely did not want this life, and this life truly didn't want Rhys. He had grown up surrounded by a cold indifference that made his childhood even worse than my own, and he deserved so much more.

Since I had been here, Rhys had been one of the few people to show me genuine kindness, and he deserved that in return.

I didn't particularly care whether I lived or died, so I didn't need protection, should anyone decide to come after me again, but I wasn't so sure they would anymore. Tove had explained that the Vittra numbers had been damaged, and another attack anytime soon would be highly unlikely.

But somewhere out there, I knew that my brother Matt was worried sick about me. He and Maggie would welcome me back with open arms, and they would be delighted to have Rhys. I didn't know how I would explain him to them, but I'd figure something out.

I was not a Princess, and I didn't want to be one. It would feel so good to be home again. That wouldn't really fix the Finn thing, but Matt and Maggie would know the best way to mend a broken heart.

Rhys wasn't convinced that leaving was the best thing for me, pointing to the cut on his eye from when he'd been unable to protect me or himself. Reluctantly, I resorted to using my persuasion, but I didn't really have another choice. Besides, I was only convincing him that he didn't need to worry about me.

In the middle of the night, I decided to act. I gathered Rhys and we snuck out of the palace, which was more difficult than I'd expected. Guards and other Trylle walked the grounds in case of another Vittra attack. Even though they thought another one would be unlikely, they weren't taking any chances.

Rhys and I went through the kitchen and out the back door,

to the secret garden that bloomed even in the middle of the night. Scaling the high brick walls that surrounded the palace compound would've been impossible if I didn't have Rhys to give me a boost . Once I pulled him up, we both jumped down on the other side.

Without even brushing the dirt from our clothes, we ran along the wall. Rhys led the way because he knew the area better than I did. We'd nearly made it to the garage when we had to duck behind a bush to wait for a guard to pass.

Once the guard moved on, we hurried to the garage. Rhys found his new motorcycle but didn't start it. He pushed it out of the garage, leaving the engine and lights off so as not to attract attention.

At the edge of town was the gate manned by a guard, and I doubted he'd let the Princess through. Rhys had a plan, though. He knew of a weak spot in the fence a ways down the embankment. He'd heard of other mänks getting through it when they ran away.

I had to help Rhys steady the motorcycle so it wouldn't go tumbling down the hill as we made our way through the trees and the brush. Apparently the hole in the fence was even larger now than it had been before. That's how some of the Vittra had broken in, and the Trylle hadn't fixed it yet. Typical of them, to be more focused on securing the palace than making sure the town of Förening was safe.

We were able to get the motorcycle through without much trouble, and it was then, as we pushed it up the hill, that I started feeling the exhilaration and relief of escape. I ignored any pangs of sadness or longing for some of the people I'd met here, like Willa and Tove, and I just tried to focus on the fact that I was getting away. I was free.

Once we got to the road, Rhys started the motorcycle. We sped off into the darkness, and I sat on the bike behind him, wrapping my arms tightly around his waist and burying my face in his leather jacket.

The sky had that eerie blue glow of very early morning when we pulled up in front of my house. Rhys hadn't even turned off the motorcycle before Matt threw open the front door and came jogging down the porch steps.

Even in the dim light I could see how stricken Matt looked. I jumped off the bike, and, completely oblivious to Rhys, Matt threw his arms around me. He held me so tightly to him, it hurt. I didn't care, though. I buried my face in his shoulder, breathing in his familiar scent and relishing the protection of his arms. I was finally *home*.

Turn the page for the new,
never-before-published bonus short story

The Vittra Attacks

by Amanda Hocking

The Vittra Attacks

(A Trylle Story)

ONE

Loki leaned back in the seat, his head against the headrest. It was too damn early for this kind of thing, but the only way he'd convinced Jen and Kyra to let him wait in the SUV was because he'd sold himself as the getaway driver.

If they came back, hauling that girl along as a prisoner, and Loki wasn't alert enough to speed off, he'd be in serious trouble. Not with Jen or Kyra, since he outclassed them, but Jen wouldn't hesitate to tell the King about any of Loki's shortcomings.

So he waited in the car, listening to the Hugo album on his iPod. He'd been lucky he thought to bring it along. The SUV they'd stolen only had rap in it, and Loki had tossed the entire CD collection out the window as soon as he'd gotten in.

A few miles from the Vittra palace, the car the King had given him had died. That was just par for the course lately. Loki had been forced to steal the SUV to keep them on track, because the King wouldn't allow for a missed deadline. He wanted the girl, and he wanted her *now*.

Loki had busted out the passenger's-side window, and Kyra had tacked up his black jacket to keep the wind out. It didn't do much to keep in sound, though, so Loki kept the music low enough so as not to wake the neighborhood.

The clock on the dashboard said it was after five in the morning, and Loki glanced over his shoulder, back toward the girl's house. He'd parked almost a block away and across the street, so he was actually at a horrible angle to observe her.

But that was just as well, since he didn't want to watch her. He wanted no part of this stakeout.

The sky was beginning to lighten, looking more blue than black now. Loki couldn't see where Jen and Kyra were hiding. He didn't know how they did it. He wouldn't have been able to stand sitting out there all night, crouched down in the cold grass, waiting to kidnap some stupid girl.

Jen lived for that sort of thing. It was the thrill of the hunt that got him going. But Loki had never been into it. The one thing in his life he'd always been grateful for was that he'd never been a tracker.

It seemed solitary and tedious, but more than that, he hated the idea of tricking people into coming back to the Vittra palace, to being forced to live a life like his. They would be so much better off in the human world, away from the King's iron fist and the totalitarian troll society.

Loki had fought as hard as he could to get out of participating in this abduction. The King was always looking for a reason to kill him, and if Loki refused an order like this, that would be reason enough.

Sitting in the SUV, it occurred to Loki that he could escape. He'd thought of escape almost incessantly since the day he was born. But it had never felt so possible. He was alone in the car. He could just drive off, leaving Jen and Kyra behind to deal with the mess.

But the same problems always stopped him. Where would he go? What would he do?

The King might track him down and kill him, just because he could. And even if he didn't, Loki didn't have anybody on the outside. He'd always believed in fighting for the things he loved, but he'd never found anything he loved enough to escape for.

For now, he didn't really see any other options. He'd have to wait and do what the King said.

From outside the car came a noise that sounded like shouting, but he didn't think Jen and Kyra would be stupid enough to draw attention to themselves. They knew how important this girl was to the King—to the Vittra as a whole—and they wouldn't mess it up.

He leaned back in the seat, closing his eyes and humming along with "Hurt Makes It Beautiful."

"Go!" Kyra shouted as she yanked open the passenger door.

"What?" Loki sat up and turned to the backseat to see Jen hopping in. Alone. "Where's the girl?"

"Just go!" Jen snarled.

"Seriously?" Loki rolled his eyes but did as he was told.

He started the car, and when he didn't speed up fast enough, Kyra pushed her hand on his leg, forcing his foot to press harder on the gas.

"Easy there," Loki told her. "Just because the King is going to kill you two doesn't mean we all need to die now."

She let up, and Loki turned a corner just in time to see the police cars with their flashing lights approaching.

"Hey, you're in this as much as we are," Jen snapped.

Loki glanced in the rearview mirror at him. Jen's eyes were black, and every time Loki looked at him, he was afraid that Jen saw into his soul and stole a bit of it.

"If anything, you're in worse, Loki," Kyra said. "The King put you in charge."

"Yes, he did, but I delegated to you two." Loki gestured between Kyra and Jen. "You both promised me you had this in the bag. It's one girl who has no idea how to harness her powers. How could she possibly have eluded you?"

"Finn took her," Kyra said through clenched teeth. "She's probably on her way to the Trylle palace as we speak."

"I'll kill that bastard if it's the last thing I do," Jen muttered.

"Finn?" Loki shook his head, not understanding what they were talking about. "What is that?"

"He's a Trylle tracker," Kyra explained. "But he's the best they have."

"You know him?" Loki raised an eyebrow. "I didn't realize you socialized with the Trylle."

Kyra shot him a glare and said, "We've run into him before. He's tried to stop us from getting other changelings."

"But he's just a tracker?" Loki asked, watching her from the corner of his eye.

"He's not *just* anything," Kyra insisted. "He's strong and a really good fighter."

"So? You should've been able to crush him like a bug," Loki said. "That's what the King will say, and he's right. There's no reason why a damn Trylle tracker should ever get the upper hand in a fight."

"I'm sure *you* could've taken him, but you weren't there," Kyra pointed out.

Jen crossed his arms and grinned with smug satisfaction. "And that's what we'll tell the King."

"Oh really?" Loki looked at Jen in the rearview mirror again. "You'll tell the King that you're weak and useless and you need *me* to do your job for you?"

Jen's smile faltered. "I don't *need* anybody."

"That's what you just said," Loki countered, his own smile growing. "Just admit it. Admit that I'm stronger and better than you, and I'll take the fall for this, Jen."

"Screw you, Loki." Jen narrowed his dead eyes at him, and Loki couldn't help but laugh at his displeasure. "When the King executes you—and he will—I will spit on your grave."

"You've been on her for three weeks, Jen." Loki dropped his playful tone, and his words were hard. "Three weeks, and you haven't done anything. The King sent me in to finish the job you barely even started, and I let you take the lead out of respect for your position—"

"Oh bullshit," Jen interrupted him. He leaned forward in the seat, so he could yell more directly at Loki. "You were lazy and didn't want to do any of this. You 'let' me do it because you don't want to get your hands dirty."

"Oh, I'm sorry that I don't get my jollies by kidnapping young girls," Loki snapped back. "You realize the King is either going to torture her the way he has the rest of us or kill her? You're bringing her back to get slaughtered."

"Who cares?" Jen leaned back in the seat. "She's not my problem. And she's not yours either."

"Since when do you have a conscience anyway?" Kyra asked.

"I don't." Loki paused, thinking of why he didn't want to be a part of this. "I've just never been one to advocate murder."

"Well, it's her or us." Kyra shrugged. "If I have a job to do, I'm going to do it."

"You mean, except for this job, which you completely ruined, and now we'll all die horrible, painful deaths?" Loki asked.

Jen kicked the back of Loki's seat, and Loki slammed on the breaks, causing Jen to lurch forward, hitting his head on the seat.

"Dick!" Jen hit Loki in the back of the head, and Loki turned around to fight back.

"Guys!" Kyra yelled, grabbing Loki's arm to keep him from hitting Jen. "Knock it off! We have real problems here, and you two fighting won't help anything."

"Nothing's going to help," Loki said grimly. "Nothing we can say will make the King go easy on us."

TWO

"It's all Loki's fault," Jen said as soon as they'd reached the King's chambers, and Loki rolled his eyes and sighed loudly.

"It is *not* all my fault," Loki said dryly. "I had nothing to do with their failure."

On the long ride back to the Vittra palace in Ondarike, Loki, Jen, and Kyra had gone over their stories, deciding what exactly they meant to tell the King. Even though they all agreed that no matter what they said, the King would be royally pissed, the right excuse could mean the difference between torture and execution.

They'd finally agreed on something that sounded plausible and would almost get them off the hook. They could tell the King that the Trylle had gotten a jump on them. By the time they arrived to kidnap the girl, the Trylle were already running off with her.

All of that completely went out the window, though, as Loki had known it would. Jen was only out for himself, which was how he'd made it that far in the Vittra army. The King seemed to respect backstabbing.

"He did nothing," Jen insisted. "That's the problem."

The King had his back to them, his long, red velvet jacket flowing down to the floor. His dark hair went down almost to his waist, and while he was a rather slight man, his presence was so imposing, even Loki found it hard not to cower around him at times.

Kyra had curtseyed when they came in, and she hadn't bothered to fully straighten up. Jen had his arms folded behind his back and stood rigid, like a soldier, while Loki had his arms folded over his chest.

Other than the three of them and the King, the only other person in the room was Sara, the Queen. She sat in one of the chairs, her small Pomeranian Froud on her lap, but neither of them had made a sound. They all waited with bated breath for the King's response.

His chambers had high ceilings, but the dark mahogany walls made it feel smaller. There were no windows, so every time Loki went in to see the King, he always felt vaguely claustrophobic. The room was sparsely furnished, too, with only a large desk and few red high-back chairs.

One wall was covered with floor-to-ceiling bookcases, and most of them were on Vittra and troll history, but he had a few other choice titles. Once, when Loki had been left alone in the chambers, he'd gone over to inspect them. He'd found a copy of *Mein Kampf*, as well as a book that had graphic pictures of precisely how to inflict the worst torture and how to fillet living people.

"Is that true, Loki?" the King asked, his voice booming like gravel and thunder through the room.

"That I did nothing?" Loki shook his head. "No, Sire, of course not. I led the team, but I delegated—"

"He waited in the car while we went after her," Jen interrupted with an unpleasant whine in his voice. "He did nothing while the Trylle took her away."

Loki looked over at Jen, his caramel eyes hard. "Yes, I waited in the car, but I told you to call for me if you needed me." He was nearly spitting out the words as he spoke. "And you never called, not even when you let a lone tracker run off with her."

"We didn't let him do anything!" Jen shouted. "And if you were there, you could've helped fight him off!"

"But you said you didn't need me," Loki countered. "You didn't even want the King to let me go along with you. You insisted you could handle this without me, so I gave you the benefit of the doubt."

"Did I send you along to give them the benefit of the doubt?" the King asked, finally turning around to face them for the first time.

"No." Loki lowered his eyes. "But I was right there in the car. I thought they could handle a simple stakeout."

"But I told you they couldn't." The King stepped closer to Loki, his dark eyes locked on him. "I told you they were incompetent and incapable of handling this, and while you aren't much better than either of them, you are stronger. Not to mention that mind trick of yours."

"I know, but I didn't think they would let her get away." Loki dared to look up at the King and gestured to Jen and Kyra standing beside him. "I mean, there's two of them, and one stupid girl! I didn't think they could screw things up that badly."

"But I did." The King stood right in front of Loki, his eyes burning into him. "And I told you to fix it. Did you fix it?"

Loki swallowed hard. "No, Sire, I did not."

The King nodded once. He turned, as if he meant to start walking away, but instead he flew back at Loki, smacking him so hard across the face that Loki saw white for a minute and fell to the ground.

Sara gasped but said nothing. After years of this, she'd learned there was nothing she could do to prevent the King from taking out his anger on Loki.

Loki lay on the floor, rubbing his jaw. For a moment, he'd been certain the King had shattered his jaw, not that that would be the first time the King had shattered one of his bones. But even though he hadn't, that didn't mean it felt good.

Jen started chuckling, laughing at Loki's pain, but the King stopped him.

"Get out!" the King roared, turning to Jen and Kyra. "Get out before I do the same to you!"

They hurried out, muttering their apologies as they did, and slammed the heavy oak door behind them.

He was still in pain, but Loki could get up, though he chose not to. Staying on the floor was safer. Getting to his feet would just give the King an excuse to knock him back down again.

"This will be the last time you fail me," the King growled. "I've given you everything, and you've let me down far too many times. You're just a lazy, brat prince."

"I'm not the prince," Loki corrected him quietly.

"And you never will be!" the King shouted, like it was some kind of threat.

Loki rolled onto his back and sighed. "I don't want to be."

"Good! Because you're never going to be anything!" The King swore under his breath, then walked over and kicked Loki in the side.

Loki balled himself up, wrapping his arms around his stomach. For a moment he couldn't breathe or move or do anything other than feel the searing pain running through him.

"Oren!" Sara gasped. Her hand clutched the arm of her chair, but she didn't get to her feet.

The King shook his hands at her in exasperation, as if he didn't know what to do anymore.

"I'm using restraint, my love," the King said, and Sara could hear it in his voice. He repressed his urge to yell, and he kept his words even. "I want his head on a platter." He gestured to where Loki lay writhing in pain. "But it's not. He's alive. Out of respect for you and for his title. But he won't be for much longer if he keeps failing me."

"I know." Sara stood up and set the dog on the chair behind her. "And I thank you for that, my King." She walked toward her husband, keeping her tone soothing. "I understand how frustrated you are and how badly you want the Princess. You know how much I want her, too."

The King let out a deep breath and seemed to soften a bit, or as much as the King could soften.

"I know." He nodded. "I do sometimes forget how much the Princess would mean to you, too."

"Perhaps your anger at Loki is a tad misplaced," Sara said. When the King opened his mouth to argue, she held up her hand. "Not at him. He has let you down. But perhaps it could be better directed at the Trylle, and not at your own people."

"What are you proposing?" The King narrowed his eyes at her.

"Nothing that you haven't proposed already, my love." She put her hands on his chest and smiled up at him. "You said you would stop at nothing to get her, and all is not lost yet. She's with the Trylle, but you've waged wars on them before. This will be no different."

The King nodded, considering what his wife said.

"Loki," the King barked without looking back at him. "Gather all the best trackers we have, all of our powerful Vittra. We'll launch an attack on the Trylle."

Loki got to his feet, still holding his side. He stretched his jaw, which throbbed dully, and cracked his neck.

"Even the hobgoblins, Sire?" Loki asked.

"No, not yet." The King shook his head. "We'll hold them back until we absolutely have to use them."

THREE

Loki stood in the back of the room while the King went over his plan for the attack on the Trylle palace in Förening with the army he'd assembled. The King had launched attacks on the Trylle before, some of them quite successful, and there was no reason for him to think this one wouldn't go the same way.

This wasn't his last measure, though. Sara had convinced him to hold a few things back, namely, himself and Loki. The Queen thought sending them into that kind of danger was unnecessary. Oren and Loki were the two most powerful Vittra they had, but the army that the King had mounted should be sufficient to take down the Trylle.

The Trylle had grown weak and complacent in recent years, which was part of the reason the King felt such contempt for them. So the King wouldn't give the attack all he had. He didn't think he would need to.

He knew enough of Trylle society to know that the girl's

coming-out ball would be soon, and he had spies in neighbor camps that could tell him exactly when it would be. The King could go after her before that, when security was more lax at the Trylle palace, but he wanted to make a big show of it. He wanted all the trolls from every tribe to know exactly how powerful he was, so he planned the attack for that night, even though there would be far more Trylle guards on duty.

After the meeting ended, the King went out with his Vittra army to work them on a few training exercises. Since Loki wouldn't be going on the mission, he stayed behind, leaning against a bookcase in the back of the King's chambers.

"How are you holding up?" Sara asked when it was only the two of them in the room.

"Oh, you know, as well as I always do after a good beating." Loki smirked at her, and she pursed her lips.

She walked over to him and put her hand on his side, meaning to heal him from where the King had kicked him, but Loki squirmed away from her touch.

"Loki, I know how strong the King is. Better than anyone," Sara said.

Over the years, he'd seen her with her fair share of bruises, probably even more than Loki himself had earned from the hands of the King. He glanced over at her but quickly looked away.

"I'm fine," he insisted, even though he wasn't.

"You should let me heal you." She stepped closer to him, but he just moved away. "You might have a ruptured organ or a broken rib. Why won't you let me help you?"

"Because." He sighed and ran a hand through his sandy hair. "I deserve it."

"Loki, you can't mean that. You know you don't deserve it. Oren lashes out over everything, and you can't take it to heart."

"But I should've helped them," he said quietly. "Jen and Kyra. Oren told me to. He said they couldn't handle it. And I knew it. But I didn't help them enough. I knew that she would get away."

"You couldn't have known that," Sara said, trying to reassure him.

"No, I did." He paused. "I even hoped for it."

Sara's jaw dropped and her eyes widened. "Loki!"

"Oh, come on, Sara!" Loki looked at her, exasperated. "I know how much you want that girl, but what good will it do bringing her here? Do you really think it will make your life better? Or the King's?"

"We'll both be happier," Sara said, but she lowered her eyes. "Everything's better when the King is happy."

Loki laughed darkly. "You really think she'll make him happy? I've lived under the service of the King my entire life, and in twenty-three years, I've never seen him happy. *Nothing* makes him happy."

"You don't understand." Sara shook her head and stepped away from him. "And I can't believe you'd purposely let her get away."

"Why is that so hard to believe?" Loki asked. "The King will treat her the same way he does you or me, and you know it. For once I wanted to see somebody get away. I wanted somebody to escape from the trap you and I are stuck in."

Sara kept walking away from Loki, the train of her long red gown dragging on the floor behind her. Her black hair had been pulled back in a severe ponytail, the way she usually wore it. She did everything she could to seem as strong and imposing as her husband, but there was something soft and frail about her.

Sometimes Loki was surprised that the King had not broken her, but when she looked back at him, her brown eyes swimming with tears, Loki realized that he had. Physically, she may have looked the same, but inside, Sara wasn't the same woman he'd met fourteen years ago.

"You don't understand," she said emphatically. "The Princess will change things, and not just for me. For all of us. She has that power."

"Sara." Loki sighed and stepped over to her. He put his hands on her bare arms, and she stared up at him, her lips quivering. "You've been trying to change things since you married Oren, and I've been trying to for as long as I can remember. But nothing we do makes anything better. He's never going to relinquish his power. And one girl isn't going to change anything for us."

"Maybe you've given up, but I haven't." She wiped at her eyes and pulled away from him. "I will never stop believing that we can be better."

"I'm not . . ." He trailed off. "Never mind."

"But I don't understand. If you think you did the right

thing letting her get away, then why did you say you deserved what Oren did to you?"

"Because of all that mess out there." Loki motioned vaguely to the door, through which they could hear the grunts and groans from the soldiers. "They're going to war over her. People will get hurt, some even killed, and I could've just brought her back and avoided this whole thing."

"Yes, you could've," Sara snapped. "You don't ever think anything through."

He groaned and flopped into one of the King's chairs. "I don't need a lecture, Sara. You're not my mother."

"Your mother was a good woman, and she'd give you a lecture much worse than this one," Sara shot back. "You have to stop being so rash. The things you do have consequences."

"I was trying to do the right thing!"

"You thought letting her getting away would be the right thing?" Sara asked dubiously.

"Kind of, yeah," he admitted.

Sara rubbed her forehead, as if talking to him gave her a headache. "You're so foolish sometimes."

"I screwed—"

"I don't want to hear it!" Sara shouted suddenly and held her hand up to him. "You let her get away! And that's unforgivable."

Loki didn't say anything. Her voice trembled with hurt, and he couldn't take that away. Swallowing hard, he stared down at his lap and let her finish.

"This attack on the Trylle should work," Sara said. "But if

it doesn't, you will do whatever the King asks of you to bring her back. No, that's not enough. You will do anything and everything you need to do, even if that means going above and beyond the King's orders.

"Because so help me, Loki, if you let her get away again, I will not stand in the way of his wrath upon you." She took a deep breath. "Do you understand me?"

"Yes," he said quietly, still looking down.

"Loki?" Sara snapped. "Do you understand me?"

"Yes!" He lifted his head, and he could see the conviction her eyes. She would let the King kill him if he didn't bring back the Princess.

"Good." She smoothed back her hair and looked away from him. "Now get yourself together. They could use you for their training exercises."

Loki did as he was told, too afraid to argue with her. The bizarre part was that he'd told her the truth because he thought she'd understand. He thought she'd agree with him that he'd done the right thing by letting the Princess escape from all this, but Sara was too blinded by her own needs.

With no allies, Loki had no choice. If the King didn't get the girl with this attack, then Loki would have to get her later.

FOUR

"We should've heard from them by now," Sara said, pacing the King's chambers with Froud at her heels.

"It's a long drive to Förening," the King told her, his gritty voice doing its best to come across as soothing. "Give them time to attack. The coming-out ball only started a few hours ago."

Loki sat behind the King's desk, flipping through a book of Vittra lullabies. All of them were surprisingly disturbing, usually involving a disobedient infant being dragged off by hobgoblins or rival tribes to be eaten or turned into a slave.

He found the one his mother used to sing to him, and it was the least horrific of them all. It still involved a human turning into a bird to try to steal a Vittra baby, but at least the baby lived in the end.

In reality, he'd rather be anywhere but in these chambers, waiting to see how the battle turned out, if they got the Princess. But both the King and Queen had commanded him to wait with them, and the whole time the King sat stoically in his chair while Sara paced.

The tension in the room was exhausting, and the book of lullabies wasn't distracting enough. He thought about getting the book on torture, because that would definitely take his mind off things, but he didn't want to see all the horrible acts the King would eventually do to him someday.

"What if they don't get her?" Sara asked, turning to her husband. She wrung her hands, and her smooth skin was uncharacteristically ashen.

"They'll get her," Oren replied, staring past her at the doors to his chambers.

"But if they don't?" Sara sounded as if she might cry, and Loki looked up from his book. "Oren, this might be our last chance to ever get her."

"It's not like they're going to kill her," Loki tried to reassure her. "Even if we don't get her today, the Trylle won't hurt her. They'll just hold her for safekeeping. So you've got nothing to worry about."

The King motioned to him. "Loki's right, for once."

Sara nodded, but she didn't look convinced. She returned to her pacing, with Froud practically tripping over the train of her gown.

Loki went back to reading the lullabies, but he didn't get much farther in the book when they heard a commotion in the hall. Footsteps running, and then the door to the chambers was thrown open.

When Kyra burst into the room, Loki stood up. She looked positively horrid. Her short hair had been singed. Dirt and blood stained her skin and clothing, except for two streaks down her cheeks that were clean from her tears.

"We couldn't get her." Kyra's voice trembled, and she shook her head. "They overpowered us. They killed Jen."

"They killed Jen?" Loki asked, surprised. He'd never cared for the guy, but Loki'd always thought he was a fairly good tracker.

"They're much stronger than we thought," Kyra continued.

"Where is she?" Sara asked, as if she hadn't heard anything Kyra had said. "Where's the Princess?"

"She's still in Förening." Kyra glanced nervously at the King, afraid of when he might strike her down. "She's fine, but they still have her."

"How many casualties did we have?" the King asked, so far sounding unfazed.

"I don't know," Kyra admitted. "A lot."

"Hmm." The King stood up, folding his hands behind him. "Very well then. We'll have to do something more drastic to get her."

He smiled, and Kyra cringed, finding that more frightening than his frown.

"We'll do whatever it takes," the King went on, "but I assure you, Wendy will belong to us."